THE DEADENING

BOOK THREE IN THE
SISTERS OF SPIRITS TRILOGY

Praise for Yvonne Heidt's Work

Sometime Yesterday

"*Sometime Yesterday* kept me glued to the pages! Ms. Heidt has written a spellbinding novel of love, loss, tragedy, and triumph!" —*Bibliophilic Book Blog*

The Awakening

"Oh my goodness and be still my beating heart, a book completely immersed in parapsychic phenomena with potent female talents. Best of all, the handling of the psychic elements is wonderfully believable, incredibly detailed, and delightfully balanced with friendship, love, and multi-dimensional sexual heat. Not to be lost in the mix is the satisfying police procedural elements and a host of subsidiary characters who probably deserve their own book one of these days. In short, there was practically nothing missing from this brilliant book!"—*Rainbow Book Reviews*

The Quickening

"These characters, their world, and the enormity of the tasks placed before these three women is simply spellbinding. As much as I loved, laughed, and was enchanted, I found the heat, intensity, and thrilling battle with a terrifying and stupefying villain completely breathtaking. This is a winner!"—*Rainbow Book Reviews*

Visit us at www.boldstrokesbooks.com

By the Author

Sometime Yesterday

The Sisters of Spirits Trilogy

The Awakening

The Quickening

The Deadening

THE DEADENING

BOOK THREE IN THE
SISTERS OF SPIRITS TRILOGY

by

Yvonne Heidt

2015

THE DEADENING

ISBN 13: 978-1-62639-243-4

THIS TRADE PAPERBACK ORIGINAL IS PUBLISHED BY
BOLD STROKES BOOKS, INC.
P.O. BOX 249
VALLEY FALLS, NY 12185

FIRST EDITION: FEBRUARY 2015

CREDITS
EDITORS: VICTORIA VILLASENOR AND CINDY CRESAP
PRODUCTION DESIGN: SUSAN RAMUNDO
COVER ART BY SHANINA CONWAY
COVER DESIGN BY SHERI (GRAPHICARTIST2020@HOTMAIL.COM)

Acknowledgments

I don't know why the Universe put Sandy and me together—but I am blessed for each marvelous minute of every day that she's in my life.

Thank you, Radclyffe and Bold Strokes Books. I am grateful your belief in my imagination kick-started this wonderful journey.

It's been an amazing ride writing The Sisters of Spirits series. I'd like to extend my appreciation to my readers for their encouragement, kind words, and the occasional poke (and more) to get me back on track! I'm still in awe when I read your notes and e-mails.

Thank you to all of the outstanding women at BSB who work specifically with me behind the scenes and manage to effortlessly make me look good. Cindy, Sandy, Ruth, Toni, Kathi, Sheri, and Stacia. I sure hope I haven't forgotten anyone. According to the rules in Vonnie-Land, I'll remember after I turn this in.

Shelia Powell, thank you for your friendship, knowledge, and compassion. What started out as a phone call to a stranger several years ago has turned into a cherished and unforgettable sister-bond.

I am so blessed to have met so many incredible women this year while attending the Golden Crown Literary Society's conference in Portland and the Lone Star Literary Society in Austin. Thank you for making me feel so special. I wish I had room to name all of you!

Mom and Papa, I'm still making it up as I go along.

Special shout out to my awesome buddy, Jove Belle. Thank you for knowing me—and my things—well enough to know when to use encouragement—and when to kick my ass. I'm so glad that you are in my life.

Love to my kickass editor Victoria Villasenor. Who knew we'd get here together? Your dedication to my writing is so appreciated. Your friendship—even more.

A big curtsy to Suzie Krelle, my underpaid (read: as-in-none) big sister, publicist, and cheerleader. Your support and love are appreciated more than you could ever know.

Andi Marquette, R. G. Emmanuelle—thank you for your confidence and friendship. I wouldn't trade knowing you both for anything (Well, except maybe a million dollars, I might have to reconsider!) Laydin Michaels for her early thoughts on Shade, her willingness to be there for me, and a beautiful pep talk when I needed it most.

Connie Ward, Shelley Thrasher, Sandy Thornton. You make my heart smile. Thank you for that. Any room I walk into always feels better when ya'll are in it.

Andrea Bramhall—for the freaking story board. I kicked, bitched, and threw a hissy fit, but hey, it worked. I guess you *can* teach an old femme new tricks!

Shanina Conway, for her beautiful cover art. I stumbled upon her work, instantly fell in love, and gained a new friend on the other side of the world.

Stephanie Keeler, Sisters of Spirits Ninja. Thank you!

Last, but never least, I'd like to thank my tribe of women in Bremerton, Washington. Ya'll know why!

Dedication

For Maralee,
Who knows every damned one of my secrets
and loves me anyway.

PROLOGUE

A cold, fetid wind blew out of the closet Shade was frantically searching. She shook with the power of her anger. The blood curse Tiffany's dead ex-husband had left in their daughter's room stank of evil. She knew it was here. She could feel the angry buzz along her nerve endings. Shade could hear his spirit talking from the corner behind her, and she prayed Angel didn't see him the way Shade did, with half his head caved in by the baseball bat Tiffany had swung after he'd kidnapped her, with the intention to kill her.

Out of the corner of her eye, she saw Kat, Tiffany's partner, attempting to protect them by keeping her body between the bed and the closet.

Angel's sweet voice was calm. "No, Daddy, you have to go to the light now."

Mark had been a cursed time walker, holding his memories after scores of reincarnations, his sole purpose to destroy Tiffany and all who were connected to her by infinite love.

The curse he left in Tiffany's house should have died with him, but the energy of a sadistic serial killer amplified his power as a dark witch. The box she was looking for would contain a mass of blood and hair, filled with malevolent energy.

She could feel the force of it crawl along her scalp, and she knew she was close.

Tiffany screamed. "Leave her alone, you bastard! Get out!"

Shade tripled her effort, throwing stuffed animals, plastic toys, and boxes of outgrown clothes over her shoulder, digging her way to the bottom corner.

"But if you don't feel good, the light will make you better," Angel said. "I promise."

Shade kept her panic at bay while Angel continued to talk, but Mark's voice was now blocked from her, leaving only a one-sided conversation that was freaking her out.

"I can't go with you now. Next time, maybe."

"Oh God," Tiffany said. "Shade?"

Shade's fingers closed around the small wooden box. "Found it." She rose from the floor, clutching it to her chest and away from them. "I'm leaving. I'll take care of it.

Tiffany nodded. "Please hurry."

"S'okay, Mommy," Angel said. "Daddy says he won't bother us anymore. He's almost done."

Mark's bloody face appeared in front of Shade, blocking the exit. "Your choice, necromancer." His teeth were jagged and broken. "I'm taking one of you with me tonight. And you know I can do it."

His power was stupendous, and she knew without a doubt he would choose the baby. Shade telepathically answered instantly and without hesitation. "Then it's me, asshole."

The doorknob turned before she touched it, and she ran down the hall.

Kat pushed past her to open the front door. "Be careful."

Shade thought about how much she loved these women, this child, and their images played a frantic slideshow in her mind as she silently said good-bye to them. She was grateful her chosen sisters had found love, and she knew that Jordan and Kat could, and would, protect them.

Shade was the expendable one.

Her heart cracked with each step she took away from the porch. She turned to look at Tiffany and Angel one last time. "Good-bye, guys. I love you." Her words felt stilted and robotic because her throat was already tight with grief. Knowing they would find each other again in another life wasn't any consolation.

She shook her head as though to dislodge the thoughts. Where did that finality come from? *Fuck that.* She would fight whatever was coming, and she would kick ass.

She opened the driver's door, stood on the sideboard, and watched Tiffany blow her a kiss before she put one knee on her seat, pivoted, and leaned into the van to place the horrible box behind the passenger seat.

In her mind's eye, she saw the bomb at the exact moment she heard the horrifying click of the device's trip wire.

She had a millisecond to register the tremendous blast that hurled her body back through the open door and into the night.

CHAPTER ONE

One week ago...

Shade opened her eyes in the dark and sensed she wasn't alone. She encountered warm skin when she pressed her hips back and heard a woman's soft sigh. *Who did I pick up last night?*

Does it matter?

She was still buzzed, and the electric energy of sex lingered in the room. For the next hour or so, she could forget that tomorrow always comes, right along with generous side helpings of despair and loneliness.

The woman's name still escaped her, but images of sliding against the woman's hot skin the previous night returned in a rush, filling Shade with a desire for more.

She turned and crushed the woman against her. Warm skin burned against Shade's own, the softness of full breasts heated her chest. A tangled mass of long hair spread around her, and Shade entwined her fingers in the curls to draw her partner forward. She followed the soft sighs to seek her mouth and lost herself in a deep kiss.

Shade nudged with her knee, and her thigh was accepted between smooth legs. She inhaled sharply when heat shot through her clit, causing her to shift forward, closer to the source, while never losing contact with the dizzying kiss.

Shade pushed her hips against the warm body under her. She felt the sharp sting of fingernails scrape down her bare back, and the pain drove her to a quicker pace. The sounds of the woman's heavy breathing increased until it became a steady whimper for release, stimulating a burning urgency of her own.

This was the place she could forget the darkness within the darkness. Her loneliness could be forgotten in this space where her heart beat in rhythm with her pumping hips, leaving no room in her mind for stray thoughts. The woman under her whispered words Shade couldn't quite understand. She felt completely flesh in the moment, entirely focused on the friction against her swollen clit. The thigh between hers became hot and slippery. The temperature and tempo increased, became a battle of dueling hips and warring tongues. Time stopped in this moment where no rational thought existed. It might have lasted two minutes or two hours, Shade didn't care.

This respite from reality was rare for her, and she welcomed it as she would a long lost friend.

When she reached her orgasm, her muscles strained with delicious tension until Shade thought her tendons might snap with the force. She came several times in succession while the woman shook and trembled beneath her. Shade dropped to her side on the bed, feeling the erratic pulse beating in her throat. She considered trying to speak, but didn't want to break the moment with awkward words. She kept her eyes closed and focused on trying to take full breaths. The energy in the room coiled and snapped with an intensity she hadn't felt in so long, she'd wondered if it even existed anymore.

She felt a thundering heartbeat behind the soft breasts pressed against her back while an intoxicating mixed scent of sex and earthy spice surrounded her.

Shade felt guilty she couldn't remember the woman's name, but didn't want to break the silence to ask. Before she could consider whether she needed to know it, she slid back into a deep sleep.

❖

Fuck. She was late for work.
Again.

It didn't keep Shade from grinning. When she'd woken up for the second time that morning and rolled over, the sheets were still warm. That elusive earthy scent continued to surround her and invaded her senses. She stretched and waited for the morning-after crash that always followed within the first few moments of opening her eyes.

When it didn't appear and her spirit didn't twist in turmoil, she was shocked. Her muscles didn't bunch up around her neck and shoulders, her head didn't hurt, and—*what is that fucking fragrance?* It tickled along her nerve endings, evading description but invoking a deep sensual response.

Shade tried to remember how last night started, but all that came forward was the sensory experience she'd experienced a couple of hours ago. The feel of her movements within and against separate beautiful body parts, attached to a woman whose face she still couldn't recall.

She braced herself on her elbow and looked at the empty side of her bed. Several long, dark strands of straight hair lay on the pillow. That gave her pause. Blondes, whether natural or from a box, were her attempt to replace what she'd lost. She knew it wasn't logical, but after the liquor, or whatever else might be handy, hit her bloodstream, she could usually pretend until the next morning.

She picked up the hair and inhaled, rubbing the strands between her fingers. When the woman's face didn't appear, she tried again and attempted to read the energy signature left behind. The only image she caught was a large black bird soaring in a stormy sky. When she didn't feel any more answers forthcoming, she shrugged it off and then headed for the shower.

She carried that good feeling all the way to work, a sensation both foreign and welcome.

When she arrived, Shade slipped into the building quietly to avoid detection.

Sunny had too many damn questions lately. At least she'd had some reprieve when Tiffany and Kat were on their extended, well-deserved vacation after Tiffany's horrific stalking nightmare. Shade knew they worried where her nocturnal activities were leading her.

Even if their nosiness came from a loving place, it bugged the shit out of her.

Her habits, her problem.

Both Tiffany and Kat were far too polite to hound her. Shade had become somewhat of a regular at their house for dinner, and although she knew they wanted to pressure her about her life, they respected her boundaries.

Although Sunny wouldn't push, she would get that familiar look of disapproval on her face, and Shade was tired of always coming up short. A little acceptance from them would let her keep up the illusion her life was just fine.

From her position at the bottom of the stairs, she saw a new receptionist on the phone, but her mass of long dark hair kept Shade from seeing her face.

Aura's replacement. Shade sighed. Sunny's mother was the one who kept them all on schedule and grounded. Plus, if they ever ran into something they couldn't handle, she'd always been readily available for help or advice. Shade hated social niceties, they made her uncomfortable, but she supposed she should go talk to the new girl. She usually left such things to Sunny and Tiffany. Now *they* were sweet. *Me, not so much.*

Shade thought nothing of cutting people to pieces with her sarcasm. If that didn't make them leave her alone, she readily shared what it was she did for a living. The gruesome title of Necromancer ensured most people would give her a wide berth. She liked it that way.

As she approached the desk by the window, the woman's energy signature grew stronger with each step. This wasn't just anyone off the street; the new hire possessed power of her own.

She heard the flurry of beating wings from somewhere above her and stopped. The air shifted and stilled, but the receptionist didn't appear to notice the disturbance.

Shade mentally filed the sign away. She might as well set the tone right away and assert how she liked things done at work, the quicker the better. Shade approached quietly so as not to draw attention to herself, and tapped her fingers on the large desk. She smiled when the girl startled. "I'm Shade. Are there any messages for me?"

"Oh, you scared me! I've been waiting for you to show up."

Shade was distracted by her striking looks, and more than a bit disarmed by her big smile. It wasn't a normal, how-do-you-do-smile—it was full of sultry recognition. Her mind raced to fill in the blank when the woman stood up to come around the desk. "Sorry I left in a hurry this morning. I didn't want to be late on my first day."

Shade's feet felt frozen to the floor as the woman hugged her and she was enveloped in the tantalizing mystery scent that filled her bedroom that morning. "Um..."

The woman pulled away and looked at Shade, her nostrils flared slightly, and temper fired in her eyes. "You're kidding, right?"

Uh oh. She thought of the beating wings and took a leap. "Raven, right?"

❖

Raven answered three phone calls and hung up on a crank caller before she had a chance to process how Shade leaving so abruptly affected her. She'd had high expectations this morning, and every one of them had been crushed with Shade's shocked utterance of her name as a question.

Raven, right?

The absolute look of horror on Shade's face when Raven stepped away flustered her. *What was that about?*

Raven had been at a table with her cousin Lyric when Shade entered and sat at the bar. What were the odds that the object of her passion would come into the same place Raven was celebrating becoming an adult? She'd considered it a sign. She and Lyric decided to split up, and Raven tried to gather more confidence; the feeling of butterflies low in her belly only made her more nervous. Finally, after managing a quick internal spell, she found the courage to take the stool next to her. Shade's dark, enigmatic energy swirled and danced with her own earth magic, creating a level of sexual tension Raven had never reached before.

The bar had been giving her free drinks to celebrate her twenty-first birthday, and she'd been a little drunk herself, but she'd no idea Shade was so inebriated she wouldn't remember who she took home.

So much for signs and feeling special and unique.

Shade's energy still echoed through her and hummed along Raven's skin. It was better than she'd imagined over the years. As she thought back to the first time she'd met her, she recognized the exact moment the seed of fate had been planted. Raven had never forgotten the rush of power she'd felt that day.

She'd been nearly twelve, and had run to answer a knock on the front door. She'd heard her mother's pounding footsteps in the hall behind her before Raven was ordered to stop, and it was her mother who answered the door.

Shade had walked in wearing a long, leather trench coat, her hair the color of midnight and chopped into different lengths and spikes. She was fascinating, but it was her eyes that drew Raven in. Dark, rimmed with black eyeliner, they almost looked too big over her sharp cheekbones, and they appeared fathomless, like Cleopatra's, whom they were studying in history class.

Raven had felt her power sizzle in the air around her, electrifying the tiny hairs on her arms. In contrast, her mother's body language was stiff and controlled. She greeted the stranger respectfully by her title, Necromancer, then by name, Shade.

Even then, Raven had recognized the thrill that rushed through her along with a tiny prickle of fear.

Her mother had ejected her from the room, but she promptly hid in the hall to listen through the wall in their old house. Shade had come to discuss a spell that would bring someone named Sunny back to her. Raven heard her mother's warning of backlash, and if she loved this woman, she would let her go.

The rest of the conversation between Shade and her mother was lost to her over the years, but she'd never forget the vow she'd made to herself.

Shade had been on her way out the door when she'd locked eyes with her. Raven couldn't look away from the painful fire behind her gaze, so she'd continued to look back, turned it into an old-fashioned staring contest. Finally, the corner of Shade's mouth twitched, and she winked at her before she'd left.

I'm going to marry her one day.

Even at that young age, she'd felt the certainty of the promise. Raven's heart pounded in her chest long after the front door closed behind Shade.

But right alongside what she'd deemed a moment of fate, was the warning her mother spoke that afternoon.

"Never tangle with a necromancer, mija. They walk a hard life with one foot here, in this world, and the other in the land of the dead. Nothing but darkness surrounds them. Heartache is a way of life, and no one ever loves them enough to stay."

Raven held that moment in stasis. She'd known the only course for her was to wait. Even at eleven and a half, she'd known.

As she grew older, she worked in the family's metaphysical store, Whispering Winds. Her sister, Lark, ran the online sales; her brother, Hawk Jr., marketing; and her mother the spells, rituals, and candles. Her oldest sister, Starling, married and moved away, but was still involved in merchandising, making charms and talismans. Raven usually worked in purchasing, keeping their elusive vendors up-to-date, and buying rare supplies from places that would never be found on any of the Internet search sites.

Shade came into the store occasionally, but if her mother noticed her entering, she sent Raven off to do something else. Regardless of how frustrated that made her, she knew her future rested with Shade.

As Raven got older, and her cousins and siblings were dating members of the opposite sex, she held herself apart. She hadn't met anyone she wanted to get close to.

Once, when she was sixteen, she'd bent under peer pressure and accepted a date from a boy in high school. Everything about the evening felt *wrong*. Raven rarely did anything she didn't want to, and after a short dinner, she'd had him drop her off at Whispering Winds.

Shade had been walking out the door with a bag under her arm. She'd nodded slightly as she passed. Raven had stood in the middle of the sidewalk and watched Shade get in her car and drive away. She'd been sure *that* was a sign as well.

The phone rang, and Raven came back to the present. "Good afternoon, this is SOS. How may I help you?" She raised an eyebrow when she heard the whispered reply.

"I see dead people!"

"Really?" Raven grinned when she heard muffled giggling. "Me too," she whispered back dramatically. "And just so you know—my dead people can kick your dead people's butts." She chuckled when the line immediately disconnected.

She didn't have time to sift through her memories or continue to reminisce. She picked up the receiver before it rang. "Hello, Lyric."

"How did it go when Shade got to the office? Was she worth waiting for all those years?"

"It was wonderful," Raven said. "But when she got here she didn't remember taking me home. She dismissed me, then walked out."

"Ouch." Lyric drew the word out into three syllables.

"Right?" Raven hated the gathering tears.

"Well, maybe it's because you were in a work situation."

Raven looked out the window and noticed it was raining again. "Maybe."

"Good thing I have a distraction for you then," Lyric said.

"What are you talking about?"

"There's a DJ party at one of the new clubs downtown tonight. You can ride with me."

"We went out last night. I don't think—"

"We're young, sexy as hell, and single. I'm not taking no for an answer. We can sleep when we're dead."

Raven knew that to change Lyric's mind would involve a long argument. She was too tired to engage, not to mention it was her first day at work, and she didn't want to seem like she was loafing.

"Fine, I'll go with you. Bye." She could think of a good excuse between now and then.

❖

What the fuck had she done?

Shade ran out of the building as if three banshees from hell were following. And if Juanita, Raven's mother, found out that Shade had slept with Raven? It might be one of the nicer consequences.

After she pulled back into her driveway, she realized she had the balled up pink messages in her lap. She unwrinkled the first to find she hadn't had to go into the office after all.

Seth had cancelled his appointment to reach his great-great-dead uncle. Just as well, she thought. He was creepy. His uncle times-two had died in an airplane crash, and those sessions were never pretty. And they sure as hell weren't the first thing she wanted to deal with after drinking so much tequila last night.

With Raven.

Shade's head hurt. It was like trying to think with oatmeal stuffed into her brain. She had no business even thinking about Raven in that way. When had she grown out of her ponytails?

How could she do something so stupid? It was a good thing she left the building. If she'd stayed too long, Sunny would hover, asking questions about how Shade was doing, asking if she could help. It was a nice and civilized way for her to let Shade know Sunny was on to her and knew what she was doing in her off hours. It was becoming increasingly difficult to evade her. If she were honest, she held more than a trace of resentment over the fact that Sunny chose Jordan over her. It was small of her, she knew, but she couldn't help how she felt. Besides, Sunny would perceive in a second what happened between Shade and Raven.

Shade cringed. Just how pathetic and needy was she? Forever wanting to be with someone who couldn't—wouldn't—be with her. Not because Sunny didn't love her, she knew she did, but because loving Shade had made her miserable.

She should probably talk to Tiffany and get some help, but there was no way she would bother her with it. The last several weeks had been horrific for all of them, and she wouldn't load her with anything else.

And damn, she'd never been prouder of Tiffany. The sister they thought needed the most protection of all, had avenged herself and several other murder victims with one swing of a baseball bat. Shade wasn't sorry Mark was dead. When Tiffany had been taken prisoner, Shade thought she might literally explode with rage. She didn't know how her body had contained it all, and she couldn't help but wish she'd been the one to wield the bat. Tiffany was sensitive, and none of them knew how it could affect her psychologically or spiritually in the future, even though she appeared to be dealing with it just fine at the moment.

The whole past life thing she vaguely remembered being a part of was fucking cool, but thinking about Mark reminded her of Beenie, the woman she'd been with who had been paid to set Shade up so motherfucking Mark could hit her in the head with a pipe. She hoped Beenie had enough drugs to keep her hidden for a while, because Shade was going to find her.

Sooner or later.

Great. The adrenaline releasing with her anger was causing her head to pound. She got out of the van and went into her dim house, where the drapes always stayed closed.

She made a beeline down the hall to the master bathroom. She leaned on the counter for a moment and looked in the mirror. Her eyes were bloodshot and belied the fact she'd been relaxed and feeling excellent this morning. Her reflection was proof she was back in familiar territory, stressed out, hating herself, and balled up with tension.

She could fix that—temporarily. Shade reached for the orange prescription bottle she'd had refilled the previous day and shook out two oval yellow pills. After Mark had bashed her head in, the doctor had no problem prescribing them for her headaches. In addition to relieving the migraines, Shade had fallen in love with the way they made her feel.

From experience, she knew twenty minutes or so after swallowing them, a little burst of sunshine would flow through her bloodstream, filling her with hope and a rush of happy feelings. The effects were utterly foreign to her usual nature, and oh, so welcome.

She felt as if she could accomplish anything put in front of her. Even better, the dead quieted down. They didn't disappear entirely, but they were much easier to ignore, as if the volume had been turned way down on a loud stereo that had been playing full blast since she was a child.

Shade was aware her problems weren't going away, and that the drug-induced feelings were an illusion. But the peace she found far outweighed the possibility of becoming dependent on the pills.

Shade dry swallowed the two in her hand, and with only a moment's hesitation, shook another one out of the bottle and popped it in her mouth as well, before heading into the kitchen to grab a beer to chase them with.

That third pill just might squelch the anxiety she felt about sleeping with Juanita's daughter.

Maybe.

After getting a cold one, she flopped in her recliner, tipped her bottle in a toast to the dead musician staring at her from the corner, and turned on the television. She flipped through the channels and stopped on the show about a forensic anthropologist who read bones.

She could totally relate. Except, of course, the bones Shade talked to—talked back.

❖

At ten to five, Raven saw Jordan come around the corner of the hallway just as Sunny was descending the stairs.

They met in perfect unison at the front of her desk.

"Hey, she lasted the whole day." Jordan chuckled. "Major points for that, by the way." She smiled at Raven. "I didn't hear any screams."

"It was great." Raven returned the smile. "Sunny, here are your messages."

Raven hoped the blast of cold air she felt was a stray breeze and not from Sunny. She really wanted this job.

"Thank you." She read the one on the top of the stack. "Oh, damn. It's Layla, for the Bristol Terrace investigation." Sunny shook her head.

"It's not like we weren't caught up in a serial murder case or anything," Jordan said. "She'll understand we need to reschedule."

"Can I go too?" Raven asked.

Sunny looked up from her message. "Have you done an investigation before?"

Raven stared at her blue eye, then her green one. Sunny's gaze was intense and probing. Raven smiled inwardly and tightened her mental blocks, but not before pushing back slightly.

Sunny tipped her head. "Very good," she said.

"Are you kidding?" Raven asked. "On Dia de Los Muertos? All of our dead relatives officially show up for three days once a year, but in reality, they're always hanging around."

"We'll see," Sunny said. "We'll have a few cases between now and that one, and you can familiarize yourself with our routines during an investigation."

"Seriously?" Raven couldn't hide her wide smile or the excitement from her voice. How awesome was it that she joined a paranormal society that included a ghost hunting team?

She silently thanked Aura once more for the opportunity to work here, but Shade's rejection still stung, dampening her enthusiasm. The second Raven thought of it, she watched Sunny's eyebrows rise, as if she'd read her mind, and had questions.

Jordan also appeared to have noticed it and put her arm around Sunny's shoulder. "Time to go, babe." She steered Sunny toward the front door, which she held open for her. "See you, Raven."

"Bye." Raven was sure she discerned a pinch of jealous energy from Sunny. As far as she was concerned, Sunny had no right to be. She'd been the one to throw Shade and her darkness away years ago.

Shade's demons didn't scare Raven one bit. She had a few of her own.

CHAPTER TWO

S hade leaned against the back wall of the club and watched the people gyrate on the dance floor. She'd thought about staying home, but habit drove her out of the house. She'd also received a personal invitation from the new owner. Tara was one of the few girls she'd gone out with more than once, and they'd remained friends over the years. How could she resist a club named The Devil's Divas? The hard rock music settled in her chest, and her heart beat rhythmically right along with it. Loud music, alcohol, and beautiful girls. There was little chance she would leave alone tonight.

She had already made nice with Tara's new wife, and was on her second drink when Raven walked in the door arm in arm with another woman. Shade tracked her path over to the bar, while she talked with her date. The sharp twist in her gut rattled her. Was it jealousy or anxiety? She couldn't decide.

Neither was acceptable.

Awesome. Now she needed a distraction from her distraction.

She deliberately looked away, back to the dancers. Not more than four feet away from where she stood, a woman made eye contact with her as she danced with a group of women. Shade let her gaze travel from her face to her breasts, and down to her bare legs and the killer red high heels. The woman smiled at her, licked her forefinger, and ran the tip of it down her neck and between her cleavage.

Blatant. Shade liked that. She blinked slowly then nodded. The twinge she felt this time was much better. Cleaner, without any kind of problems attached, and no need to fake small talk.

How the hell had she gone home last night with Raven anyway? And at the intrusion of her name, Shade's jaw tensed, and she sought her out again.

She told herself it was ten times ten stupid, and she should quit while she was ahead, but the second she found her, she couldn't look away. Raven was sitting at the bar laughing, and her hands moved gracefully while she talked with her date, touching her shoulder often. Shade had no right to be jealous. She was the one who ran this morning.

Work was going to be awkward until it blew over. She would have to shut her down and make Raven dislike her. She didn't want to hurt her feelings, but it was best for all concerned, and it would save Shade a whole lot of pain later. She hoped it wasn't too late to avoid a horrendous mess.

"Hi!" said the dancing blonde, sidling up to her. "You're Shade, right?"

"Yep." Shade welcomed the distraction but inwardly cringed when she giggled, actually giggled. From her tone, she expected her to start snapping a piece of gum. *Jesus. How old was she?*

"I'm Bambi. Don't you remember?"

Shade didn't answer. She couldn't. That didn't stop Bambi from talking.

"I met you last week. I was with my friend Stacy." She pointed to another blonde sitting at a small table a few feet over. "Well, the next day, after, you know." Bambi blushed and giggled again. "She told me you liked having a good time." Bambi leaned closer to whisper in her ear, making sure to brush her breasts against Shade's arm. "She also said you were very, very good. Do you want to play?"

She'd never even noticed this girl before. Worse, she didn't remember Stacy, the girl Bambi had pointed to.

Shade pulled back and stared down into her blue eyes to read her emotional energy. Bambi's beauty was only surface. Underneath lay competiveness and ruthless manipulation. Deeper than that was a determination to latch on and win Shade. As if she were a fucking prize.

How come they never believed they were better off without her?

❖

Raven's body moved with the beat of the music, but she kept Shade in her peripheral vision. She'd noticed her the second she'd walked in with Lyric. Out of the hundreds of different scents in the room, Shade's CK One stood out to her. Even if she hadn't scented her, her body recognized Shade's energy. Raven carefully avoided looking at her. That worked until a woman edged up to Shade. Raven raised her hand slightly and stopped Lyric's one-sided conversation. "Excuse me," she said.

Raven watched Shade disengage with the woman, then saw her reach into her pocket. She pulled something out and swallowed it before she scanned the crowd again. When she met Raven's eyes, she quickly looked away.

Oh, no, you don't, thought Raven. You *will* notice me. She picked up her water glass and put on her hip-swinging, sexy walk to cut through the crowd of dancers toward Shade until she stood in front of her.

Shade nodded curtly. "What are you doing here?"

"You were looking for me."

"What makes you think that?" Shade waved a hand to indicate the crowd. "I have no shortage of company."

"Really?" Raven asked. "Are you going to be that immature? Are you just going to pretend last night didn't happen?"

"Look, kid—" Shade began.

"I'm twenty-one."

"And I'm not." Shade shrugged. "I've got at least ten years on you."

"You didn't care about my age when I was naked underneath you last night."

Shade blinked. "I was drunk. Everyone looks good at closing time."

Ouch. Raven's temper spiked, and she reached for a quick spell to slap her with, to hurt back. Before she could utter the words, Shade had her against the wall, trapped between her outstretched arms. "Don't you *ever* pull that fucking crap on me. Got it?"

Raven was too surprised to do anything but nod and hold her breath as Shade's face came closer, then stopped mere inches from hers. She could see the sharp desire in Shade's eyes, just as she felt the heat of their combined energy spark between them. She tugged Shade's collar and brought her closer still until the tips of their noses touched. "You're lying when you say you don't want me." She nipped Shade's lower lip.

Before Shade could step back, Raven tugged her onto the dance floor and put her arms around her neck. "I love this song."

"I don't dance," Shade said. She stood stiffly with her arms at her side.

"Liar." Raven smiled and pressed her hips tighter against Shade before swaying to the music. "There's nothing wrong with your moves." Raven felt Shade's body hesitate minutely before she took the lead and spun her around so Shade was behind her.

Raven inhaled sharply and arched her back, pushing against Shade as they moved to the heavy bass. Her inner thighs felt slick, and her desire throbbed in time with the beat. Raven put her arms around Shade's neck, rested her head against her shoulder, and absorbed the memory.

Shade's heavy breathing in her ear, the fingers of her hands gripping her hips, how perfectly their bodies synchronized and moved together.

"You can dance," Raven said.

"I didn't say I couldn't." Without missing a beat, Shade turned her again. "I said I don't." Raven tipped her head back, and Shade swept her tongue along her neck before tugging at Raven's hair to pull her back to kiss her lips with a heat that made Raven's knees weak.

The next song phased in, but Raven barely heard it. She looked up at Shade. Her eyes showed a naked lust Raven would be happy to slake. She felt a surge of sensual power, knowing she'd been the one to put it there.

The space around them became crowded with dancers, and Shade stepped back. Raven felt the intimate connection break.

"I can't do this," Shade said and walked away. Raven followed and grabbed her arm to stop her.

Shade stopped at the bar but didn't turn around. "No, Raven."

Damn it, she couldn't think straight. Her body still thrummed with sexual heat, and Shade's words didn't at all match what her body was saying. Raven felt desperate in a way she'd never felt in her life, and that in itself was humbling. She *knew* Shade wanted her. The call of Shade's power had Raven's own magic metaphysically crying out in an effort to match it. She paused before speaking past the lump in her throat. "Tell me why, then."

Shade turned to face her and leaned on the bar with one elbow. Her body language showed casual ease, but Raven could feel her heart speeding right along with her own. Shade tipped her beer and drained the entire bottle before walking past Raven and out of the club.

Raven stayed on her heels until Shade stopped at the door of her van and finally looked back at her.

The nearby streetlight eerily reflected in Shade's eyes, making it hard for Raven to read them.

"Why are you chasing me, kid?"

"Stop with the kid, dammit. I'm not a child."

Shade chuckled. "Still doesn't make you my type."

Now that...that stung. "Of course not," she snapped. "Not being a cheap blonde and all."

Shade merely blinked, opened the door, and got into her van.

"I'm sorry," Raven said. "That was uncalled for."

Shade didn't answer or acknowledge her apology. She started the engine but didn't close the door. Instead, she leaned her forehead on the steering wheel.

When she didn't move, Raven grew concerned. "Hey, are you okay?"

Shade turned to look at her but didn't lift her head up. "I'm a little fucked up right now."

"I'll drive you home." Raven pulled out her phone and sent a text to Lyric while Shade climbed over the console to the passenger side without a word.

Tkng S hm

She was in the van, snapping her seat belt when she received the reply.

Ok u hussy.

Raven smiled, dropped her cell into her purse, and put the van in gear.

Shade didn't speak during the drive, and since Raven couldn't see her face, she had no idea if she'd passed out or not. It didn't take long to arrive at Shade's house, and Raven pulled into her driveway. The instant she stopped, Shade leaned over and pushed the garage door button on the driver's visor.

Raven felt a little shiver of premonition. When the door lifted, the dark space inside looked like an endless black hole, unsettling her a bit until the overhead light clicked on. She didn't know why; she'd been here just the night before. Then again, she'd been a little drunk herself, and caught up in her fantastic fantasy of Shade.

After they got out, Shade held her hand out for the key. "I'll call you a cab to get back to your car."

"Right." Raven followed Shade into the house.

She was a little appalled at the sight of the living room. It appeared as if a wrecking ball had swung through the room. She stared at the dirty glasses, empty bottles, and clothes strewn on every available surface. She must not have noticed last night because they had barely taken their hands off each other on the way to Shade's room. It was still dark when she left early this morning, and she'd been sated and far too preoccupied to see *this*.

"I'm not here much," Shade slurred. "The maid quit." She snorted at her own joke.

"Apparently. How do you think in this mess?" Raven noticed the chaos extended down the hallway as well. She couldn't believe this mess escaped her earlier. It was a wonder she hadn't broken her neck on the way out.

"I don't. That's the point." Shade peeled off her coat and dropped it on the floor.

A dark shadow shifted, then moved across the living room. Raven felt a chill go down her spine as she tracked its movements. "What is that?"

Shade shrugged. "Some dead drug dealer who's been hanging around. He wants me to give someone a message."

"So give it," Raven said. "Isn't that your job?"

"He's an asshole."

"So why are you letting him hang out here?" Raven was confused. Didn't Shade just normally send the spirits on their way to the other side? Banish them to protect her home?

"He's amusing."

The simplicity of the statement grated against Raven's nerves, and it sent her internal warning system off.

Before she could address it, Shade cleared her throat.

"Kid...Sorry, Raven." Shade's voice softened. "I'm a little screwed up right now, okay?" She searched her pockets for her phone and squinted to see the screen. "Ah, taxi." Shade's movements were exaggerated, and she lost her balance before landing heavily into the recliner next to her.

Raven was shocked when Shade reached for a bottle of open liquor on the side table, lifted it, and took a long swig. "Eww. How old is that?"

"Stop making that face," Shade said and dropped her phone. "Don't you dare judge."

Raven paused. "I'm really not. Actually, I'm a little worried. Do your friends know you live this way? I can't imagine they do."

Shade's eyes closed. "No, and you're not going to say anything, either."

Raven couldn't stand the thought of anyone she cared about, even this currently mean version of Shade, sitting in this dirty and negative atmosphere. It wasn't right. "Here, let me help you." Raven began picking up papers and other random trash before heading back into the kitchen to find the garbage can.

Her chest hurt to discover how Shade lived. The reality was so far outside Raven's fairy tale it might as well be another planet. When she returned to the living room, Shade's even breathing indicated she'd passed out. Raven had no idea what she'd taken at the bar, but now she was out cold.

She decided to keep going and cleared the coffee table. She considered how little she actually knew about Shade. Their chemistry together was blinding, and the feeling of how much she wanted Shade overran the rational voice clamoring for attention inside her mind.

Raven made one more trip with a washcloth to wipe down the table next to Shade. She tripped on her own discarded coat then fell into Shade's lap. Raven barely managed to stifle her surprised squeal.

Shade's arms came around her, her eyes half-lidded. "God, you're so fucking beautiful." She kissed Raven, sliding her tongue past her teeth effortlessly. She tasted of beer, tequila, and power, and it pulled her lust right back to the surface until she met the passion of Shade's kiss, stroke by stroke with her own tongue, and nipped her lower lip with her teeth. Raven felt dizzy as she rode the rush of electric energy that snapped between them.

Shade stood abruptly with Raven in her arms, impressing her further when her weight didn't even throw her stride as she strode purposefully down the hall, then dropped her onto the bed.

"Okay, that was hot," Raven said. "Come here."

Shade straddled her and worked on the buttons of her blouse, parting the fabric when she was done. She rested her head on Raven's collarbone, and Raven felt her hot breath fan across her breasts. "You're going to be the death of me."

Raven heard the metal teeth on her jeans when Shade unzipped them. She grabbed the hem of Shade's T-shirt and tugged. She hadn't had any alcohol tonight, and her mind was clear enough to see the details of Shade's body, unlike the night before.

With each movement, Shade's defined biceps were accentuated, and the second the cool air hit her nipples, they hardened. Raven reached to touch her abdomen, loving the way Shade's skin was soft on the surface, but coiled with muscle beneath.

With a quick tug, Raven's jeans were on the floor. The swiftness of it took her breath away, and when Shade spread her legs and settled between them, she had a moment of feeling vulnerable while completely exposed. That ended the second Shade's lips and tongue touched her.

❖

Shade had a moment of déjà vu when she woke in the dark surrounded by Raven's scent, despite her earlier resolve not to put herself in that position again. Raven sighed in her sleep and pressed her breasts tighter against Shade's back. The last thing Shade remembered was laying her head on Raven's thigh after she...

No!

...Before she'd passed out on her.

Shade was mortified. She gently lifted Raven's arm from around her waist and moved slowly to the edge of the bed to go to the bathroom. Cold air filled the heated space between them.

What was she going to do? Obviously, she couldn't let this continue, because whatever it was between her and Raven was best left untouched. But the little vixen knew she'd been lying. How had she gotten past Shade's mental gates?

She didn't want to think of how steamy and incredibly hot the sex was. Yet, she couldn't seem to stop herself. She respected Raven's mother, and *knew* she was treading treacherous ground.

Shade finished in the bathroom, and then crossed back to the bed. The living room lamp was still on, and in the glow of the yellow light Shade studied Raven. Her mass of dark hair spread across the pillows, framing her beautiful, sleeping face. The smell of her arousal stirred Shade's, and she wanted nothing more than to get back in bed and taste every inch of her. When she realized what she was feeling was close to tenderness, she was troubled. She'd locked away those emotions long ago, and ran before they even had a chance to surface.

Raven sighed and turned over. The sheet shifted and uncovered her naked breasts. Shade's pulse accelerated, and then she heard mocking laughter in the living room.

Shade stalked naked down the hallway and used her rage to build energy powerful enough to confront whatever spirit had taken this opportunity to appear. She didn't care who it was; she was going to kick ass.

The dead drug dealer, Travis, reclined in her chair.

He laughed again. "Dude, that was hot, right up until the time you started snoring between her legs."

Not so amusing now. Shade's jaw tightened. She was beyond pissed. "What did you say?"

"Why the hell do you think I hang around? You get more action than I ever did, and I had quite a few sluts putting out."

Shade felt each word as if she'd been physically slapped by them. Had she really held her own life and privacy in such cold disregard that she'd allowed him his voyeuristic behavior? She had to accept this was her fault, but instead of shame, it was jealousy that fueled anger.

"Dude, the way she whimpers when she comes for you, and that hip action? It makes me want to rise from the dead—for reals." He grinned nastily. "Is there a way to join you?"

Shade's eyes narrowed and she reached for the power she'd built. "Get the fuck out of here." Instead of flicking it at Travis, as she normally would have done when she was annoyed, she blasted it in his direction. When it hit, Travis didn't fade away, he was totally annihilated.

Shade stood in the middle of the room, shaking with the rush of adrenaline. "Anyone else want to fuck with me tonight?"

Shade closed her eyes and searched the house. "Don't test me. Here's your only warning. You stay the hell away from Raven, or I'll destroy you."

She sat in her chair to calm down. Her heart contracted painfully with the reality of her situation. Even if she could brave

Juanita's wrath about her seeing Raven, she would never get past the darkness. In her world, the shadows always won in the end.

Shade felt a tiny spark of hope she hadn't even been aware she'd been guarding, flare up and then extinguish within her. She had to make Raven hate her. She couldn't see any other way to avoid the pain that would inevitably follow if she even entertained the idea of allowing Raven in. When her emotions ebbed and she successfully tucked them behind her metaphysical brick wall, she returned to the bedroom.

That wall wavered at the sight of her, and Shade wished like hell she would have turned off the lights so she couldn't see her, couldn't want her.

Raven was dreaming, and her thoughts were easy to read. Shade saw herself through Raven's eyes throughout the years. The Shade that Raven was dreaming of had never even existed. She was some kind of idealized version of what Raven wanted.

She was dreaming of happily ever after, and Shade knew from experience that wasn't possible. Raven deserved much better than she could ever give. She was fiery, passionate, and incredibly open to receive love.

"I'm not capable of that shit. I'm broken," Shade whispered. When Raven stirred and cried out, Shade got back into bed and curled around her, hoping Raven hadn't met one of her demons. Regret snuck past Shade's barriers. She was going to have to break Raven's heart in order to save her.

And in turn, add one more dance with the Devil on her dance card.

❖

When Raven woke up, Shade wasn't in bed. The appearance of the room was worse now that she could see it in the daylight, and she mentally added cleaning it to her ongoing to-do list.

She'd just gotten out of the bed and was just on her way to the bathroom when she heard a crash in the kitchen. She raced down the hall.

Shade stood in the center of the room and shook an empty bottle at her. "Where is everything? Dammit—I knew where things were before you cleaned it."

Not the flowers and sunshine reception she'd hoped for. Shade's angry energy was evident in her tone of voice. Raven was initially stunned but quickly squashed her reaction. It wasn't in her nature to back down. "Good morning, and you're *welcome.*"

"I didn't ask you to do this."

"Oh, you'd rather live like a pig?

Shade glared at her. "Didn't I call you a taxi last night?"

Raven stared right back and bit her tongue. Again, it appeared Shade didn't remember making love to her.

"Jesus!" Shade yelled when she opened the refrigerator door. "Where's my fucking beer?" She crossed to the kitchen trash can and opened the lid.

"It's eight in the morning," Raven said calmly.

"So? You know what—I don't need to explain myself to you."

"*Madre de Dios*, are you always this ungrateful?" Raven bit her lip to control it, but the intention formed in her mind anyway, and an instant later, the empty bottle Shade was holding flew out of her hand and smashed against the wall.

Shade didn't even flinch. "Two-bit magic, got anything better?"

Raven was stunned. Who was this stranger? She'd wanted Shade as long as she could remember, and she'd never seen this side of her. She'd viewed her as a reluctant necromancer, a James Dean misunderstood type. Not this horrible and rude version in front of her.

She felt her temper dangerously close to the surface. How dare Shade treat her this way? There had to be something else going on, but with her emotions screaming *charge*—she wasn't exactly clear-headed.

"I can hear you," Shade said. "And you're speaking Spanish. If you want to fight, think in English so I can understand you." She drank from the milk carton, put it back in the refrigerator, and wiped her mouth with the back of her hand.

Raven's mouth fell open. Her blood began to boil. Damn her. "That's freaking gross. You're not supposed to drink from the box."

"You see my mama around here?" Shade pointedly looked at an empty corner in the room. "Well, not lately."

Raven let that remark slide. Years ago, she'd heard her mother talking to one of her aunts about how Shade's mother had been murdered. Then she heard Shade mumble something else.

"What did you say?" Raven crossed her arms across her chest.

Shade looked down at her feet. "Nothing."

"Look, I didn't come here for you to be nasty. I'll leave you to your chaos." Raven would be damned if she'd put up with this shit. She needed some space to think.

She went back to the living room, avoided looking at the leather armchair, and grabbed her shoes and purse. When she came back out, the kitchen was empty but the door to the garage was open. She quickly put herself together and went out the door.

Shade was waiting in the van. "I'll drive you to your car."

Raven didn't want to get in, but it was a long way to walk, and a taxi would take at least another forty-five minutes. She didn't want to be late for work either.

She neutralized her expression, gathered her dignity around her boiling temper, and reluctantly got in the van.

"Thanks for the ride home," Shade said. "I appreciate your concern, but I don't need it."

Oh, but you do.

Shade burned rubber in the driveway. "I don't need your fucking pity!"

"Stop doing that. It's rude!" Raven turned to look out the window, seething inside. It was just a short drive to where she'd left her car and she didn't want to argue anymore.

Shade pulled up behind it.

"I'll see you later," Raven said quietly.

"What is wrong with you?" Shade asked. "Why are you hounding me?"

Raven was shocked. Is that what she looked like? *Oh. My. God.* Now, she was utterly embarrassed and didn't know what to say. She searched Shade's expression for something, anything, to lessen the bitter taste of her question. Was she serious? She was horrified to find that tears were ready to fall, but there was no way in hell she was going to let Shade see them.

"Don't flatter yourself. I meant at work." Raven slammed the door shut when she got out.

La Diabla, Raven thought, and hoped she shouted it loud enough in her head for Shade to hear her.

She got in her small economy car, a gift from her mother at graduation. It wasn't until she looked into her rearview mirror she realized she hadn't even brushed her hair yet.

The long strands were snarled, giving that messy look some girls craved, but not her. She loved her long, straight hair. She noticed someone peeking out the window of a nearby house, so she started the car and then headed across the Manette Bridge toward the other side of town.

Now she'd have to deal with her mother and her questions about why she hadn't come home last night.

The "I'm twenty-one" argument didn't work with her. As long as she lived under *her* roof, it was mother's rules. She could recite the lecture verbatim.

Raven sighed. There was no use stretching the truth, or even outright lying. Her mother always knew. It had already been a draining morning and she didn't want to argue with her mother any more than she had with Shade.

She ran up the walkway and entered the house to find her mother standing in the hallway with her hands on her hips.

"Where have you been?"

Raven's throat tightened and she knew she was on the verge of tears again. She tried to keep her voice steady while she evaded. "Um, just out. Nowhere important, Mama. I'm sorry I didn't call. I didn't mean to worry you."

Her mother looked surprised, as if she'd been resigned for one of their fights. Raven didn't blame her. She had been a difficult teenager at best, and even though she was now of age, they still possessed that same synergy most of the time. Raven always fought fiercely for her independence, but now she could see the toll it had taken over the years.

She was ashamed to see the weariness in her mother's features, to know she was responsible for most of the anxiety her mother wore in and under her eyes, along with the lines of resignation around her mouth. Her older sister, Lark, had always been day compared to Raven's night. It had been hard trying to live up to Lark's reputation, her perfect grades, looks, and sweet disposition.

Raven had lived most of her life trying to be the exact opposite. She was sure that none of the gray hair on her mother's head had come from Lark or any of her other siblings.

"Take your shower," her mother said gently. "You'll be late for work and I have to go."

Raven nodded as her mother turned. "Mama?"

"Yes?"

"I love you."

"I love you too, *mija*."

She stood in the hall and watched her mother walk away. In the space of two days, it seemed her world turned upside down and backward.

It left her feeling lost, as if she didn't belong in her own space.

❖

Shade's regret twisted inside her on the return trip home as she thought of her behavior. In another time, Lacey, the girl she'd once been so long ago, would have been a better match for Raven. But there wasn't anything left of her, and Shade wasn't made for relationships. They came with a cost she refused to pay.

She'd seen too much, had done too much, to be worthy of anyone to love. Besides, she liked her life the way it was. She didn't answer to anybody, she did what she wanted when she wanted, slept with whom she chose, and then walked away with no ties and no regrets.

Nope, she'd done that feeling thing. And look how *that* turned out. The one person capable of loving her had walked away.

Because she was broken.

Still, she wasn't going to lie and tell herself she wasn't disappointed at what might have been possible if her life had been different. The look on Raven's face nearly undid Shade's resolve to send her away.

Raven's earth scent hung in the air, and her energy still wavered in the atmosphere. She probably could have handled that better. She could have explained and listed all the reasons that she shouldn't stay. But something told her Raven would have just argued back.

She was puzzled about the depth of Raven's feelings for her. The only contact she'd had with her over the years had been when Shade shopped at her family's store, Whispering Winds.

More often than not, Shade would smile or wink at her. Raven was a cute kid.

Kid.

That's all. At that point in her life, Raven was the only child Shade had met that didn't cringe from her when she walked into a room. Most children subconsciously knew she favored the dark side, and automatically kept their distance.

Shade had worked very hard on her persona. She relished the whole necromancer thing—wearing black, wearing dark makeup— and fed on fear. Quite frankly, the only women it attracted were weird ones, into all that death shit.

She still couldn't figure out why Raven even looked twice at her, let alone dreamed last night of a happily ever after with her.

It could be her death sentence, as far as Shade was concerned.

Her life before meeting Sunny and Tiffany held nothing but agony. Her friends had pulled Shade through her most painful memories of the past and showed her what love was.

But as it turned out, Shade's love was dark and dangerous. If Sunny, the woman who professed to love Shade most, couldn't live with her, then there were no more options, and no chance for any others to attempt to get close to her.

Raven's energy was impulsive. And if she really knew Shade, she wouldn't stay—she'd run far and fast in the other direction. She was too young to know better.

The standoff in the kitchen had been a surprise. When Raven stood up to her, she hadn't even blinked before the bottle went flying. Shade was impressed and just twisted enough she found the angry energy stimulating.

Once upon a time, Shade might have taken a chance and explored what might happen next, but not at the expense of Raven's feelings. She couldn't, in good conscience, hurt her later when she knew how Raven felt now.

She almost welcomed Juanita's impending consequences. She certainly felt as if she deserved them.

A familiar ache in her temples traveled down her neck, and settled in her shoulders, balling up between her shoulder blades.

That, at least, she could fix. She walked back to her bathroom where she kept her pain pills.

Three ought to do it, right? Shade shook them out into her palm. Almost as if her hands answered the question for her, the bands around her heart tightened, and the corners of her eyes burned.

Four would work better.

Chapter Three

Raven watched the last of the fire dim, until only one small orange ember was left. She remained in her cross-legged position on the floor with her hands on her knees, inhaling the last of the spicy scents. It burned her eyes, a small price for feeling the success of her spell. Her skin tingled with seductive heat.

The intention needed to complete the ritual was easy—she'd only needed to remember being naked with Shade. Too bad Shade didn't remember being naked with her.

This ought to fix that. A small, innocent spell to help Shade remember their time together. Well, that and a little you-know-you-want-me-again thrown in for good measure.

Shade had stayed away from the office for three days, and so far, Raven managed to not drive by her house. Her pride kept her from checking the clubs and bars.

Barely.

She was going crazy with the not knowing. It disturbed her that she had tendencies and more than a little insight on stalking behaviors. She kept running through the memories of her time with Shade over and over again, trying to find where she went wrong. Raven wasn't made for one- or two-night stands. But when she had seen Shade on her birthday, the dam of feelings she'd held for so long burst, and she had no idea how to put them back away again.

Once her head cleared from that awful scene in the kitchen, Raven knew Shade was lying to her and being mean on purpose. She could feel it. But why?

She also realized what she was doing under the full moon tonight was impulsive, but she felt compelled. She rationalized it by telling herself Shade just needed a nudge. Nothing wrong with a little nudge, right?

She heard the door open behind her, and Raven rushed to clear the remains of her ritual.

"What are you doing?" Lark asked.

"Nothing," Raven snapped. "Couldn't you have knocked?"

"I can smell the herbs you used. Don't let Mama catch you." Lark bent over to look at what Raven was hiding.

"Catch what?" *Busted.* "She knows I'm practicing." She hoped she sounded casual.

"Does she know you're casting a spell *on* someone else? Not good, Raven." Her sister's tone softened. "You realize that can backfire, right?"

"Okay, how do you know what I was doing?" Raven pointed to her clean, small, cast iron cauldron, where no traces of the ashy incense remained.

Lark sighed. "Clean the rest of your stuff up and we'll talk, okay?" She left the room, closing the door gently behind her.

Another awkward conversation, Raven thought. Lark actually seemed concerned, though. What was up with everyone in her life showing different aspects of themselves? First her mother, and now her sister. It was as if they changed overnight.

Maybe it's you who's changed.

She quickly put her tools away, cleared the floor, and then put her rug back in the center of the room. She opened the window and turned on the fan, letting the chilled air clear away the last of the smoke. When she finished, she did a double check of her room to make certain everything looked normal.

She crossed to her personal altar and lit some sage. Their house always smelled of the sweet grass. It was a scent she associated with home and love. Satisfied with her work, she went off to find Lark, hoping against hope she hadn't misjudged her kindness.

Lark may have her mother fooled, but Raven knew all too well that her sister had many masks, and you never knew which one was in use until Lark chose to show you. She wasn't as goody-goody as most people thought. She was just much better than Raven at getting away with things.

She admired that about her, even as it pissed her off. Especially when Raven got blamed for Lark's actions. But she never told on her; it wasn't in her nature. She might be the only one in the family to know what her sister kept buried deep inside her, but she would never betray her.

Lark sat at the small red Formica-topped table. Raven loved that kitchen set. It was a throwback from the fifties, and her mother had owned it since it was new. The chairs had been re-covered a few times over the years, but the table was constant. They'd learned to cook, done their homework, laughed and cried at it.

All serious family conversations started and ended there.

Raven rode the rush of nostalgia. She was so sensitive lately, her emotions felt raw. It was easy to blame Shade and her rejection, but everyone around her was acting weird. She was sure of it.

"Sit down, *hermana*." Lark pointed to the chair across from her.

Raven was uncharacteristically nervous but sat anyway.

"How's the job working out for you?"

Although it appeared to be just small talk, Lark had a way of winding the conversation to her own advantage. You would relax and think you were safe, and then bam, she'd nail you, putting you on the defense. "It's great." Short and sweet would be the safe way to answer until Lark made her point.

"And the women who run it? How do you get along with them?"

"Sunny is amazing, so is her partner, Jordan. Tiffany and Kat just got back from their honeymoon in Hawaii, so I'm just getting to know them."

"How's Aura doing?"

"Oh, she breezes in and out to make sure I'm doing a good job for SOS."

Lark grinned. "I'm glad that Mama's good friend thought of you when she retired."

"Me too." Raven's anxiety kicked up another notch. The tension in the air was building as Lark finally came to the point.

"And Shade?"

Crap. She knew. Raven tread carefully and shrugged nonchalantly. "Shade is Shade, you know?"

"Raven. I'm not mad. I'm worried."

"Why?"

"Because I know how long you've had a crush on her."

And Lark had teased her mercilessly about it over the years. Why did people always say the word "crush" as if it weren't a serious thing? As if the pain of longing and angst was less than real somehow and didn't measure up to what they considered real love? It made her angry. Raven felt her cheeks heat up but tried to keep her composure. If she reacted at all to Lark's statement, it would only get worse. She wiped her hand across the table, searching for invisible crumbs. It was spotless already, but it gave her something to do, and she kept silent even as she felt the ache in her heart. It matched the empty feeling she felt in the area of her stomach. She was tired of hurting because she wanted Shade. And when she'd finally got her, she'd been rejected. Damned if she didn't, and damned if she did.

When she looked up, she was startled to see the look of compassion on Lark's face, and not the expected one of judgment or worse, sarcastic derision. Now she knew she must be in an alternate reality.

"I know exactly how you feel," Lark finally said. "Do you remember Joe Martinez?"

"Wasn't he the guy you used to sneak in your room at night?"

Lark blushed and nodded. "You knew that?"

"I'm only six years younger than you. The gap between us shortened as I got older."

Lark nodded. "Well, you were only eleven. That's a huge difference when I was seventeen."

"I'll give you that one. What about Joe?"

Sadness filled Lark's eyes, and Raven wasn't quite sure she wanted to hear what she had to say. She reached out to touch her hand.

"I cut school one day and did the very same spell you just played with upstairs."

Uh oh. Now Raven was certain she didn't want her to continue, but Lark kept talking.

"Oh, I was so full of myself back then. I was recklessly selfish."

"Yes, you were," Raven said, "and mean, too."

"I'm sorry for that Raven, truly I am. But let me finish. I cast that lust spell on Joe. I thought it would be fun and exciting, so I did. I didn't consult Mom, the aunties, or anyone else, for that matter. It backfired on me, hurtfully so."

"What happened?"

"I turned up the heat all right," Lark said. "But I forgot to write into the spell the intention that he would want *only* me. Joe ended up screwing everyone he could convince to go to bed with him."

"I vaguely remember that, the phone calls and how upset you were."

"I was devastated in the process. I broke up with Joe, the beautiful boy I loved, because he constantly cheated on me. I couldn't admit to him it was my fault. He cried and cried and told me he didn't know why he couldn't keep it in his pants. I finally told Mama. I had to. I couldn't stand it anymore, his begging me to come back."

"I bet she was furious."

"You have no idea," Lark said. "She said I was too old to spank, but I almost wish she would have rather than make me go to Joe and explain what I did."

"She didn't!" Raven couldn't remember a time her mother had been mad at Lark. This must have happened behind closed doors.

"Yes, she did. Then she grounded me for six months afterward."

"What did Joe say?"

"He was outraged. After he sat through a reversal session with Mom and the aunties, he never talked to me again. He's hated me ever since. So you see why it's a bad idea?"

Raven felt a chill. "Yes, but you were a teensy bit late with your story, as I've already finished it."

❖

Shade came home after an afternoon appointment at a client's house. When she walked in through the garage door, she took a good and honest look around. Even with the work Raven had done mere days ago, it was still a disaster zone. She'd walked around in it for so long, she didn't even see the mess anymore. This was way past clutter; this was downright dirty. What was that saying she'd heard? The home's appearance is supposed to reflect how you felt inside.

Yup, that sounded about right. She dropped her bag on the counter. Then put the half-rack of beer she bought into the refrigerator. Shit. Where to start?

It had been a while since she had done laundry; she'd get that going first. She picked up five black T-shirts and a red thong. Instead of being a little perked up at finding sexy underwear, she felt sad. She had no clue who they belonged to.

After finding a third pair, she gave up wondering, she just made another pile. It wasn't as though she brought many women home twice, or that they would come and claim them of their own accord.

She came across Beenie's faded jean jacket. Now *her*, she had no problem recalling. Nothing like a trip to the emergency room to make you remember a girl.

Bitch. Shade still hadn't found her, which was a very good thing for Beenie, yes indeed.

It took her almost a half hour to round up all the clothes in the house, and that was after the ten-minute search for a basket. She hauled it all out to the garage and started the washer. When she was done, she could already see a small difference in the living room.

Okay, now dishes. Raven had rounded up most of the empties three nights ago, so there were few to find. But she hadn't searched the back bedrooms yet. Shade sighed and opened the door to the guest room.

She took one look, closed the door, and backed away. She wasn't feeling that ambitious. Her room then. The sheets needed to be changed. She stripped her bed, picked up more dirty clothes, then headed back to the garage. Jesus, she thought, how many pair of black jeans did she own, anyway?

Two hours later, she sat in her armchair and opened her third beer, pleased with herself and the progress she'd made. She'd forgotten how nice a clean house was. The energy was lighter and without static.

She felt a slight push in the air surrounding her. Her senses perked, and she searched for the source. She picked up a trace of Raven's signature a few seconds before she felt some serious heat building between her legs. She was slightly puzzled before she realized what was happening. She reluctantly but easily pushed the effects of the spell away.

Sneaky little witch. Shade chuckled. She was proud of Raven. She hadn't expected this from her, especially after her mean performance in the kitchen. Apparently, the kid was stubborn and didn't give in easily.

Now the question remained, what should she do about it?

She would definitely have to teach her a lesson about trying to impose on someone's will, especially hers. Shade lost her train of thought as she pictured Raven's naked, slippery body grinding against hers.

What was the problem again?

She stood, then paced to clear her fuzzy head. The problem was Raven's dreams of Shade, butterflies, puppies, rainbows, and all that happy shit.

Shade had been an absolute dick to her. But all she could see right now was how Raven had looked so beautiful lying beside her. But sending a spell? Impressive as it was, she had to ruthlessly nip this behavior in the bud, and stop her from repeating it.

She was certain that Raven hadn't had much of an idea how Shade would react. The spell's energy was built from youthful longing, but she had managed to weave in a truly lustful intention. Shade could still feel the echo of it pounding between her legs.

Raven had quickly made her feel things she'd long buried under drugs and a parade of women. Ironically, years ago, when Shade had returned to Juanita, instead of the love spell she had initially asked for, she'd asked for another to keep the feelings buried instead. Together, Shade and Juanita wove an intentional shield of ice to encase Shade's heart, ensuring she wouldn't fall in love with another woman.

Shade would rather die than go through that pain again.

A broken heart felt as if it could kill you, but it didn't. Instead, Shade had walked around like a zombie; she couldn't eat, sleep, or even function in the daily world. The dead hounded her constantly, trying to tell their stories, and Shade hadn't cared. She shut them out and closed her psychic connection the best she could. She drank and whored until Sunny saved her a second time, bringing Shade into her parents' business when she took it over.

Sunny had been the air she breathed.

Shade rubbed the pain in her chest, hoping to sidestep the memory.

Juanita's spell had never taken away the stark emptiness she felt after Sunny broke up with her, but it *had* kept Shade safe from feeling that way about anyone else.

She knew she lived in a dark place, and it didn't bother her. She hated that Raven made her realize she was lonely. She hated that she made her feel, period.

Raven was dangerous. The fact that she was sitting here and thinking about her at all was proof enough of that. She was nowhere near a faceless substitute for Sunny, which is all she should have been. No, Raven brought several unique responses out of Shade all on her own.

Damn it.

She grimly hatched a plan that would have to wait until tomorrow.

Now she felt itchy and agitated. She checked her watch. It was still early, and she could hit a couple of the bars to find some easy company, someone who came with no emotional strings.

Shade realized that this time, her actions would be an attempt to put *Raven* out of her head.

Fuck.

She needed to shower first.

The clean house that she was proud of was now throwing her off. She felt as if she didn't belong in it. But that was an issue she wasn't willing to address right now, or any time, really.

When she entered the bathroom, even the shiny nickel finish of the faucet seemed to mock her. The mirror was clean, and she could see herself clearly. She hadn't enough of a buzz for the edges of reality to become softened.

There she was, in all her glory. Shade, the necromancer, with her hard reputation and kick-ass attitude.

What a fucking joke.

She reached into the vanity drawer and pulled out her bottle. There were still several left.

Hallelujah.

Behind her reflection, she saw a shadow move to the left. Shit, the last thing she wanted to do was converse with a spirit. She blinked slowly, but the vision remained. A young woman sat in her bathtub, fresh from some kind of bloody accident. She could always tell the ones who had just died, or the people that died very quickly. They always had that look of abject shock on their faces.

Can you help me? The spirit reached out.

"Not today."

Please. I don't know where I am. I'm lost.

"You're not lost, honey." Shade popped the pills into her mouth and then chased them with the last of her beer. "You're dead."

She saluted her with her empty bottle. "Go away."

She tried not to notice the hurt and confusion on the spirit's face before she faded away.

God, she was tired of them coming in and out of her house. It never, ever stopped. Shade prayed the pills would kick in quickly enough to waylay the shame of what she'd just done.

It was just one more thing to add to her multitude of sins.

She stripped and got in the shower, letting the water hit her in her face to distract herself. But she knew she would never feel clean. Just as the lump in her throat threatened to travel and open her tear ducts, the opiates began working. She relaxed in increments and was able to detach from her reality.

It was just where she wanted to be.

❖

Raven finished making copies of the schedules and headed upstairs to leave them on Sunny's, Tiffany's, and Shade's desks after she turned on the lights and opened the blinds in each room.

When she reached Shade's dark office and opened the door, someone pulled her in, spun her around, and put a hand over her mouth to stifle her scream.

She reacted instantly and bit down, maneuvered her body to face the attacker, and then kicked up to connect with the groin area.

The body dropped heavily to the floor with a grunt. Raven turned to run out of the office but her ankle was grabbed, and she fell hard on her stomach. The breath whooshed out of her lungs, and she couldn't get enough air to scream again. She began striking the attacker and dug her nails into his flesh.

"Stop it! It's me. What the fuck is the matter with you?"

Raven froze. "Holy shit," she exhaled. "I thought you were a rapist." She'd kicked Shade's ass, and her fear turned into a satisfied thrill.

Shade rolled into a seated position, put one hand between her legs, and the other to the scratches on her neck. "I'm bleeding!"

"You're tough. You can handle it. That's what you get when you attack someone in the dark. What's *wrong* with you? That's not even remotely funny." Raven got up to turn on the lights. She had a horrifying revelation. Was this the result of the spell she cast? Her intention had been that Shade would be attracted to her, not jump her in the dark because she couldn't control herself.

Shade finally gained her feet then limped to the door. "It sounded like a good idea at the time. It never entered my mind you were going to go all ninja badass on me." She stopped a foot away from Raven.

She was so near, Raven could smell her. Shade's gaze was hypnotizing, intoxicating. Her dark eyes held her own in an unspoken challenge, and Raven's adrenaline continued to increase the pace of her breathing.

When Shade put her hand on the doorjamb next to Raven and leaned in, her heart continued to thump against her ribs. Shade exhaled, and Raven felt her breath feather against her mouth and cheeks.

She closed her eyes when she thought Shade was going to kiss her, but instead, she felt her body push past hers and into the hall.

What just happened?

❖

Shade looked in the mirror and poured antiseptic on her scratches. She should have put a little more thought into setting up Raven's retribution. She had intended to come on like gangbusters and teach her a lesson about putting spells on someone. Instead, Shade had ended up bleeding from a bite, several nail gouges, and aching between her legs. Raven kicked her ass and not only had Shade not expected it, she hadn't known Raven had it in her.

Damn, she'd almost kissed her. Worse than that, when she'd first landed on Raven on the floor, she'd been turned on by the struggle. She'd wanted to take and possess her, to *own* her. This was exactly why she couldn't be with Raven in the first place. The way Raven looked at her made her feel like she was an imposter keeping dirty secrets.

Which, of course, she was.

She briefly considered the possibility that Raven's spell might be stronger than it first appeared, but dismissed the idea and put the blame squarely back on herself. It was up to her to control her impulses. She was the decade older, supposedly wiser, woman. She tried not to think about how Raven felt underneath her while she squirmed. It didn't help. Raven's energy still burned from two floors down. Shade needed to leave and get away from her.

She hated being mean, but she didn't see another way to make Raven leave her alone. If Shade told her the truth, that she was a hot mess and beyond repair, Raven would want to fix her. As appealing as it sounded, Shade knew better, and in the end, they'd both end up hurt and broken.

With her mind made up, she applied a bandage to her bitten thumb, and then left the building through the back exit.

She drove to the seedier side of town where she stood in front of a badly repaired door that had been kicked in several times, and knocked. Sylvia opened it, half-dressed, bleary-eyed, and disheveled. She motioned Shade inside, where she paused to let her eyes adjust to the darkness before following Sylvia down the hall to her bedroom.

She'd been in it many times, but she only just noticed what a wreck it was after cleaning her own yesterday.

Sylvia reached from her position on the bed to the nightstand and pulled out a large white bottle.

"You're in luck." She shook the bottle. "I just got refilled yesterday."

"Sweet," Shade said and put her hand out.

"Nice foreplay."

Shade grit her teeth. She just wanted the goddamn drugs. She was so tired of wanting things she couldn't have. "I don't have time to play today."

"Today is a trade only. I'm flush and I don't need the money." Sylvia pouted and then gave her what Shade thought to be a pathetic come-hither look. She took a hard look at the reality of the situation, and what she saw made her sad. Sylvia's brittle, fake blond hair was snarled and knotted. She was too thin, and looked as if she hadn't showered in a few days. Raven's sultry curves and clean scent bombarded Shade in stark comparison.

Oh, fuck no.

She wouldn't let Raven enter this dirty room. Something menacing in Shade's expression must have been apparent, because Sylvia opened the bottle, and with shaky hands counted some pills out for her.

"That's all I can spare. You can let yourself out now."

Shade had scared her, but she didn't feel much regret over it. Sylvia had tried to manipulate and play her. She tucked the pills into her coat, tossed some money on the bed, and left the same way she came in.

God, she was tired of this shit. She didn't want to troll the bars tonight, and she didn't want to call anyone she knew. There was no fucking way she would compare every woman she came across with Raven. Damn her. She just wanted to kick back and enjoy some good company with people who didn't expect anything from her.

She called Tiffany on her way home, made plans for dinner, and to spend the evening with her, Angel, and Kat. Plus, they could talk more about their past lives. That shit was cool.

❖

Raven managed to make it through the rest of the day in a professional manner. She took calls, answered e-mails, and checked in with Sunny, who was taking the day off.

She seemed to know instinctively how to differentiate between those who really needed help and the ones who were screaming for attention.

The people she felt concern for, she put to one side. So far, the poltergeist call kept the top spot. The caller had sent pictures and a short video of the midnight activity in her kitchen while she and her family were sleeping. Raven watched it several times to analyze its authenticity. With all the fancy editing programs in the market today, it was imperative.

She detested posers and liars. Whispering Winds received their fair share over the years. If they didn't believe, why didn't they just avoid the store?

One time, unbeknownst to her mother, she'd once cursed one of the horny, sarcastic college boys who wouldn't leave her alone, with a severe case of night terrors. Raven even kept a straight face when he returned four nights later for something to make them go away.

She kept waiting for the spell's backlash, but after three years, she hadn't received any. She either slipped under the radar or, more likely, the Universe decided it was an apt punishment for the way he treated her. Karma could be an awesome thing as well.

It was past closing time, so she switched the phone to the answering service, gathered the stack of messages together, and headed upstairs. Tiffany had already left for the day, and Shade had never come back.

Raven walked cautiously through Shade's door, a little apprehensive, but really hoping Shade would be waiting for her.

The office was empty, as she knew it would be.

Raven stroked the end of Shade's desk absently. It smelled like her, the CK One had left a permanent imprint in the fabrics of the room. The scent stirred a physical reaction, but it also tweaked her embarrassment. Raven had to go find Shade and hope she would forgive her. Like her sister had, she needed to come clean.

She turned the lights off on her way out.

Raven did a drive-by, the one she swore she would never do, of Shade's house. Her van was in the driveway. Raven turned her car around at the next intersection, pulled to the curb, and prayed for strength and clarity. She actually knew a spell for that—but there was no way she was going to try it right now.

The door opened before she reached it. Shade stood backlit from the hall light. The longing in her soul tripled, and then doubled back again, twisting inside her painfully.

Shade simply stepped aside to let her in. Raven brushed against her, and the contact sent tingles along the right side of her body.

She stopped. The house was clean, and surfaces sparkled. She felt her mouth drop open. Shade put a hand to the small of her back to prompt her forward into the living room.

"Wow."

"I know, right? It seems you woke a sleeping giant." Shade wrapped an arm around her hip and walked her into the living room.

In more ways than one. She had to tell her right now, before something happened. "I have to tell you something."

"Tell me back here," Shade said.

Raven wanted Shade, but not like this.

She twisted to the side and stepped away from her. "I said I have to tell you something."

Shade grinned and threw herself down on her recliner. "So talk."

Raven sat on the arm of the chair. "Please don't be mad at me."

Shade's half smirk kicked Raven's senses into overdrive. Oh God, she knew already. Raven was so embarrassed. "Why did you jump me if you knew?"

"Lessons, young grasshopper. Be careful what you wish for." Shade's voice was slurring slightly. Raven wondered how much she'd had to drink before she arrived.

She felt like a fool, and when she felt stupid, she got angry. "You attacked me and laid hands on me knowing what I did? Do you think I'm a joke?"

"Turnaround is fair play. Don't do your mojo shit on me, Raven."

Red temper spots appeared in Raven's vision. "But—"

"I'm not going to play games with you."

"How could you?" Raven sputtered before cussing her out in Spanish while she stalked around the room and pointed at her, then colorfully swore at her some more in an effort to wipe the stupid smile off Shade's face.

"What? What are you saying?"

Raven switched back to English. "I can't believe how cruel you can be."

"Wait a minute, let me break this down for you, sweetheart— you cast a spell on *me*, which I recognized. I do exactly what *you* wanted me to do—and *I'm* the bad guy? How screwed up is that? If you want to fuck again, Raven, you could have just asked, and got in line."

Ouch, that hurt. Raven lowered her voice. "You were lucky to have me. I've seen the trash you've slept with."

"Yeah? Well, *you* slept with me."

Raven gathered her power. She was going to hit her with something, anything that would match the way Shade's horrible words had just cut her.

Before Raven let her energy loose, Shade's power came out to meet hers, spiking the ozone in the room, leaving a faint trail of red lightning discernible in the air.

Her temper was beyond the flashpoint, but Raven made a huge effort to pull back because she knew she wasn't nearly strong enough to win this fight.

"That all you got, kid? Because I have a dinner date with someone else."

"I hate you." Raven picked up her purse and left.

Chapter Four

Ten days later

A sickly green glow lit the tunnel that stretched endlessly into the distance. The walls seemed to expand and contract with her labored breath. Shade had been trapped and lost in the dark for an eternity. She wasn't alone, of course. She was never alone. The dead screeched and moaned, reaching for her with bloody hands as she ran.

They were the least of her problems. Other things lurked in the shadows as well. She could hear them, slithering and hissing in the background. Maniacal laughter echoed off the walls, always keeping her off balance, her nerves on fire.

She was exhausted, and though she didn't want to admit it, terrified of what was happening. Time kept twisting around itself as she struggled to grasp reality. She knew who she was, but couldn't remember anything of her life or anyone in it.

When she couldn't run anymore, she slid down the slimy wall to sit on the spongy floor. The feeble light went out, and the dark settled in around her, forced itself into her pores, suffocating her.

Where the fuck was she?

She was everywhere, yet nowhere.

The deafening rhythmic pounding was driving her crazy, and she held her hands over her ears. The thumping continued and increased in volume until she wanted to scream, but she was afraid if she started, she would never, ever stop.

Her sweat-soaked hair stuck to her neck, and the muscles in her legs cramped from running. As soon as she closed her eyes, a hand gripped her neck from behind and squeezed.

❖

Raven was sitting in the chair next to the bed and startled when she thought she heard a loud exhale in the corner, though she couldn't see anything. She searched Shade's face for any signs of awareness, but found none. The monitors continued their beeping, reminding her that if there had been any changes, the intricate machines would have picked them up.

She dismissed the noise and smoothed Shade's dark hair back, running her fingers through the uneven lengths. If it weren't for the purple bruising under her eyes, Shade would look almost peaceful, a direct contrast to the tough image she presented to the world at large.

The jagged wounds and bruises from the bombing had mostly healed, thanks to Aura's and Tiffany's sessions. But it remained to be seen if her fractured spine would ever heal enough to allow her to walk again. Raven refused to consider any outcome that wasn't for Shade's greatest possible recovery.

Raven traced the contours of Shade's face lightly with her fingertips, silently begging her to wake up. She smoothed the covers around her legs, as she'd done at least sixteen times that night.

Her hands saw what was hidden from her eyes. Shade had lost weight, and the hard muscles in her thighs were already weakening from her forced inactivity.

The door opened, and Mary, the night nurse, walked over to the bed, her soft-soled shoes gliding noiselessly on the linoleum floor. "Still here? Visiting hours were over hours ago." Mary winked at her.

The nurses were well aware she spent every night here with Shade, but she usually wasn't awake when Mary came in during the wee hours. "I don't ever want her to be alone."

Mary looked at her thoughtfully. "I've always believed that some part of the patient's consciousness can hear us."

"Yes," Raven said, stroking the back of Shade's hand. "I believe she knows I'm here."

"I don't think she's been alone since she got here." Mary scribbled in Shade's chart.

"No. And she won't be either."

Mary smiled. "How long have you two been together?"

"Not long." For the thousandth time since Shade's accident, Raven wished she could take back her words. *I hate you.* It broke her heart to think those words could be the last thing she ever said to Shade, even if she *had* deserved it at the time.

I love you. Please come back. I didn't mean it.

Raven had gone over that fight over and over. If she hadn't been embarrassed and flustered, she'd have known Shade hadn't meant the horrible things she'd said either.

Shade had been trying to protect Raven—from Shade.

During the long days and nights that Shade had been hospitalized, Tiffany often sat with Raven. She was a good listener. Though she was reluctant at first, she agreed that when Shade showed her fangs, the behavior came from her absolute fear of commitment.

The time they spent together watching over Shade was in close quarters, which meant there wasn't any hiding from Tiffany's mind reading abilities. Raven didn't mind much, as she was grateful she finally had someone to talk to about Shade's side of things, someone to give her insight and hope.

More than anything, she wanted a spell to wake her up, but her mother, Sunny, and Aura expressly forbid her to use any. Raven burned to defy that order, but promised she wouldn't after she was told that Shade could bring something bad back with her from the other side.

No one wanted to take the chance that Shade's consciousness would remain in the dark, possibly leaving her body and mind open to possession. The only person who knew if it could happen was Shade, and they couldn't ask her.

"In any case," Mary said, "I'm sure that *when* she wakes up, she'll be glad to know how many people love her."

Raven sighed. "I hope it's soon."

"Well, then." Mary rechecked the IV line. "Good night. The morning shift change is in an hour and a half or so. I'll see you tomorrow."

"See you." Raven waved halfheartedly while she settled back into the armchair next to the bed. She'd already been up for twenty three hours, the charm she'd done on herself was wearing off, and she was too tired to replenish it. Magic required energy, and it was the one commodity she had too little of right now.

She let herself drift off to the interminable beeping of the machines around her.

❖

Shade frantically tried to pry the icy hand off her neck, but it was too slippery. She was dangerously close to losing her grip, and the phantom fingers dug deeper into her esophagus. She felt her eyes bulge from the pressure, and her vision began to dim.

She wasn't going, not without a fight. In a last-ditch effort, she gathered what little strength she had left, forced her screaming muscles to work, and gained her feet. With a sharp twist of her torso, she tore free. The air she gulped felt like fire in her lungs.

The faint whispers in the dark became louder, and she tried not to pay attention because they were meant to be a distraction, to scare her. If she could get a grip on what was happening, she could find a way out of this nightmare.

No way out.

No, no.

Not for you.

The giggle that followed the creepy voice chilled Shade to the bone. "What the fuck is going on?" she yelled. "Show yourself."

Heavy footsteps pounded toward her from behind. They grew louder, until the vibration of them caused loose rocks to tumble from the curved sides of the tunnel to settle around her feet. Shade's gut clenched.

She knew she didn't have the energy in her current condition to fight whatever was approaching. She took another ragged breath before she turned and fled in the opposite direction.

Into the blackness.

Her legs were too tired to run in a straight line, and she continued to stumble and bounce off the walls. She strained to see but remained blind.

The dark was complete, final.

There was a flash up ahead. A small weak light in the distance flickered on and off twice before growing marginally brighter until it was constant.

With something to focus on, Shade forced herself to keep moving. The jarring footsteps were gone, but she wasn't going to look back or take any chances. She would keep going until she dropped from the effort.

She ran for what seemed like hours, but the light never grew bigger, it stubbornly stayed the same size. She'd briefly lived in Arizona once, and the mountains produced the same illusion. They appeared to be close enough to reach in a day, but in actuality, the peaks were miles farther than she ever thought.

As soon as she thought about the desert sands, the ground beneath her shifted. Deep drifts appeared, slowing her stride, until she fell forward. Shade managed to get her hands in front of her, but she still ended up with a mouth full of granules. She tried to get up again, but her muscles refused to obey.

In the distance, she could hear the thunder of approaching footsteps again.

She couldn't run anymore, but she'd fight on her back if she had to.

God, she was so thirsty. She would give anything for something to drink.

The sand vanished from underneath her, and she dropped into icy water. The cold temperature forced what little breath she had left from her lungs. She searched for the surface, but she dropped like a stone into the inky depths.

Her limbs jerked and convulsed, as she fought for oxygen. Though she knew to take a breath was to die, reflex took over, and she inhaled deeply, gulping liquid in a frantic attempt to breathe. The water burned as it traveled down her throat, into her lungs to suffocate her.

Her terror lifted as she stopped struggling and allowed the water to take her.

Dying wasn't so bad, she thought. She felt weightless and completely without pain. She was so damn tired of fighting.

A sense of peace and well-being filled her, and wonderful emotions replaced her doubt and fear with warmth. If she'd known it felt this good, she'd have died a long time ago.

She opened her arms and let go.

❖

Raven stood at the edge of a high cliff. The large canyon below her spread out like a gargantuan red blanket. Her hair lifted in the wind, and she spread her arms wide to the setting sun. Vivid hues of fire burned across the sky in its wake, painting the sky with dark red, yellow, and purple. The perfect beauty of it ached in her chest, and she gave thanks to the wonders of Mother Earth.

Her foot slipped from underneath her, sending rocks, then boulders, tumbling down the mountainside. She windmilled her arms to catch her balance, but the edge crumbled, and she fell. It happened so fast, the scream in her throat never materialized. Raven smashed against the rock face, bounced off it, and continued her descent.

Trees and brush went by in a blur as she frantically tried to grab something to stop her fall. Faster and faster she slid, until she hit the end of a ledge and bounced out into nothing but air.

Rising up to meet her was a rushing river, and she knew that to hit it at this velocity would be like hitting cement. She braced herself for the impact.

Don't panic. It's a dream, only a dream. Take control.

Raven slowed her fall and slid into the river effortlessly.

She tread water while the current took her over the rapids and into a deep pool. She used a powerful sidestroke to reach the bank and then pulled herself out to catch her breath.

The large rock she sat on had been worn smooth from the river, and Raven watched the full moon rise slowly, until the area was lit by its glow. She could see a small clearing of grass on the other side of the river, framed by tall trees.

The night air felt alive with the song of crickets and the rushing river. She watched a small fallen log float downstream until it was almost parallel to her. It twisted in the eddy, and Raven saw a flash of pale skin.

It wasn't a tree; it was a person. Without hesitation, she threw herself back into the water. She cut through the current until she reached the body. Her heart thumped in her chest. She couldn't make out her features, but Raven would know that Led Zeppelin T-shirt anywhere.

Shade.

Raven's adrenaline powered her into action. She pushed Shade's limp body to the opposite side of the bank, until she had her footing and was able to pull her out of the water. She dropped to her knees beside her and checked her pulse.

Nothing.

Shades skin was icy cold, and in the glow from the moon, her lips were a dark purple. Raven began CPR, drawing deep breaths to fill Shade's lungs with life. She carefully counted the chest compressions before repeating the process.

Once, twice, three times.

Again.

Raven refused to give up. *With this breath, I give to thee, life to live, and part of me. Eyes shall open, heart shall beat, as I will it, so shall it be.*

When there was no response, tears fell and she started the process from the beginning. It didn't matter that this was a dream. If Shade believed she was dying here, in this place, she would die in both worlds.

One second, she was peaceful, floating, happy, and the next, her nose was being pinched and she couldn't breathe again. Shade struck out blindly but stopped when she heard a cry. She tried to open her eyes, but instead turned and leaned on her side while water came up from her stomach in streams, nearly choking her again while someone pounded on her back.

She was confused. Her brain felt fuzzy. She couldn't remember where she was or who else was here.

She sensed echoes of the fear she'd held while being chased, but it felt as if it were eons ago. The coughing fit finally ended, and she dropped onto her stomach.

A soothing, trilling noise sounded from her right.

It took enormous effort, but Shade finally opened her eyes and saw a giant black bird hovering over her. The sound of beating wings thundered in her ears. The bird cawed, raising the hair on her neck.

Shade tried to talk but couldn't manage any sound and couldn't move.

Panic crowded her consciousness, accelerating her pulse, closing her throat. A loud growl erupted from the trees near the side of the clearing.

It was too much for her to process, and she let herself slip back into the darkness.

Again.

❖

Raven felt tears on her lashes before she opened her eyes. She'd brought the acute feeling of helplessness back with her from the dream. Why hadn't she been able to tell Shade her name?

She'd saved her, had in fact put hands on Shade's astral body before she was thrown back into her own. She ignored her lightheadedness and got out of her chair to stand next to Shade's body lying in the bed. Raven's arms still had goose bumps from the chill on the other side.

"I won't give up. I promise you. I'll keep trying." Raven knew she didn't have the energy to try again this morning.

Daily visits from Aura, Sunny, and Tiffany had ensured that physically, Shade's body was continuing to heal at a rapid rate. The results of the brain scan the doctors ordered yesterday still showed brain activity. Her synapses showed they fired at a rapid rate and appeared normal. All of this still gave her hope.

But she didn't want to wait, damn it. She wanted to help now.

The day nurse came in to take Shade's blood pressure. The interruption and her seemingly careless handling of Shade's body pissed her off. Raven wanted to smack the bored expression off her face.

She forced herself to take a breath, then another. It wasn't the nurse's fault. Raven was exhausted and frustrated, and looking for a target to shoot her helplessness at.

"It's a tiny bit higher than it was," the nurse said and checked her chart. She placed her fingers on Shade's wrist to take her pulse. "If I didn't know better, I'd say she'd been up and walking around today."

Raven was elated. If Shade was physically reacting to Raven's presence *there*, by the same token, didn't that mean she was getting closer to her *here*—on this side?

The nurse left just as Aura walked in. Raven felt a rush of relief and quickly told her about the successful dream walk, and the change in Shade's vital signs.

"I had an idea that a force might be keeping her there against her will," Aura said while brushing Shade's hair back before kissing her cheek. "Good morning, sweetheart."

"What do I do now?" Raven asked.

"We wait. I don't recommend you try again until you've had a good rest. Your colors are very pale, and your mother is worried about you." Aura sat in the chair closest to the bed and rearranged her skirt before reaching into her big bag for her crocheting. "As am I."

"My mother just came home from her trip, and she's made it very clear she doesn't want me here at all," Raven said and looked at the floor.

"She doesn't have to like it, but she does understand why, Raven. That's what's important."

"The last two days, every time I try to talk to her about Shade, and ask for her help, she shuts down."

Aura smiled sadly. "Then she's only seen one side of our girl now, hasn't she? The necromancer, not the woman she is. I'll try and talk with her again."

Raven stretched and stifled a yawn. "Why did you and my mother want me to work at SOS? I mean, if she has such a problem with Shade?"

"Your mother and I have been good friends for almost twenty years, since you were a baby, but that's a discussion you'll have to have with her. After that, if you have more questions, just come and see me." Aura's crochet needle was twisting the yarn with lightning speed, even though Raven hadn't seen her look down once at the project in her lap.

"I'm afraid to go home," Raven said. "I want to be here when she wakes up."

Aura's head tilted slightly to the left, a mirror image of what Sunny did when she appeared to be listening to a voice no one else heard. "I still can't hear her," she said.

"You love her."

"Yes," Aura said. "Like my own daughter."

"What happened to her? Why is she so sad inside?"

"Honey, that's Shade's story to tell and something you should hear from her. I'll only say that she had a horrific childhood until we moved her into our home."

Raven nodded. There was no use in trying to wheedle any more information. This family of women stuck together like glue, and their loyalty was stellar. She would do the same in their position and she wasn't completely inside the circle, yet.

"Honey, go home now. Get some rest."

Raven yawned and leaned down to kiss Aura's cheek. "Okay," she said. "But call me immediately if something changes, promise?"

Aura put down her crocheting and hugged her. Raven felt a tiny surge of electricity flow through her body. "Thanks," she said.

"Just a little something-something for the ride home." Aura smiled gently. "Drive careful."

"I will. Don't forget to—"

"Call you, yes, I know. Don't worry. I'll be here for a few more hours, then Tiffany and Kat are coming in for their shift."

"Bye." Raven walked down the hall to the elevator and leaned against the wall while she waited. She was soul tired, even with the healing energy Aura had given her. She didn't want to take the time to rest, but the lower the elevator descended, the more exhausted she became, until when she got out in the lobby, she knew she had no choice but to sleep when she got home.

It was either that or pass out cold in public.

Raven was in her car and pulling out of the parking lot when she felt another psychic push to keep her awake. *Thanks again, Aura.* She made it home safely, if not entirely lucid. After entering the house, she went straight to her room and fell across her bed fully dressed. She was asleep within seconds.

❖

Wolves stirred in the underbrush, just beyond the light of the fire. The eerie howls tickled the hair on the back of her neck, and made her chest ache with their yearning.

Shade opened her eyes slowly, and a full moon in a night sky full of thousands of stars shone brightly above her. She took a few deep breaths to prove she could. She didn't sense anything or anyone, but the nagging feeling everything was wrong and out of place didn't leave her. Her head was clearer than it had been, and she didn't feel disoriented, she just wanted answers.

She felt a raindrop hit her cheek, then another, but no clouds were above her. *Shade, come back to us. Please. We miss you so much.*

Shade's stomach twisted with grief. She knew that voice. Another drop hit her face, and she reached up to brush her cheek, tasted the drop on the tip of her tongue.

Salty. Not rain, she realized, but tears.

You have to fight. Don't give up. We're here for you.

Something in her mind shifted, and she attempted to sit up, but was once again knocked flat by the pain shooting through her spine. "I can't see you!" Bits and pieces of the past came back to her, and loving memories attached themselves to the melodic voice she could hear, but not reach.

"Aura?"

Thrashing erupted in the bushes. Branches bent, then broke and the air filled with the sounds of snarls and howls of pain. Shade shot a wary look to the left, away from the smoldering fire. The wolves looked frantic as they backed away from the forest, the hair on their backs stood straight up. *Shit. That can't be good.*

Two excruciatingly loud sonic booms vibrated the ground under her. The trees that encircled the clearing shook, and leaves showered to the ground before limbs began to crack and fall around her.

The wolves whimpered and scattered, leaving Shade alone with the dying fire. She managed to get onto her side and pull herself along the forest floor by her elbows toward a large boulder almost twenty feet away. She was nearly there when the malicious laughter began, and the evil that emanated within it froze her blood, and paralyzed her.

You didn't think it would be easy, did you?

Shade felt her eardrums strain and pop from the volume of the voice. She was scared out of her skull, but she wasn't going to die until she faced whatever it was that came for her. She bit her lip against the pain and rolled over again.

She had two seconds before she passed out again to wish she hadn't bothered.

❖

It was dark outside. Raven checked her clock, surprised to find that she'd been out for almost ten hours. She should have been back at Shade's side by now.

She hadn't taken two steps toward her door before she staggered and leaned against the wall. She didn't feel refreshed at all. If anything, she felt the same as she did before she went to sleep.

Maybe a shower would help. When she'd finished, she was on her way back to her room when her mother stopped her in the hallway. "No, mija. You need to stay home tonight. You're too drained to be out on the roads, or to help anyone."

Raven couldn't argue with the tired part. The cold water hadn't helped wake her up either. Still, she felt a spark of temper. "Why are you so against me being with Shade in the hospital? She needs me."

"No, Raven."

Her mother's expression was closed off, and her tone matched the finality of her statement. Once again, she felt like a small child being told she couldn't do something, though she felt an absolute need to do it. This was where the fights with her mother always started. And the more her mother pushed against her doing something, the faster Raven ran toward it.

Dios, she had no energy to argue right now. Instead, she sidestepped her mother, entered her room, and opened a drawer to find a pair of yoga pants to make sure she was comfortable while trying to rest in such a hard environment.

"Why are you so stubborn?" Her mother sat on the edge of Raven's bed.

Raven smiled in spite of her irritation. "I came by it honestly."

"Sit down, *por favor*."

She finished dressing and then sat next to her mother, who wrapped an arm around her shoulders. Raven was struck with the familiarity of love and laid her head on her shoulder. Her mother began rocking and humming an old traditional lullaby she'd used to put the children to bed. The soothing motion and melody had her melting into her mother's side. It brought Raven to a lovely place, when things were simple, and they weren't at odds all the time.

Unexpectedly, she began to cry. The self-imposed pressure she'd heaped on herself after Shade's accident began to lift. She hadn't realized how scared she'd been because she'd refused to acknowledge it. That was the thing about fear and denial, both bit you in the ass when you least expected it. It was time to face it head on.

"Mama, do you think she's going to die?"

Her mother's grip around her tightened, but she remained quiet. Her silence caused Raven's stomach to cramp, and she cried harder. "Please tell me."

"Only if you get back in bed and stay there until morning."

Raven shook her head. "No, it's my job."

"It is not. Your job is as a receptionist, not a babysitter."

Why did her mother sound so cold? How could she talk to her about how she felt if she wouldn't listen? Raven needed to throw down a virtual gauntlet, set an adult boundary. She wasn't a child anymore. "Mama, I love Shade."

Her mother's expression remained closed and she stayed silent.

"Did you hear me?" Raven asked.

"Sí."

"Aren't you going to say anything?"

"I'm thinking of how I'm going to say it."

Raven's cell phone vibrated on the nightstand, and she jumped to answer it. Tiffany's number appeared on the screen. "Hello?"

"Hi, Raven. I wanted to call and let you know I'm taking your shift at the hospital tonight. Kat took Angel to the city, and I don't want to stay home alone."

"Weren't you supposed to move back to your old house today?"

"Originally. Jordan's friend completed the remodeling, but we decided to put it on the market instead. We'll be looking for a new place to live in the next couple of weeks."

Raven thought that was a good thing. Of course Tiffany and her family wouldn't want to stay in that house. A fresh start would be good for them.

"So, listen," Tiffany said. "How about you come in the morning, and we can have breakfast together."

"Are you sure?" Raven asked. She hadn't missed a night since Shade was hurt, and she was anxious to see if she could reach her again.

"I'm positive. In fact, I'm already here with her. Take a break, Raven. I'll call you if anything changes."

What could she do but agree? "All right. I'll see you about seven thirty?"

"That sounds fine. Good night."

"Good night." Raven placed the phone back on the table.

"So, you're staying home tonight?"

"Apparently." She looked down at her clothes and then went back to her dresser for pajamas. She was disappointed, but a full night's sleep in an actual bed was undeniably appealing.

"I'll make you something to eat," her mother said. "Go on, get in. I'll bring it to you and we'll talk."

Raven finished changing and got into bed, under the covers this time. Blanca, her white cat, joined her. She petted her absently, noticing the tangles in her normally pristine coat. "I'm sorry. I've been neglecting you."

There was no recrimination coming from Blanca, who continued to purr and knead Raven's comforter while she combed the cat's fur with her fingers. She rested with her eyes closed until her mother came in with a plate for her.

To Raven's surprise, without a word, her mother climbed into bed with her. Her energy was heavy with—what? It was unfamiliar. "Is everything okay with you?"

The silence lasted.

"Mama?"

"I tried everything to keep this from happening." Her mother's expression was one of sadness.

Raven shivered as her mother continued.

"All those years ago, I saw this, and I prayed for it not to be true."

"What?" Raven asked the question, but she knew the answer. Her mother knew she'd been with Shade. Of course she would. She briefly wondered what it would have been like to grow up in a normal family, where such things were kept secret.

But her mother didn't answer. She kept talking to the wall and didn't meet Raven's eyes. "I kept the two of you apart by any means necessary."

"Look at me," Raven said. "Mama, please, I need to know."

Her mother wiped her eyes with a tissue she'd pulled from her pocket, and finally looked at her.

Resignation.

That's the energy her mother wore, and that—more than anything—scared her the most. Her mother was never defeated; she was the strongest woman Raven had ever met.

"What did you see?"

Her mother sighed heavily, her entire manner one of reluctance.

"The necromancer and the witch."

CHAPTER FIVE

Shade came back to consciousness slowly.

She was back in the tunnel.

The agony was omnipresent. It took on a life of its own and became the only thing to exist during, and between, each breath.

It was cold and she was soaking wet. The pain and the nagging feeling she was missing a critical piece of information wouldn't ease. She felt a sense of urgency, and she knew if she didn't solve the puzzle soon, she'd be here forever.

Lost inside a demented board game, do not pass go, do not collect...

She managed to turn her head to look down the tunnel and saw a light in the distance.

Realization came in tiny degrees, until her location was clear. The astral plane she traveled as a necromancer. The place she used to kick ass, take names, and force the dead to give up their secrets.

Her short-term memory told her she'd been here for an eternity. She closed her eyes and strained for more answers. *Come on...how did I get here?*

In her mind, she saw fire, burning with intense flashes of orange and red, but attempting to look past the black smoke only intensified the stabbing pain in her temples.

She couldn't find her lifeline, her connection to her physical body. Trapped in this nightmare, she tried not to give her fear validity, but trembled at the thought she might be dead after all. *Is this it, then? Is this what hell is like?*

A nasty hissing noise came from the other direction.

"Lay-see."

Fucking awesome. A tortured spirit who knew her name.

"Ish Mommy!"

"Oh, hell no." Shade fought the ball of nausea forming in her stomach and turned away from the light.

Story of her life.

"Waiting for you."

"Wait a little longer, would you?" Shade was furious and forced herself to her feet, surprised at the lack of pain in her back.

A cacophony of blood-curdling screams pressed in on her eardrums, and the reverberation through the tunnels intensified the pressure until she was sure they were going to burst.

Clods of dirt hit her in the back, and hands burst through the walls, waving maniacally in their blind attempts to grab her.

One made contact with her arm, and it burned along her skin like a razor blade. The claws left three bloody scratches in their wake.

She backed away from the attack and into a body, and she whirled to face her mother.

Bile burned in the back of her throat when she got a good look at her. In the decades since seeing her first dead person, Shade had been spared seeing her mother's death mask.

Now she saw the full impact of her murder. The left side of her face was sunken from what must have been a powerful blow that appeared to have broken her cheekbone. Her head tilted at an odd angle, the result of having her throat cut from ear to ear, a gaping tear that left little to support the weight of her skull.

Her mother smiled at her obvious discomfort, but Shade found it impossible to spare even an ounce of pity for the woman who had sold her when she was eight years old.

"Ungrateful leech. You were lucky I waited that long."

Shade's body shook with the force of her anger. "Did you really just fucking say that? No wonder you're stuck here."

A whistling, sucking sound resembling a laugh erupted from her mother's open throat. It was just wrong, Shade thought, vile and wrong. She had to get away while she still had respite from the pain in her back.

Shade dodged left and right as she ran back toward the light. She looked back once, to see her mother's body twitching and convulsing while she continued to laugh.

"Hey, Lacey! Ask yourself why you're here."

Shade's step faltered, and a screeching roar from her right nearly cost her her balance before she shifted and ran straight into a giant set of talons that had materialized and sideswiped her into the spongy wall. She slid to the rocky floor, the force of the blow knocking the wind out of her lungs, and though she tried, she couldn't move.

Her body trembled against her will, and she wanted to throw up. A dragging noise drew near from the dark, and the closer it got, the farther the light withdrew. The tiny source was nearly imperceptible when her mother reappeared and toed her in the ribs with one bare foot. The other was still clad in a broken high heel.

"This is insane," Shade said. "Get away and stop looking at me. Your face is freaking me the fuck out."

"Not happening." Her mother clapped. *"You can't control the demons you need to face. They are the consequences of the life you chose to live."*

"I didn't choose you." Shade's jaw clenched.

"Yes, you did."

Shade cringed at the sight of her broken teeth behind the torn lip. "I fail to see why or how I would choose a selfish, narcissistic bitch who would never love anyone but herself."

Rage boiled alongside her exhaustion, and Shade was surprised to find power sliding along her skin. It was warm and loving, and so out of context of where she was currently trapped. But it wasn't nearly enough. She still couldn't find the strength to get up.

Shade knew her mother also sensed the new intrusion, and she turned and sniffed the air, obviously looking for the source.

One second, she was standing in front of her, the next, a hurricane force wind blew her mother back the direction she'd come from. It hadn't even moved a hair on Shade's head.

The silence that followed unnerved her a little, but the anticipation of waiting to see what would happen next was worse.

A large beacon of light spun in a circle a few yards away, and each time it swept past her, she could hear the sounds of women weeping softly.

"Come back to us."

"We're waiting for you."

And just that quickly, between one heartbeat and the next, Shade recognized Sunny's and Tiffany's voices. More portions of her adult memory returned. Her love for her chosen sisters swelled in her heart, and a small spark of hope ignited.

"I'm here," Shade yelled. "Right here!" She attempted to stand, to look for their energy lines, to find her way back. She braced against the wall, but when she was halfway up, the beacon disappeared and she heard the double click of a shotgun being locked and loaded.

Fire shot up from the ground.

Shade froze, and the flames consumed her.

❖

Raven stared at her mother. "What about the necromancer and the witch?"

The question hung in the air for a few seconds. Finally, her mother answered. "Later. First, mija, ask your questions."

"All right. Why is Shade stuck on the astral plane and how did my dream tie into it?"

"Spontaneous. It's been known to happen when there is a strong connection between couples. It was your intention to meet with her. Your subtle body, your dream self, creates a reality like a movie set that you build with your beliefs and psyche."

"So, I created the river Shade was drowning in?"

"Sí," her mother said. "By your intention and longing to save her." Her mother cleared her throat. "And because of the physical bond you share, you merged into her reality."

Raven didn't feel the mortification she assumed she would when her mother acknowledged her sexual relations with Shade;

she only wanted more information. "Yes, our realities combined, but she threw me out of it."

"It only seems so. The coma keeps her trapped between this world and the next."

"How do I help her, Mama?"

"You can't, mija. It's her reality now. Shade must decide if she wants to return. It's her own demons that keep her trapped."

Raven didn't like that answer one little bit, as it continued to leave her feeling helpless. If knowledge was power, she wanted more.

"I'm angry with Shade," her mother said. "She didn't come to me before knowing you intimately."

"Why on earth should she?" Raven's defensiveness triggered. "I'm an adult now."

"Respect, mija. She should have stated her intentions."

"Mama, she does nothing but push me away."

Her mother blinked. "That's not what I see, and I feel the pain she leaves you with. Had I known of it, I would have forbidden you to see her."

Raven was both angry and embarrassed, and the word slipped out before she considered the impact. "Whatever."

Instantly, her mother's lips tightened into a line, and the worry lines in her forehead deepened.

Raven was aware, and instantly regretted the petulance in her tone. "I'm sorry I hurt you, Mama. I don't mean to."

Her mother's eyes widened slightly, and Raven was once again reminded of the difficult child she must have been over the years. She'd never given much thought previously on how her words and attitude had affected her until this last week. "Por favor, tell me what you saw regarding the necromancer and the witch."

It was a long minute before her mother began talking. "It started with a vision of clouds in the crystal ball. They rolled violently with thunder and lightning for a long time, then the mist began to part, revealing a cold and dark place. A cave carved in rock, a fire in the middle of the space. Wolves howled in the distance, making my heart ache. A woman limped wearily out of the tunnel in the back of the cave and sat down to warm herself. Dark energy surrounded her, heavy and stagnant. I could feel her dilemma. It held her heart in a vice and burned her mind.

"The necromancer faced the flames, while behind her I could see a young witch, inexperienced, but powerful. Impulsive, but full of fiery passion for life."

Raven hadn't been aware she was holding her breath until her lungs burned, and she was forced to draw in a breath. Her mother's voice was trancelike and quiet. She didn't want to interrupt with any questions yet.

"On the other side," her mother continued, "was a seductive demoness, representing all the darkness the necromancer held inside. It was a time of choosing. She could no longer walk with a foot in each world."

The anticipation was killing Raven. She whispered, "What did she choose, Mama?"

Her mother took her hand. "She chose the dark, *mija*."

"Oh." Disappointed and hurt, Raven looked down at her blankets. "Oh."

"Then the witch followed the necromancer into the darkness with the demoness, and I watched the light of her soul extinguish, swallowed into the other realm."

Raven's first impulse was to argue, to alter the vision her mother had had, so Raven could win in the end. But she didn't. Instead, she spoke carefully, addressing her mother's feelings. "That must have been terrifying for you."

"Who are you and what have you done with *mija*?"

Raven shrugged. "Maybe I'm growing up."

"You will always be my beloved baby."

Raven didn't want to give up just yet. "Can you tell me more please?"

Her mother shook her head, but Raven felt the undercurrent of unsaid words, something her mother wasn't willing to share. "I assumed, if I kept you two apart, I could prevent what I saw in my vision. Aura and I discussed the possibility of her version of the vision."

"That's another thing," Raven said. "Exactly how does Aura tie in to this?"

"She called me after Shade came to see me years ago. She'd had the same precognition of events, but interpreted it with her own perception."

Raven still had a chance then. "But you wanted to protect me."

"Aura loves Shade. Of course she would predicate toward her best interest. As your mother, I wasn't willing to take the chance, and nothing she could say would make me change my mind. I was determined to keep you two apart."

"Mama, you should have known better. The harder you pushed, the more I ran to do whatever it is you didn't want me to."

The laugh lines around her mother's eyes appeared. "Just like your father. You are the one most like him you know, the tiny image of him I looked into each day. He was so contrary."

Raven's throat tightened. Her father had committed suicide when she was four. "I'm sorry for being the one who reminded you of him."

Her mother patted her hand. "No, never be sorry for that. Your father was the love of my life."

"But he chose to end his life."

The air in the room turned sad and bitter, and Raven saw the tears gathering in her mother's eyes. She'd only seen her mother cry a handful of times in her life. "Mama?" Surprise turned to concern. "What haven't you told me?"

❖

With each step Shade took, she felt as if hours passed. The walk toward the light was unending, as she knew it would be.

During the eternity, she struggled to put together the pieces of memory she could recover.

Thanks to the visage of her mother, she recalled her childhood. Yay, Shade thought, she damn well could have done without that chunk. Those memories settled on her shoulders, a thousand pounds of resentment and betrayal, slowing her down even further.

Abruptly, the light in the distance turned red and grew larger. Shade continued to plod on, exhausted, but determined to reach it. The tunnels weren't safe, and although she hadn't been attacked again, she was still acutely aware of the sounds and scrabbling noises within the walls.

By the time she reached the source, she realized the light was coming from somewhere beyond a twist in the tunnel. Shade walked around the corner and saw yet another turn up ahead.

It could be a trap, but at this point, she didn't much care. She was going to reach her destination one way or another.

The journey continued on with its creepy Gothic effects. Intermittently, she would hear the sound of wings beating in the air above her. She shut them out the best she could, trying not to imagine how large the creature must be to cause such a wind in her face.

Icicles formed stalactites that dripped onto the spongy surfaces, and her breath was clearly visible as she folded her arms to tuck her hands under them.

At last, she walked around the last twist and came upon a chamber in a cave, where a fire burned within a sunken circle framed by stones.

Shade pushed herself the last twenty feet and sank gratefully beside it, holding her frozen fingers dangerously close to the flames to warm them.

In her mind, memories shuffled like a deck of cards and fought themselves for their proper order, until those that didn't make sense or fit flashed as insistently as a neon sign.

Beating wings.

Click. Fire. Pain.

Pain. Click. Fire.

Fire. Pain. Click.

Like a skipping, scratched CD repeatedly playing a string of chords over and over again.

Shade forced herself to quit trying. She should rest, as she had no idea what might happen next. She didn't have much of a choice anyway, after the forever-walk.

She'd depleted her last reserves, and reluctantly, she laid her head on her bended knees, hearing only the crackling sounds of branches on the fire.

As her thoughts began to drift, she heard birds calling in the distance. They were so out of context, she knew they had to be a clue, but it didn't stop her from sliding into sleep.

❖

"You're holding something back," Raven said. "I know you think you're protecting me, but I can handle it."

"Let me start at the beginning." Her mother sighed heavily and pulled her hand away from Raven's in order to cup her cheek. "But first, I want you to know, really know, that all of you were conceived in deep love."

Raven's face tingled where her mother touched her, and she felt the energy of love between them swell. But along with it, was an underlying current of grief.

Her mother's.

Raven didn't remember much about her father, since she'd been a toddler when he'd died. Her brother, Hawk Jr., had been her father figure for most of her life. She realized, as she felt the depth of her mother's pain, how blessed she'd been to be so young when he passed, she'd been spared the ache of missing him.

They never talked about it. Her older siblings were as closed on the subject as her mother. When Raven would question the aunties they would smoothly change the subject.

The weight of unspoken words hung between them. Raven recognized the moment as being monumental, certain to alter the way she perceived the world and her place in it.

"It wasn't the first time I'd had the vision," her mother finally said.

CHAPTER SIX

R aven walked into the hospital room and hesitated when she saw Sunny sitting next to the bed. She had only expected Tiffany to be present. She knew that Sunny was aware of her relationship with Shade, and although she knew it was absurd, Raven couldn't seem to help being deeply jealous. Not the in-your-face-get-away-from-my-lover jealous, but because Shade had loved Sunny so much. Something Raven wanted for herself.

"It's okay," Sunny said. "Jordan feels the same way."

Raven wanted a hole to open up right in the hospital floor so she could fall into it. She thought she'd put up excellent mind blocks this morning. It was discouraging. Why bother with it if Sunny and Tiffany could read through them? It was quite rude, actually.

What if someone wore something hideous to the office and it made their butt look big? That could get her into big trouble if her inner voice couldn't be stifled.

Tiffany laughed, lowering Raven's anxiety a bit, but when it subsided and trailed off, the room fell silent again.

"So," Sunny finally said. "I've brought something to see if it will bring Shade around."

"What?" Tiffany moved from her perch on the window seat.

Sunny reached into her bag. "I've brought the documentary my father made. Jordan took it to a place that transfers VHS tapes into DVDs."

Raven knew the circumstances that brought the friends together in the past, but she'd never seen the movie itself. She was excited. They'd all been eleven years old, the same age she had been when she met Shade for the first time.

"Do you really think it will work?" Tiffany asked. "God, I haven't seen that in ages."

"Jordan found it in the attic when she was moving boxes around."

"Have you watched it yet?" Tiffany placed her hands on Shade's legs and began to stroke them in long, smooth motions. Raven knew Tiffany was using Reiki to heal the muscles as best she could.

"I couldn't bring myself to," Sunny said. "But I thought it might help her come home, give her an anchor somehow."

Raven held her hand out for the video. "Here, sit down. I can do it."

"Thank you." Sunny touched her shoulder, and Raven felt her sincerity. There was no need for any hard feelings on either side, and for that, she was grateful. She inserted the disc and became engrossed when a distinguished man appeared on the screen.

Raven heard Sunny's sharp intake of breath as she saw her father. Her heart went out to her, but she had little to no memories of her own.

The camera panned left and stopped on a young girl with a riot of blond curls who was jumping up and down. "I'm so excited, I can hardly stand it!"

"You look exactly the same," Raven said.

"Thank you, but ssh." Sunny hushed her.

Raven dimmed her enthusiasm. Of course, it must be difficult for Sunny and Tiffany to see this. She could kick herself for seeming so blasé about something that meant so much to them. Raven had to remember she wasn't the center of this group of friends, the way she was with her own group. Sunny, Tiffany, and Shade were the primary trio, and as much as she hated it, she was still an outsider. She forced her shoulders to relax and turned her attention back to the screen.

The scene cut to an outside view of a driveway, and Sunny was running down to an old sedan that just pulled in. A woman got out and walked past her and up toward the camera.

"Oh," Tiffany said. "That's my aunt Darleen. She passed away not long after we filmed this. My mother didn't want me to do this documentary, and my aunt lied and told her we were going to Portland for the weekend."

"Why?" Raven asked. "I mean, why would you have to lie about it?"

"I'll tell you later. Let's watch," Tiffany said.

Little Sunny was leaning into the car, talking to someone who appeared to be reluctant to get out of the car.

"I was painfully shy," Tiffany said. "But God, the minute I saw Sunny, I felt connected. I may have been too young to articulate it then, but I knew there was something special about her."

Raven knew exactly what she meant. She'd felt it when she'd met Shade, but didn't bring up the similarity.

On the screen, a tiny red-haired girl finally got out of the car, holding Sunny's hand. The audio wasn't very good, and Raven had a hard time making out what they were saying. "What were you talking about?"

"I think that's when I saw her bi-colored eyes the first time." Tiffany smiled. "She told me she was an empath and could see spirits. I'd told her I had place memory, the ability to see things by touch."

"Ssh," Sunny said. "Here comes our Shade." Her voice choked off at the end of her sentence.

A large van that had clearly seen better days partially entered the camera's viewfinder. The side door opened, and a tall, skinny girl jumped out with a cigarette in her hand.

Raven noted the wrinkled, black clothes and the dark eyeliner that made her eyes look too large for her face. She looked haunted.

"Don't ever call me Lacey," young Shade said and flicked her cigarette to the curb.

Raven wanted to drink in every inch of her and commit it to memory. Even then, Shade wore her wounded, badass attitude. Her heart was breaking for her, the young girl who had to develop that protective persona at such a young age.

The van's loud muffler was still idling at the curb. Tiffany's and Sunny's voices were too low to be picked up, but Shade's came through loud and clear. "Necromancer," she said.

Raven heard a screech of tires and watched the van in the background speed off. Shade looked angry, Sunny looked puzzled, and Tiffany hid behind her. She leaned forward in her chair to hear better, but the screen shot went black.

Sunny hit the pause button. "God, how young we were. I'll never forget that day."

"Me either," Tiffany said. "It was the first time I had ever met anyone with psychic abilities, and neither of you appeared to be the spawn of Satan, as my mother warned." Tiffany continued to stroke Shade's legs. "Though at first, I was scared to death of Shade."

"I could never understand why her mother just dumped her there. Well, at that time anyway." She looked at Raven. "This next part has the scenes with my father talking to each of us about our past, when and how we realized we had powers. Don't get upset, but I'm going to skip them, as counseling sessions are extremely sensitive, private, and subject to doctor-patient rules of confidentiality."

"But wasn't this film released to the public?" Raven was curious, but she didn't want to press, as Sunny seemed very emotional about it.

"It's a documentary," Sunny said. "Various doctors and professionals in the field of parapsychology were invited to view it, but it wasn't seen on any public network, and it was long before reality television. I don't mind, really, but Shade can't give her consent right now."

"Thank you," Tiffany said. "I don't want to relive any of my mother's horror today either."

Raven totally understood but was more than a little disappointed to not have any more insight into how Lacey Stewart had become Shade. "Is there more to see?"

"Yes," Sunny said. "We have some experiments that my parents set up, and a ghost investigation." She stood abruptly, crossed to the bed, and touched Shade's cheek. "We're here, honey. Please come back to us."

"We love you," Tiffany said.

The day nurse came in and ordered them to move back. "Sorry, girls, time for vitals, blood draws, and clean sheets. I need some room. Wait outside."

The clipped tone of her voice had Raven sizing her up. She was young, slender, and just Shade's type. "You're new," she said between clenched teeth.

"Randi," she said. "I just transferred from another hospital." She whipped the curtain around the bed, blocking Shade from view. "Now, shoo. You can come back later."

Oh, hell no. Jealousy tightened her stomach muscles, and Raven narrowed her eyes at her. "I can change the bed."

"Sorry, hospital policy." Randi parted the curtain and smirked at her before disappearing behind it.

Raven took a step forward. She'd show Randi some *policy.* She reached for an intention to gather power and quickly tried to think of an appropriate spell, maybe some super-acne to make her less attractive? Yes, she decided, that would work.

Sunny hissed, grabbed her arm, and pulled her out of the room. "What's the matter with you? She's just doing her job. *And harm none.*"

Raven blustered and felt blood rush to her cheeks. "I…"

"Let's go now." Tiffany took hold of her other arm, and they marched Raven between them to the elevator. No one spoke as they made their way to the cafeteria.

She was embarrassed that she'd overreacted. It wasn't until they were seated with their drinks and food that Raven felt tears slipping down her cheeks. Her emotions were in freefall, and she was exhausted.

"So," Sunny said. "Do you want to tell us what that was about?"

❖

Shade opened her eyes. The last thing she recalled was the eternal run down the tunnels and curling up by the cave fire that was now almost ash. The dying embers gave little light to see by.

It was dark. Dark enough she couldn't see the walls of the cave. The air smelled singed, as it did after lighting off big firework displays on the Fourth of July.

She rested her head back on her knees. The movement sent shock waves up her spine and into her temples. Her sciatic nerves were on fire, spreading flames through the muscles in her lower back and down into her thighs.

Shade waited for the agony to plateau, to become manageable, but it didn't. It continued to increase, building a scream in her throat that would soon have to find its way out.

A disturbance from the back of the cave sent rocks to the ground, and Shade bit her lip to keep quiet. She felt the foreign energy increase around her. Menace skittered along her nerve endings and twisted her stomach into knots.

Her senses went hyper alert and kept her on the edge. The air shifted and moved, creating a barely perceptible breeze. She kept her gaze toward the sounds she couldn't see and finally saw movement in the dark, revealing a female form as it rose from a crouch. Dark wings spread into the space, blacker than the cave. Shade wanted to think this was an illusion, but she knew better.

This was true danger. Shade curled her hands into fists but was acutely aware her fighting skills were currently non-existent, and gave her a distinct disadvantage.

"Lacey."

The voice hissed her name out into two long syllables.

"Fuck off," Shade said.

A low, guttural sound came from the intruder, which she assumed was a laugh, but it still caused the hair on her body to rise, and chilled her to the bone.

"Fine then, *Shade*." The creature stepped closer, and the fire reappeared in the pit with a roar.

She was tall, Shade thought, at least six and a half feet. Her skin was bronzed by the firelight, but her hair was pure white, framing her face and cascading down her body to the back of her knees.

"Like what you see?"

Shade watched the demoness as she held her arms out and turned in a slow circle, flicking a whip into the air, producing a sharp cracking sound as she did so. Another log caught fire, illuminating more of the cave and the creature.

Not a whip, Shade realized, but a tail.

I am so fucked. She stared in disbelief as the creature drew closer.

"What's the matter, necromancer? Is the sight of my glorious body too much for you?"

Actually, it was the way she talked that disturbed Shade, the hissing at the end of each word. Well, that, the wings, and the goddamn tail. Other than that, she was exquisitely perfect.

Succubus.

The creature grinned and nodded. "Oh, you're very good."

"That's what they tell me." Shade hoped it came across as sarcastic, because she didn't want to admit, or show, the total terror she felt building. "What do you want?"

"The better question is, what do *you* want Lace—oops, Shade?" The succubus moved quickly, becoming a blur when Shade tried to gauge her distance. She crouched next to Shade and stuck out her hand. "Where are my manners? I'm Phaedra."

Her fingernails were extremely long, sharp tipped, and painted blood red. She ignored the extended hand, and instead closed her eyes, willing Phaedra to go away. When she opened her eyes again, she was still next to her staring at her with pale, ice-blue eyes. It freaked her out to see the diamond-shaped pupils. Like so much in this place, Phaedra was just *wrong.*

Phaedra sighed dramatically. "I so hoped we would be friends." She ran one pointed claw down Shade's cheek. "Oh, your skin is so delicate. My bad, you're bleeding. Sssweet."

Shade felt the wetness trickle down her face and cringed when Phaedra's long tongue swept out to lick it away.

"We're going to be good together." Phaedra sniffed the air and giggled. "You know, I can smell the fear. It makes me hot."

Shade looked away. She didn't have enough strength left to block her emotions, but she made a weak attempt anyway.

"That doesn't work in my house," Phaedra said. She pointed to a dark corner in the cave, and a wolf howled in pain. "All things here obey me." She pulled Shade's hair to turn her back around to face her, leaned down, and licked Shade's lips. "As will you."

Shade tried to loosen Phaedra's grip but couldn't budge it. "Let me loose."

"What's my name?"

"Why?" Shade asked.

"So you know whose name to scream out when I take you."

"That is so not fucking happening," Shade spit out between her teeth. Even as she refused, she felt her dark side spike with desire.

"Really?' Phaedra sat back on her heels. "What makes you think you can stop me? This can be as easy or as hard as you make it, but either way, I promise you'll love it."

That's exactly what Shade was afraid of. "I'm not just going to give it up."

"We're going to fight then?" Phaedra clapped with obvious glee. "Even better." She snapped her fingers. "Bring it on."

Shade felt a rush of energy fill her entire body, the pain disappeared, and she could move freely. But she was so stunned at how rapidly it happened, it was a full ten seconds before she stood. This was more like it. She grinned and started toward Phaedra, who'd moved to the center of the cave.

She managed two steps before she was flat on her back again. Shade rose and tried again, with the same result. Phaedra had barely flicked her wrist, and it felt as if she were hit with a ton of bricks.

"You disappoint me, necromancer. I thought you'd be full of fight." The hiss at the end of Phaedra's sentence turned to a purr.

Shade should be horrified but found she wasn't. "Just finding my bearings."

"From your back? Please."

Shade took the distraction as an advantage, rose again, threw a roundhouse punch, and hit Phaedra in the side of the head. She knew her fist connected, but Phaedra hadn't even moved with the force of her blow. Shade stood chest to chest with her and felt a shiver of fear when Phaedra's eyes turned red.

Shade's entire body lifted into the air, and she slammed against the wall on the opposite side of where she'd been standing. Her gasp of pain cut itself off as the air rushed from her lungs. Phaedra's hair stood virtually on end, snapping with electricity, along with her tail. "No quarter, no mercy."

With those words, Shade was pinned and unable to move again. When she felt her eyes begin to bulge with the effort she exerted to break free, she forced herself to relax and breathe. There had to be another way out. She could back off now and live to fight another day.

Phaedra smirked while she stared down at her with her reptilian eyes, and their hypnotic effect mesmerized Shade. When Phaedra pushed the darkness into her mind, Shade let herself fall back into unconsciousness.

❖

Raven wiped her face and squared her shoulders. She was embarrassed, but angry tears were the hardest, if not impossible, to hold back. She wished for the ten thousandth time that she had more control of her emotions.

"It comes with time," Tiffany said. She held Raven's hand in her own. "May I?"

Raven watched Tiffany close her eyes and felt a warm tingle along her scalp and the hand being held.

"Oh," Tiffany said. "Oh."

The urge to snatch her hand back was strong. Raven knew Tiffany had already seen her intimate encounters with Shade in great detail, but what bothered her most was opening up her family's business to someone else.

The sisters could read her thoughts, innermost desires, and secrets. After growing up in her own family, whose members could do the same, she'd thought she'd finally have some privacy.

That expectation just went out the window. "I'm having a hard time with this. It borders on rude."

"Don't be angry with us," Sunny said softly. "We have your best interest at heart. Truthfully, Shade is our first priority, but you're becoming part of the sisterhood we hold at SOS, and therefore, new family."

"I know we can be an intrusion." Tiffany let go of Raven's hand. "It's always been this way with us."

"It was small of me," Sunny said. "And I'll apologize for my snotty attitude when you first started working with us. I just didn't—and don't—want Shade to hurt again."

"I can totally understand that," Raven said. "But—"

"Jordan and I talked about it, and once I let that go, I could feel your genuine emotion, Raven. Shade's hospital room is full of your love and concern."

"You talked to Jordan?" Raven was stunned. "About how you felt about Shade? Doesn't she get jealous?"

Tiffany laughed. "That's a long story, for another time. The key to how this circle works is communication. We may be gifted, as you are, but talking things out is still the best way to handle it. Emotions can be all over the place, and they're not always clear until you vocalize them."

"Well," Raven said. "It's something to work on. And back off a little, would you?"

"Absolutely. Sometimes, I can't control it, and we're all exhausted. I'll make an extra effort, okay?"

"Me too," Tiffany said.

Sunny stared at Raven and lowered her voice before speaking again. "Raven? Do you really know what it would mean to love her?"

Raven wanted to snap back at her, and say that she wouldn't run like Sunny did. Then instant mortification hit her. "I'm so sorry. I didn't mean that, really."

"It's okay," Sunny said. "It will get easier with time, controlling impulsive thoughts. You're still young."

"She's attached to a need I have deep inside," Raven said quietly and placed her palm high on her stomach, beneath her breasts. "It seems as if I was born loving her. Does that make sense?" Raven shook her head. "It seems to mean so little right now, and she's made it brutally clear, she doesn't want me."

"You scare the crap out of her," Tiffany said. "That's why."

Sunny nodded in agreement.

"Let me tell you something I know." Tiffany tapped the table. "The night of the bombing, Kat had mentioned to Shade that she'd met you. Shade got this funny look on her face, and I began to sense something different in her energy, but she was able to shut me out of her head. Then Angel screamed in the bedroom." Tiffany's face paled, and her eyes filled with tears.

Sunny put a hand on her shoulder. "Don't go there right now. Later, when Shade wakes up, okay? This is not your fault."

"I wish I could kill him again," Tiffany said. "This time, I'd make him suffer."

"Be careful, very careful, of what you wish for with strong emotion and violent intent," Raven said. "It can affect our situation."

Sunny's and Tiffany's puzzled looks reminded Raven she hadn't yet told them of her dream walk, or the eye-opening conversation with her mother. "Yesterday morning, I fell asleep and woke in a dream. I was standing on the top of a mountain. You know how your heart aches when Earth's beauty is manifested, and you feel plugged in to the Universe?"

When they both nodded, Raven continued. "I was on the edge when I slipped, and started a rock slide. I fell into the air and knew I was going to be pulverized on the cliffs. It was the very next moment when I realized I was dreaming, spread my arms, and became the raven, soaring over the boulders and down to the river in the canyon below.

"I returned to human form and was watching the sunset when I saw Shade in the water and dragged her to higher ground. I gave her CPR until she could breathe again. She began fighting me when she came to, and I stepped back. She looked at me with empty eyes and wouldn't, or couldn't, acknowledge my presence.

"The next thing I knew, I was waking up in the chair next to her." Raven felt guilt ooze out of her pores. "I had my hands on her and couldn't bring her back with me."

"Raven," Sunny said quietly. "I've told you the dangers of bringing her back by force. She could bring something dark with her."

"I hear your internal stubbornness," Tiffany added. "But Shade has to choose."

"I don't want to just leave her there!" Raven said loudly, several other diners seated around them looked over, and she lowered her voice. "I *won't* abandon her."

"Neither will we," Sunny said, her expression tight with determination. "Now we know a little more of what we're dealing with."

"It's the head injury," Tiffany said. "It must be. Otherwise, she'd come back. If she doesn't remember who she is, she's lost and *can't.*"

"So," Raven said. "What's our plan of attack?"

Sunny held up her forefinger. "First, we're going upstairs, and we'll throw Randi out of the room."

Raven smiled at her bitchy tone. "Let's go."

CHAPTER SEVEN

Time twisted around itself here, and Shade didn't know how long she'd been out this time. It could have been ten minutes or ten years. But she knew the longer she was trapped here, the less likely it was she could return home.

Home. Back to her fucked up life where she felt she didn't deserve anything good or the the love of anyone. The thought brought a tremendous ache to her heart.

The sound of harsh laughter startled her. "Just go away," Shade whispered. God, she was so tired of this shit.

"Spare me the self-pity," Phaedra hissed. "You're just another drug addict looking for redemption, and don't even pretend you didn't love being bad, Lacey."

Shade heard the snapping whip of her tail before Phaedra came into view, stepped over the flames, and stood in front of her.

Shade reluctantly found herself drawn to her physical perfection, the lines of reality blurred, and any pretention of morals went right out the nonexistent windows. The building lust was almost enough to make Shade forget what Phaedra was.

Who the fuck was she kidding anyway? Phaedra was right. More often than not, Shade enjoyed playing on the dark side. It, at least, welcomed her with open arms.

Shade stared at Phaedra's feet. Her toenails were painted a polished steel color, shining against her bronze skin. She let her gaze travel up her long, long legs, to the silver scrap of material resting on her hips. She didn't have to see between Phaedra's thighs, the scent of desire was a delicious ambrosia inviting her to sample. She licked her lips and continued to look up, registered first, her small waist, then the full breasts, and her gilded nipples.

When she finally met Phaedra's eyes, she felt captured.

In any fantasy Shade might have had of a perfect seductress, Phaedra could slide seamlessly into it. Shade wanted to flip her onto her back, force open her thighs, and give Phaedra what she so obviously wanted. Make her scream.

Remember the fucking tail.

Shade quickly looked down and cursed under her breath. She used to know better, to never look a demon in the eyes.

Undeterred, Phaedra purred seductively in her ear. "You know you want me." She placed a hand against the crotch of her jeans, and Shade was horrified when her hips bucked toward the pressure, and her own body welcomed Phaedra's touch. It shot straight to Shade's core, tripping a vibration of need, creating an empty space that begged to be filled.

And it terrified her.

❖

Sunny and Tiffany had taken a detour to the ladies' room, so Raven was the first to get to Shade's door. When she opened it, she heard a woman talking, and assumed it was Randi until she heard the actual words spoken.

"I only wanted to love you. Why wouldn't you love me back? Look at what you made me do." Hysterical sobbing was followed by an eerily gleeful giggling. "Now look who's broken. Not me. Nope!"

Raven rushed to the divider and then threw the curtain open with a force that broke several of the hooks. "Who the hell are *you*? You're going to want to step away, right now."

The woman ducked and pulled her ball cap lower over her forehead to hide her face. She backed up to the wall, where she tried to slide by Raven, who blocked her exit.

Raven was distracted when she noticed Shade was completely exposed. She rushed to her side to fix the sheet which was indecently pulled down to her knees, while her gown had been scrunched up and gathered under her chin. "How *dare* you!" She was livid and ready to kick her ass, but the intruder had disappeared when her back was turned.

Tiffany's screech echoed down the hall. "It's her, it's *her!*"

"Catch her!" Sunny yelled. "She's the one who tried to kill our Shade."

Raven's hair crackled with electricity and swirled around her face. She closed her eyes and pushed for a spell, but she was too furious to concentrate. The commotion in the hall grew louder, and she quit trying.

Tiffany ran into the room. "Is she okay?"

"Who was that?" Raven was calm because she'd already made a vow that as soon as she got home, she'd perform a blood spell, and Raven *would* find the woman who'd molested Shade while she was helpless. She imprinted the intruder's energy signature into her mind.

"Her real name is Sabrina-something, nickname Beenie, and she was the one who orchestrated my ex-husband's attempt to kill her a few months ago." Tiffany's voice wavered. "Omigod, she may even be responsible for the bombing."

"Is that so?" If Raven had known what Beenie looked like before she caught her in this room, she'd never have gotten away. Then again, maybe it was better for Raven that she hadn't. Hospitals were a very public place, and for what she had in mind…Raven kept herself from finishing the thought. All of the women worked consistently on keeping their energy pure when in Shade's room, to keep the atmosphere full of love and healing light. It wasn't always easy to do because the hospital, as inanimate as it appeared, possessed an aura of its own, a smorgasbord of death, regret, despair, and hopelessness, all wrapped in a smothering, pervasive blanket of fear.

Sometimes, the walk from her car to Shade's room made Raven feel as if she were running a gauntlet. It seemed to her that each day she came, there were more ghosts in the hall, looking for someone to help them. Raven needed to talk with her mother about the increase in her abilities, as she'd never been aware of so many spirits at once.

But that would have to wait. First, she had a score to settle for Shade.

And for herself. Raven wouldn't have any problem carrying out any retribution if it were deserved. She didn't have a clear line in her mind that said "don't cross" when it came to her magic. She would do what she thought needed to be done and deal with whatever consequences came back threefold into her lap. It was a very good thing indeed for Beenie to have disappeared quickly. This way, Raven would have time to calm down and plan advantageously.

She still brimmed with nervous energy, and her hands shook while she brushed Shade's hair.

"Okay, let's breathe this out. We'll get her." Tiffany rubbed her back, and a welcomed soothing rush of energy followed shortly after.

"Thank you," Raven said. "And yes, I will."

"I'm not even going to ask any questions. We all love Shade, Raven, but I have a feeling you're the one that's going to make her happy."

"I hope so," Raven said. "I really do."

The remnants of Sunny's rage spiked the energy in the room when she returned. Raven realized she was getting better at reading their little group as a whole, but she refused to crawl when she wanted to run. "I'm so done with this," Raven said. "I'm going to use Shade's necromancy to call her back."

Sunny's eyes widened. "I've told you. In Shade's unconscious state, we'd run the danger of bringing something back with her."

"Can't we just banish it if it does?" Raven asked. "I mean really, we're all strong here."

Tiffany shook her head. "That's a dark magic. I can't do it. Neither can Sunny."

Raven wasn't going to give in this time. She was getting stronger every day, becoming more like her father than she ever realized was possible. "Well, *I* can. So can my mother and my family."

"Are you sure?" Tiffany asked.

Raven nodded. "After what just happened, she's in danger here, and I'd rather be proactive than sit and wait for something to happen. The waiting is driving me crazy."

"I think it's time," Sunny said. "We need a plan." She dug her phone out of her purse and walked out into the hallway.

"I also have some calls to make," Raven said. "I'll be back."

Tiffany nodded and took her place at Shade's side where Raven knew she would resume sending healing energy into her body.

In the space of an hour, her insecurities masked as fear had been replaced with a quiet confidence. The battle lines had been drawn, her enemies revealed, and it was time to fulfill the prophecy.

❖

Shade was disoriented when she opened her eyes, but the feeling was quickly replaced with humiliation when she remembered riding Phaedra's hand. She tried to move, only to find her back seized up again.

"What's the matter, cat got your tongue?" Phaedra crouched next to her. "I've got a good use for it."

If she hadn't been currently paralyzed, Shade knew she would have been crippled with self-loathing and hatred. As it stood now, she could barely turn her face away. "No, no. Can't have that." Phaedra grabbed the back of Shade's hair, covered her mouth with her own, and slid her tongue past Shade's teeth.

Shade's lust was instant, and she raised her hands to stop Phaedra from topping her, but came in contact with her breasts instead, filling her palms with soft, hot flesh.

Phaedra hissed and arched against her. "Yesss."

The pain disappeared, and Shade experienced a rush of endorphins better than any high she'd yet to experience. The euphoria Phaedra's kiss released pumped through her bloodstream; two things remained in her consciousness: her hatred of Phaedra, and the fire between her thighs.

Shade lunged against her, and the momentum flipped Phaedra onto her back. Shade forced her thigh between her legs and pinned her arms above her head.

Phaedra laughed, and her hips danced beneath Shade's while she ground against her.

Slick with sweat from the heat of the fire, Shade was a little surprised to find her clothes were gone, but it didn't stop her rhythm. She was going to fuck her straight into the ground. Each time Phaedra moaned, Shade felt more of her strength return. Sharp teeth bit into her shoulder, and she cried out when she felt sharp claws digging furrows into her back. The sting and the smell of blood brought her back to her senses.

I don't want this. She heard the crack a split second before she felt a blow behind her ear. Phaedra's tail wound around her, squeezed, and threw her several feet away. Shade heard her spine crack on impact, and the agonizing pain returned.

"Choose, necromancer."

"What the fuck are you talking about? Choose what?"

"You have to want me. Pick me, all I stand for, and I can make all the agony of your miserable life disappear."

Shade's will went to war with her body's need for sexual, emotional, and spiritual release. It was getting harder for her to remember why she was fighting so hard, but she refused to cower. "No, final answer."

Phaedra waved her hand in front of her face; her features shifted and changed in its wake. Her white hair morphed to blond, and she glared at Shade with one green eye and one blue.

"Don't you fucking do that." Shade hissed back at her. "You don't get to bring Sunny in here. Not ever."

Phaedra shifted back, but she'd done irreparable damage with her trick. Shade remembered why she'd been resisting. Overwhelming grief made her feel as if her chest were going to split open.

Shade screamed until the illusion shattered like broken glass, and she saw her reflection come back to her in the pieces. She felt herself slip away, growing smaller, disappearing into the shards, until there was nothing left for her to hold on to.

❖

Raven sat in the one padded chair in the space. She was both nervous and excited. Tiffany was guarding the door to make sure there were no interruptions, and Sunny sat in the other, harder chair, to combine her energy with Raven's.

She wasn't sure how to do this again. She hadn't been trying when she fell into the last dream walk. "Tell me again why you can't come with me? Wouldn't we have a better chance together?"

Sunny's expression was full of sadness. "I can't go there."

Raven's anxiety lessened. She wasn't afraid of going alone, and that's why she was meant for Shade. She could and would go to the dark places Sunny was banned from. Raven knew it was out of necessity for Sunny's spiritual light. Still, she couldn't help but feel a twinge of triumph.

"Good for you," Sunny said.

Raven twitched and stared at her, but there was no evident sarcasm in her statement. "Are we good to go then?"

Tiffany looked down the hall. "Shift change. We have time. Go."

Raven imagined the tools, herbs, and offerings she would have used, while she cast a circle in her mind. She hoped it was enough. The rituals were important for focus and intent. She felt a little lost without them, but continued anyway.

She stared at Shade's face for clarity, even though she'd already memorized every detail and shadow. She closed her eyes, held Shade's exact mirror image in her mind, and inhaled deeply before whispering and weaving the spell around her image.

"Mistress of night, open my dream eyes, and guard my flight. Find my love, bring her to sight, aide me in my attempt to fight. As I will it, so shall it be."

Raven felt a push of light from Sunny's direction. She held on to the armrest and forced her taut muscles to relax while she opened her mind to the astral plane.

Much faster than she expected, Raven was traveling down a dark tunnel. Unruly laughter echoed through the small space, rolling around her, growing in volume, until every hair on her body lifted with her terror. She realized how unprepared she was to actually walk the darkness on her own.

Look, fresh meat.

The voice hissed right next to her in the dark, and Raven startled violently while she fought her revulsion.

I get her first.

The voices were guttural, inhuman, and oh, *so* close.

She frantically searched for the small astral trail connected to her physical body, and ran a slideshow of positive, love-filled images of her family and her time with Shade.

A powerful force slammed her backward.

Raven's breath whooshed into her lungs the same instant her eyes opened and she saw Sunny's and Tiffany's concerned faces.

❖

Shade floated in the never ending black abyss, weightless, emotionless. She couldn't feel anything at all, but unlike when she was drowning, the peace she sought was unobtainable as thoughts continued to spiral through her consciousness. She wasn't at all afraid, and wondered somewhat idly if this is what it felt like to be a baby in a warm womb.

Shade became aware of a drum in the distance. The steady repetition beat against her body and brought feeling back to her skin, separating her from the safety of oblivion, and it brought her further into awareness.

The pounding increased until gradually, she felt the solid surface of the earth beneath her, and realized the drumming was her own heartbeat.

When she opened her eyes, she was looking at the tunnel entrance across from where she sat. A tiny blue orb danced in the distance. Shade willed herself to go toward the light, despite her reservation of the entities that lived in it.

The color of life was visible, tantalizing her, but staying out of reach. Just like so much of her life had been, elusive and hidden in the smoke of time.

She asked herself why she hadn't simply given up yet. Sunny had Jordan; Tiffany and Angel had Kat to protect them. Shade didn't want to continue being the one they worried about. Hell, she couldn't even function any more without chemicals of some kind.

A small breeze blew past and brought with it a nagging feeling she was still missing something. The light danced closer, near enough she could see tiny spinning stars of yellow weaving in and around the blue orb of energy.

The signature felt familiar—like the stranger you meet and you know you've met before, but couldn't quite pin down.

Shade knew there were more answers hidden in her mind, solutions she couldn't reach, but she couldn't drum up enough energy to pursue them.

The insistent caw of a crow screeched in the tunnel, unleashing another level of urgency within her, but Shade found herself slipping away again, unable to do anything about it.

When she woke again, she halfheartedly tried to consciously will herself out of this place, but she didn't budge. Her ass was numb. After she shifted her position, she looked down. Next to her was a large, shiny black feather.

The missing pieces came together like cymbals in a fancy orchestra finale.

The sound of beating wings, the crow calling, the feather.

Raven.

The bomb.

The fire.

All of it rushed back to Shade at once, making her dizzy and sick to her stomach.

The sound of clapping came from beyond the light of the fire that had just sprung up from the cold ashes. "Brava," Phaedra said. "Finally, we can get down to business."

Shade ignored her and continued to file the pieces of memory that returned. Raven had bravely come to this hellhole, not once, but twice, in order to save her.

"You don't deserve her."

Shade's jaw tightened, and her teeth ground together. She really fucking hated that hissing sound, but her words were true. She tried to swallow the shame she felt about the way she'd treated Raven.

"Pay attention," Phaedra said. Her tail cut through the air with precision and it stopped a fraction of an inch away from Shade's face.

Shade didn't flinch. "Go to hell."

"Oh, that's rich." Phaedra laughed. "We're already there." Red light flowed from within her eyes. "And the next time your lover comes, I *will* slam the gates and keep her."

The threat turned Shade's blood cold in her veins. She'd rather die than let that happen.

"Really?" Phaedra asked. "Your self-sacrifice is amusing. What happened to you?"

Shade glared at her. "You don't know anything about me."

"That's where you're wrong," Phaedra said, then leapt across the fire and landed next to her. "I *do* know you. Fucking hypocrite." Phaedra jabbed Shade's chest with a pointed claw before continuing. "You abused your power with a don't-give-a-fuck attitude, and then compromised souls with your absolute arrogance. What makes you think you're any better than me? You—with your drug addiction and pathetic depression. You positively stink of self-pity."

Shade had harsh words to spit back in self-defense, but found they wouldn't leave her throat. Phaedra was right.

"Don't you get it?" Phaedra asked. "*You* created this place, and you have no one to blame but yourself." Her voice lowered to a whisper. "Can you guess what I was before I came here?"

"I have no idea," Shade said. "Why don't you enlighten me?" She kept her voice calm and even. She didn't want Phaedra to know how much her verbal attack had shaken her.

Phaedra grinned. "I was a necromancer." She poked Shade again, accentuating each word with more sharp jabs of her claw nails. . "Just. Like. You."

The truth in her words washed Shade with a chill from head to toe. The elation she'd felt when she remembered Raven quickly faded into despair and guilt.

I'm never getting out of here.

CHAPTER EIGHT

Raven kissed Shade's unresponsive lips lightly and whispered, "I'll see you soon." She crossed to the window and watched the full moon rise from the third floor of the hospital.

She was as prepared as she could be. She had fasted, bathed in sacred herbs, and meditated in preparation. Her last experience had made it crystal clear she needed to go in with major protection, and a wealth of experience she didn't yet possess. So the little experience she had would have to suffice.

There was no way the staff of nurses would allow the painting of symbols or burning candles, let alone the smoke of incense, and Shade couldn't be moved.

Anxiety bubbled in her stomach, but Raven did her best to quell it. When it was time, the spell would set and she had to have concrete faith in herself, along with the purest intentions.

She turned from the windows and crossed back to the bed with a vial in her hand. It contained her personal scent, a special blend of oils and pheromones she'd worn since she'd been sixteen. The one Shade told her drove her crazy the first night they'd been together.

Granted, Shade hadn't remembered the conversation—but Raven did. She resisted the urge to hurry, but her sense of urgency grew with each minute she spent here while Shade remained trapped. They hadn't yet caught Beenie, and she remained elusive to Raven's magic, apparently protected by someone who must be far more powerful. That concerned her, but it wasn't her first priority.

Raven dabbed each of Shade's pulse points and main chakras with her oil and then did the same to her own. She kissed her again.

The sharp electric shock when she made contact stung her, but it also let her know she'd been successful. She finished the ritual, tucked her in neatly, and smoothed Shade's hair.

Before she put the brush back in her purse, she checked to make sure there were strands of Shade's hair remaining in the bristles. Raven secured the bag, then bent over and whispered in her ear.

"My love for thee is strong and pure, my intention is to find and cure. I weave my soul to yours with light, but use the dark to aid our fight. As I will it, so shall it be."

She repeated the spell three times and when she straightened, Raven noticed their matching goose bumps.

Excellent. It meant that Shade had heard her on some level. "Give me strength and courage." Though she wanted to stay, she went out to meet Tiffany and Kat in the hall. "This is going to work," Raven said. "I feel it in the air."

"I feel something building," Tiffany said and hugged her. "We'll be right here with her if she wakes. Sunny and Aura are on their way."

Raven blew out a breath. "Well, okay. If anything tries to piggyback Shade on the way out, Aura can handle it."

"Of course," Kat said. "And you're stalling. We've planned this down to the last detail."

Insecurity threatened her resolve. "I don't want to fail or disappoint anyone."

"Then don't. Get out of here." Kat put her arm around Tiffany. "We've got this."

Raven nodded, then hurried down the hall to leave the hospital.

❖

Each time Phaedra left, Shade felt more of her vitality go with her. She imagined herself emptied out, a mummy husk leaning against the wall of the cave by the fire pit.

She ran her fingers along the soft ridge of the feather and smelled it, inhaling Raven's scent before she tucked it under her thigh and out of sight.

It was her talisman of hope she'd used against the growing despair. Shade knew she didn't have much time left, but she also knew the window to go home wasn't yet closed. A small crack remained, but she needed help, as her own astral trail was nonexistent.

The waiting was the hardest, and she was at the point she'd rather die than spend any more time here. She remembered the peace she'd felt when she'd been drowning. Really, why was she even still fighting? They'd all be better off without her.

As if on cue with her internal thoughts, a waterfall appeared in front of the tunnel entrance, and the floor flooded within seconds. Shade put Raven's feather in the back of her jeans, at the small of her back, and startled when she felt an electrical shock against her lips. A phantom kiss.

The air stirred next to her ear, and a chill blew across her neck.

Shade knew someone spoke, but the noise of the waterfall drowned the words. She leaned against the stone wall, and waited.

❖

Raven entered her aunt Reina's home. It had been decided to hold the necromancer ritual here, as she possessed the most experience in the dark magics.

Sometimes, Raven wondered if she and her cousin, Lyric, had been switched at birth, as Raven took after her aunt the most, both in personality and appearance.

Her aunt was also the baby of her mother's siblings, and she possessed the same streak of stubborn independence. It was Reina Raven went to when she fought with her mother. Raven even had her own bed in Lyric's room.

Her mother and aunt had been pregnant with them at the same time, and Lyric had been born only twenty minutes before Raven.

Strangers always asked if they were twins when they'd been younger, and although they disputed the question or corrected the inquirer, they'd always been proud of their bond.

Raven felt a powerful rush of love and held it close while she braided it within the spell she'd been building all day. She set her purse on the entry table, took the brush out of her bag along with her vial, and brought them with her to the bedroom to change.

Here, she felt strong. Raven thought briefly of how she'd moved from acting like an impulsive teenager to becoming a compassionate, confident woman. It felt damn good, and she knew she could handle Shade when she came back to them.

When, not if.

She finished the last preparation, then walked down the hallway to where her family waited.

❖

"Since you're choosing to be a coward," Phaedra said. "There are some things we need to get out of the way."

It rankled Shade to stay quiet, and Phaedra's presence and insults agitated her, instigating, reawakening her natural instinct to fight. It was when she was alone she had the fortitude to end this torture. She had no doubt Phaedra pushed her buttons on purpose. But she didn't want to give her the satisfaction of an answer, either.

The water level had risen to lap against Shade's waistline, and she shivered. If she ignored Phaedra long enough, soon she wouldn't have to worry about being cold at all.

"Oh, come *on*, Lacey. Give me a little fight at least."

Push. Shade reacted. "Stop calling me that."

"Why?" Phaedra asked. "Lacey is alive and accounted for inside you. You may have her locked away in a cell with no light, but her screams, her torture, echoes in your soul."

"I'm not eight years old anymore."

"No, you're not. But *girl* Lacey is rattling the bars of her prison. Why do you bother to hold on to that shit?"

"I'm not." Shade's defenses went on high alert. Phaedra's insight kindled an emotional turmoil in her stomach. The water level had now risen to her nipples, and her teeth chattered. She looked around the cave to gauge how long it would take to fill, and in the corner, she spotted a blue-gray orb as it shifted into a black bird.

Raven.

Shade forced herself to stay calm and not focus on the spot. Through the chill of the water, she felt the feather heat up, and it radiated heat along her skin.

"Pay attention," Phaedra growled.

Shade looked at her. Anything to keep Raven safe while she unobtrusively hopped along the rocks near the top of the cave.

"Let's get on with it." Phaedra waved her hand dramatically at the waterfall and it disappeared into the floor, sending the standing water flushing down the tunnel.

Shade had a moment of pure terror when the resulting air current knocked Raven off a boulder before she balanced herself with her wings to keep from being sucked into it.

The fire roared to life and the dancing flames created deep shadows. Shade exhaled when, out of the corner of her eye, she saw Raven's bird image back into a nearby niche, not too far from where she was sitting. She was close enough Shade could hear an odd, muffled trilling noise from her throat, but couldn't understand what Raven was trying to tell her.

Phaedra sat on a rock and held a long wooden pointer, as if she were teaching a class and Shade was her only student. While Shade had been distracted by Raven, the entire wall of the cave had become transparent, and a street scene came into view.

"Oh, look!" Phaedra pointed with the stick. "It's little Lacey!"

Shade's heart stuttered in her chest when she saw her eight-year-old self who was huddled in a doorway during a Seattle winter storm. "I don't want to fucking see this!" she yelled. Worse, she didn't want Raven to witness her humiliation.

"Want some popcorn?" Phaedra asked.

"Bitch." Shade attempted to get up and move, but was knocked back against the wall with a flick of Phaedra's wrist. "I really, really hate you."

"Blah, blah." Phaedra shrugged. "Ssh. Here comes the good part."

A large lump filled Shade's throat and the noises of *that* day filled the cave.

The relentless rain as it hit the pavement. The sounds of cars as they whooshed past on the oily street. The sickly glow and buzz of the old streetlights.

It had poured that day. It was cold and full dark just after four thirty. Shade had been waiting for her mother to pick her up, but as usual, she was late. Or drunk, or couldn't be bothered. Shade never knew which one until her mother actually showed up, or Shade had walked the three and a half miles home.

This particular late afternoon, she'd been stuck halfway between the school and the house when the storm hit. Her thin body didn't protect her from the cold, and her hand-me-down jacket she'd been given by her teacher when she realized Lacey didn't own one, didn't help much. It was a patched red down coat, which kept her warm on most days, but not when it rained. It soaked up the water and hung like a heavy wet blanket from her skinny shoulders. She had taken her guitar to school that day for music class, and because she didn't want it to get ruined, Lacey took cover in an apartment building's small alcove to wait for the rain to let up.

If Phaedra wanted to break her, this would do it.

Shade strained to close her eyes against what she knew was coming but found she couldn't even do that.

Dark and ugly emotions bubbled in her chest. Reliving the moment was becoming inevitable, and the shock of realizing she'd have to do so, pushed Raven to the back of her mind.

The sound of the blue Cadillac as it pulled to the curb.

The armor Shade had built over the years disintegrated as the scene played out in front of her.

She watched herself startle when the car's horn blasted twice. Her heart ached for the child who looked so miserable. Shade had never realized how malnourished and frail she'd been. The guitar, how had she forgotten how much she loved to play that instrument? It had been her only solace when she was young.

Before.

The passenger window rolled down, and through the icy sleet, a harmless old man waved at the child. Shade's adult eyes registered him as late forties, early fifties. But back then, as a child, she'd thought him absolutely ancient.

"Hey," he called out. "Your mom sent me to come and get you. She said her car won't start."

The relief Shade saw on her shivering child's face nearly broke her, and she wanted to scream at her to not get in that car. Instead, twenty-five years later, she was helpless to watch the girl she was. When she was still Lacey.

The lump in her throat grew larger, and she wanted to choke on her revulsion, watching Lacey, in a wet coat that was too large, and the old guitar case that dwarfed her tiny frame, casually shrug with resignation, and climb into the car. Even at eight years old, she'd known she could never count on her mother.

Before that day, Shade had no inkling of her gifts. Realization came later that night.

After the screaming was over and done.

"Please, please, Phaedra, don't make me watch this." Shade knew the gratitude that young Lacey was feeling for getting out of the rain was going to soon turn into abject, indescribable terror in a very short amount of time.

Phaedra mocked surprise. "But this is the very best part."

The feather heated again, reminding her she wasn't alone, and Shade dared a quick look. The Raven tilted her head and stared back with one dark eye. Shade thought she saw a tear.

She'd never shared this experience with anyone other than Sunny's family, and then later, Tiffany. She certainly didn't want to relive this in front of anyone else.

Logic and the psychological "there-theres" and "it's not your fault" had nothing to do with what lived inside Shade. The shame of being so helpless at the hands of someone else tore through her.

She realized looking away from Phaedra had been a mistake the instant an unholy growling noise rumbled through the ground beneath her.

The walls of the cave vibrated, sending rocks and boulders crashing down. Phaedra stood in the middle of the chaos with red eyes and her hair snapping with the electricity building in the air.

Shade watched, horrified, as Raven's hiding place crumbled and she took flight, making her vulnerable to Phaedra's attack. Billows of smoke and the smell of burnt ozone invaded the space. She leapt to her feet, jumped between them, and took onto herself the bolt of fire Phaedra threw at Raven.

Shade was relieved to catch a glimpse of Raven as she flew down the tunnel before she fell face down in the dirt. She heard a soul-wrenching scream of pain echoing back to her, and Shade stumbled to her feet, asking herself for the thousandth time why the people she loved always got hurt.

She managed to keep her balance while she chased Phaedra over the rocky ground. Raven's cries had faded, and Shade came to the worst conclusion. Her forward motion was stopped by a gale force wind and then Phaedra's body slammed into her, curling her claws into her shoulder before she dragged her back to the cursed cave.

Shade's soaking wet clothes were freezing, and sharp stones cut into her back as Phaedra's body covered hers. The ever-present chill ached in her bones. Whoever said this place was hot hadn't spent any time here.

Phaedra's nails ripped into her skin, and Shade felt the warmth of her blood track down her sides.

Still, her first concern was whether Raven had gotten away.

Phaedra's eyes hardened. "You'll break her. Just like you did—"

"Shut up!" Shade said. She was so damn tired of feeling guilty all the time. Jesus, hadn't she been punished long enough?

She couldn't control what her gift was any more than she could the need for air to breathe or the eye color she was born with.

"You know you're a drug addict, right?"

"I can quit," Shade said.

Phaedra shrugged. "Not really—not all the way. There is always going to be that whispering temptation in your mind. It doesn't ever truly leave."

"What would you know about it?" Shade didn't like where this was going. When Phaedra smiled sadly, got off her, and sat next to her, she knew it would get worse.

"I was broken like you," Phaedra continued. "That's how I got here. You can't erase the memory of what happened. There's a part of you that will always be helpless, crying on your back in that filthy car."

Shade's stomach cramped, and she felt the echoes of the wounds and injuries she'd received that day so long ago. "No."

Phaedra tapped Shade just above her belly button. "That's the part of you that screams for drugs. To make the pain go away, take away the shame and powerlessness. It's the source of your darkness, the catalyst for your gift."

Shade turned on her side, brought her knees to her chest, and started rocking back and forth on the ground. "I never asked to see the dead."

"Not in so many words," Phaedra said. "It was dormant until that day. Some people are born knowing they have gifts, but others can go their entire lives without knowing they have extraordinary powers because nothing in their lives was powerful enough to trigger it. Your deep pain took you there, unleashing the knowledge you hadn't yet developed."

Shade thought back in time and remembered the horror of the experience had only continued when she got home. She crawled from the porch where the old man had dumped her, and knocked feebly on the door, bloody, naked, and traumatized. Her mother answered the door and yelled at her to get in the house, not to lay there like white trash.

Shade remembered trying to tell her mother the obvious; she'd been raped by one of her mother's friends. What she got for it was an order to go clean-herself-the-fuck-up.

Pain triggered it? No, it was a venomous hatred that unleashed the dead *that* night. Her mind felt splintered. Her mother had actually sanctioned and received payment for Shade's horrific ordeal. She'd sent the man to pick her up, knowing full well where she'd be. That a human, a *mother*, was capable of such atrocity was still unfathomable.

Shade didn't have the ability to articulate her condition when she was young, but now she knew that she'd been in shock as she lay in the bathtub whimpering quietly so her mother wouldn't come in.

It had been the first time she'd seen a dead spirit. While she lay in pink water, with both her eyes blackened in her swollen face.

"You're lucky," the apparition told her. He'd sat on the side of the tub and kept one side of his face hidden from her.

She'd been in shock, and she'd thought she might be dead.

The man was near transparent, but solid enough that she could see him. She should have been terrified, but Shade only remembered feeling numb when she asked through split lips what she had to feel lucky about. There wasn't an inch on her body that didn't hurt.

"You're lucky she didn't have you killed."

Shade had tried to focus better, but her eyes wouldn't work right. "Feels like I'm dead. I wish I was. Who are you, an angel to come take me away?"

The man-spirit chuckled. *"No, not an angel."* He turned his torso, and Shade saw a large gaping wound in his side, his ribs stuck out like cactus spikes. *"I'm your father."*

Shade remembered screaming. Screaming. Screaming.

But no one had come to help her.

"That's what you keep buried," Phaedra said.

Shade felt buried under Lacey's sorrow, the grief of a child who was broken, naked, huddled in a bathtub—with nothing and no one to comfort her.

Sharp, stabbing pains around her heart overrode the agony in her spine. They didn't appear to be leveling off; they only got more intense, until she could hardly breathe through them. Shade wondered if this was it. Now she could finally die.

Were these memories her life review? Sucked pretty bad if that's the only memory she had to relive. Where was her happy shit?

The pain reached a red, then white, level. Regret and anguish overwhelmed her.

She'd only wanted not to hate herself and have someone who could love her.

Shade closed her eyes. The tears she'd held back for an eternity slipped out, and the warmth of their trail heated her cheeks. From behind her lids, a bright light appeared.

A clean and pure glow, one she hadn't seen since she'd dropped into this hell.

Lacey.

The word was a whisper in the back of her mind and said with love, no mockery attached. Through the bright light, her father's features became visible, but not the shot and bloody version she'd seen as a child.

This time he stood tall, bathed in white, and surrounded by a bright yellow glow. Shade knew he was at peace, not stuck in the land of the dead and guilty.

"*Sweetheart,*" her father said. "*It's time to let go.*"

Shade was enthralled by his voice, not merely mortal, but with a background of beautiful music. Her pain slipped away, and she felt light.

"*The only way out, honey, is through it.*" Her father smiled, and she remembered his bawdy and loud laugh when she was a child rocking on his lap. A thousand smiles, the way he tucked her in at night before the fighting with her mother started.

Her father had loved her. *She'd been loved.*

Shade felt her heart skip with the effort it was taking to pump her blood. Slow and sluggish, it beat four hard times.

In the distance, an alarm sounded, screeching, insistent, but Shade ignored it.

Instead, she took her father's hand—and stepped into the light.

❖

Raven didn't remember the ride to the hospital—nor did she feel the last two of her thirty-three stitches. She *needed* to get up to the third floor to Shade.

When she'd been thrown back into her body, the dark, heavy energy in the room had overpowered the burning ritual herbs and made it difficult to breathe. She had tried to scream, but couldn't get enough air into her lungs. She became aware of her family's frantic activity inside the circle and around her, so she knew she was safe. Her mother wiped her face with a cool cloth, while her aunt held her from behind.

It took her several minutes to come all the way back to her physical body, at which time she became aware her left shoulder and breast were on fire. She had looked down to see three long, angry red slashes ripping diagonally through her skin from her shoulder to the top of her midriff. Her sister, Starling, packed the wound with homemade salve, a mixture that soothed the burn, but did little to settle her nerves. She'd impatiently batted her away. "I need some room."

"Mama," Starling said. "They won't stop bleeding."

Raven recalled being lightheaded from the coppery scent of her blood, and the amount covering her white ritual outfit had been alarming. She looked at her mother and aunt whose concern was palpable. But when she saw her brother Hawk's face, the obvious distress he was in nearly undid her.

Raven's head felt too heavy for her neck, and she remembered falling backward against her aunt while her siblings were yelling around her.

She had come to in the emergency room where her mother lied with a straight face to the admission nurse, and told her Raven had cut herself trying to climb through a broken chain link fence.

The wounds were bloody, jagged around the edges, and when the attending nurse asked if she wasn't a little old to be climbing through fences, Raven ignored her.

The second the last knot was tied, Raven jumped to her feet, causing chaos in the room as she put her shirt on and ran for the bank of elevators. On the ride, she felt a tremendous tear to her psyche, the spell she'd woven to connect her with Shade was being ripped from her chest.

The door slid open and she cut to the left. When she saw the commotion at the end of the hall, her stomach sank and she cried out. Sunny, Aura, and Tiffany were being pushed into the corridor, and the crash cart was going into Shade's room.

Raven reached the doorway, clutched Aura, and watched as the horrible finality of the long red line flattened in tandem with the excruciating sound of the alarms.

It was too much for her to bear. She backed up to the wall outside the room and slid down it.

Her flight and injuries were for nothing. What she was left with was a huge, gaping hole where Shade's essence had been.

Shade was gone.

CHAPTER NINE

Two days later

Shade opened her eyes, blinking several times to clear her blurred vision. The last two days had been a haze, and she hadn't been lucid enough to talk with anyone. She remembered being aware her sisters had been there, but she hadn't been able to stay awake long enough to talk to them much. She vaguely recalled the small army of nurses, doctors, and other folks dressed in standard hospital gear. There were mumbled conversations about what might be permanent damage to her spine. Now, she thought it was fitting that the first person she had a clear head to talk with was Sunny.

Sunny smiled down at her. "Hello, sweetheart. Are you awake?"

Raw emotion washed over Shade's body, as it had non-stop over the last two days. Somehow she'd made it out of the cave and into a hospital. Her back was in some kind of brace, which was why she hadn't been able to move. It would take time to absorb everything. She still remembered everything that happened there. It was all burned into her aching, shredded soul.

Right now was not the time to relive it.

The only way back is through, her father had told her. She'd had to die to come back.

"Hey," she said, more of a croak than a word. "I'm here."

"You gave us quite a scare." Sunny smiled. "Are you well enough to talk?"

"Yes."

Sunny's tears flowed down her cheeks as she leaned over to kiss Shade on the forehead. "I thought I lost you. I don't know what I would have done if you'd died."

"You have Jordan." Shade couldn't believe the obvious resentment popped out of her mouth. That wasn't what she meant to say at all. The worry and stress were evident on Sunny's face, and Shade was truly sorry she was so careless with her words.

Sunny stood straight. "Really? You're going to bring that up now? Goddamn it, Shade—you piss me off."

Nothing new, Shade thought. She tried to grin, play it off as if she weren't hurt—but seemingly, she'd crossed Sunny's invisible boundary line—and like many of those boundaries, only Sunny knew where they lay on any given day. Temper flared from her, and Shade could almost see the anger sparking off her aura. This was going to be serious.

"I love you," Sunny said.

"No," Shade said. "You used to love me." Again, Shade thought, with the no filter response, what was wrong with her? The words flew out before she'd even had a thought to say them.

"I've loved you since we were eleven years old. Why are you being such an asshole?"

Shade was surprised. Sunny hardly ever called her names. She tightened her lips to keep more words from popping out.

"Are you that self-absorbed? I never stopped caring. And you know it. You're my best friend, and it hurts tremendously to know you still hold that against me. How long are you going to punish me? Can you give me a date? An estimate maybe?"

"I'm not—"

"Listen here, I'm done being punished by you. I can't help that we couldn't be together. Do you know what that did to me? To feel and soak up your pain every day and know I was the one who caused it? To love you and know that my friendship wasn't enough for you? You suffocated me, Shade, and then refused to acknowledge it, to even consider my pain during our breakup."

Shade tried to interject. "I—"

Sunny was stalking around the room and didn't hear her; she just kept talking. "Have you ever tried to let go, even once? To give someone else a chance to see the awesome person you are—when you're not feeling sorry for yourself?"

Sunny answered her own question and pointed at Shade. "Noooo," she said, sarcastically drawing the word out into several syllables. "You choose to wallow in it and project your arrogance onto every person you come in contact with."

The night nurse, Mary, entered the room. "Is there a problem in here, ladies?"

Shade watched Sunny blush.

"No," Sunny said and looked down at the floor. "I'm very sorry."

"Please keep it down. There are other patients trying to rest."

Shade tried to laugh, but it came out as more of a bark instead. "Of course they're resting. They're in fucking comas."

Mary tried to keep a straight face, but Shade saw the corner of her mouth twitch. "Please," she said.

"Oh," Sunny said and turned to face Shade. "I was just awful! I'm sorry I yelled at you."

"I'm sorry I suffocated you. Hey, give me a break here. I just came back from the dead two days ago."

Sunny sat in the chair. "Of course. I have no idea where that came from. I apologize that the first words you heard from me were awful."

"I do," Shade said. "Know where that came from, I mean, and you're right. It's been my problem all along. I love you, Sunny, and I've used it as a weapon against you for years. I'm sorry for taking you as an emotional hostage." Shade's throat felt like sandpaper as she uttered the apology, but even as she said it, she felt a weight leave her shoulders. Only days out of a coma, and she was apologizing for pretty much her whole life. "That needed to be said for far too long."

"I forgive you." Sunny patted her hand. "And I'll always love you."

Shade loved that Sunny's storms of temper always left as quickly as they blew in. Her touch tingled along her skin, and with the contact, Shade was surprised at the shift in Sunny's energy. Or maybe it was the way Shade's perception had changed. What she *didn't* feel was the hurtful longing she was used to.

Shade wanted to think more about that, but she was exhausted. There was a part of her that was terrified to close her eyes, though. Maybe she wouldn't wake up this time, maybe she'd end up back in the tunnel, back under Phaedra. She quickly realized that wanting to stay awake wouldn't keep her from falling back asleep, because when she blinked, she couldn't keep herself from sliding back under. Sunny's hand closed over hers, and she let go.

❖

Shade felt her, smelled her, before she opened her eyes and found her sitting in the chair next to the bed.

Raven was curled up with her legs tucked under her, breathing softly with one hand resting on the bed near Shade's, that intoxicating scent wafting around her. She still couldn't define the scent. The ingredients weren't anything she could use her senses to identify, but she knew she wanted to wrap herself around the source and stay there.

She took the time to study Raven's features but stayed still so she didn't wake her. Everything about Raven appeared to be soft and curvy. What didn't show in her appearance was the incredible bravery she possessed. That she'd ignored Shade's horrible behavior toward her, and sought to save her anyway, at great peril to herself. It was humbling, and it made Shade ache.

A muscle in her back twitched, and Shade gasped at the pain that shot down her legs.

Raven didn't stir.

Shade inhaled quietly through the pain and became aware of what her right hand was holding.

A small plastic wand that fit in her palm. She pushed the red button on top with her thumb and felt an immediate, answering rush of relief hit her system.

Respite from the constant pain in her back, a release from the emotions that threatened to drown her every time she woke, the permission to feel good despite herself; she'd died, and life was different on every level.

Raven shifted and opened her eyes, unerringly looking into Shade's. "You're awake."

Shade nodded. "You don't have to sleep here."

"Yes, I do." Raven sat up and raked her fingers through her tangled hair.

"Why?" Shade whispered. The moment felt heavy. She could hear the squeak of rubber soles in the hallway outside the door, the rhythmic beeping of machines accentuating the stillness and expectation around them.

"I wanted to."

There went that lump again, the one that tightened her throat and squeezed her lungs, making it difficult to breathe. Shade frantically pushed the morphine button again.

Nothing. Fuck. A timer.

Raven put her hand over Shade's, and the contrast between her dark tan skin against Shade's pale, almost translucent skin, brought the reasons back. Raven was beautiful, healthy, and young.

Shade was not.

Even if she forgot that, Shade's emotions were irreparably broken, and she saw dead people. And if she managed to put *that* aside, for even a second, there still remained the possibility she might be paralyzed for life from her injuries.

Shade closed her eyes and felt Raven's hair tickle her face before she kissed her forehead. It was such a heartbreakingly tender gesture, Shade felt the corners of her eyes burn.

She could not—would not—give in to this feeling. It was against everything she'd trained herself for. Sunny's words came back to her, reminding Shade of her sharp accusations. Had she really punished her all those years? It had never been her conscious decision to do so.

Yet, hindsight showed how grief had become the self-entitled arrogance that Shade had held on to come hell or high water. The weight crushed her chest, and again, she pushed the damn button.

Crap, still nothing.

Shade had no choice but to feel the emotions she'd handed out to others. The shame covered her like a wet wool blanket, and she retched with the force of it.

Raven jumped up to get a bowl and brought a cold washrag with it. She laid it on the back of Shade's neck and made soft murmuring sounds. The kind Shade had never heard during her childhood.

Wasn't there something wrong with Raven comforting her like a mother? Shade was more than a decade older, and tough, damn it.

Memory after memory slammed her while she dry heaved over the plastic bowl. Shade was sure she wanted to die. It would hurt far less than all this feeling shit.

When her stomach felt as if it had turned inside out, she sank back into her pillows, emptied physically and emotionally. Raven continued to stroke her with the wet cloth, and Shade wanted to give in to the soothing caresses, but her guilt wouldn't allow it. She gripped the plastic wand as if someone was going to take it away.

She pushed it again.

It worked, and she was released from emotional purgatory. The burden of feeling was lifted. Shade made a humming sound in the back of her throat.

"It's the drug that's making you sick," Raven said.

"Mmm?" Shade heard her but couldn't reply out loud, as she felt as if she were floating three feet above her body. *Oh no. Not sick, sweetheart—better.* Through the haze, she could still feel Raven's hair against her skin, and she inhaled her scent again. The stench of death in the hospital disappeared.

Raven was so clean, so fresh.

So beyond what she deserved.

Shade sighed, full of chemical contentment. The last thing she was aware of was Raven adjusting the covers around her.

❖

Raven returned to Shade's room after getting another cup of horrible coffee from the nurse's station. It was too strong, but she was grateful for it anyway. The nights she spent here now weren't as hard as when Shade was in the coma. The not knowing, and not being able to help, was the worst part of the journey.

At least now, while she sat here and listened to her breathe, she knew Shade would eventually wake up and talk for a few minutes.

Raven had so much to tell her, to share with her. But she also wanted Shade to have full function of her cognitive abilities while she did so. She needed her awake, alert, and the morphine out of Shade's system before she could really talk to her about them being together.

Though it shamed her, she resented sharing Shade with Tiffany and Sunny. Raven couldn't help it; she wanted Shade to herself. She wasn't trying to be selfish, but every moment she had to leave Shade's side was hard, and they both wanted bits of time alone with her.

Sunny and Tiffany talked to Shade about things and memories Raven didn't share, and she felt left out. Logically, Raven knew it was unreasonable, but still she wouldn't lie to herself, and not acknowledge that it also hurt.

Yesterday, a woman named Sylvia had come in, and before Raven could ask who she was, Tiffany had walked into the room, whispered something to Kat, and they both escorted her out of the room.

When Raven asked, Tiffany refused to explain. It was hard to let stuff like that go, but the loyalty Tiffany held for Shade kept her silent. It was the not knowing part that made it worse, because it left the missing details up to Raven's very colorful and active imagination to fill in the blanks.

Raven set her coffee on the moveable tray and crossed to Shade's right side. Her fingers were clenched around the device that kept taking her away. Raven took care, managed to remove it, and lay it on the edge of the bed, still within reach, but not so automatically accessible.

She settled back in her chair and sipped the sludge masquerading as coffee.

Outside, it began to rain, and lightning split the black night sky. She counted one-Mississippi and made it to five-Mississippi before thunder rumbled in the sky.

Raven had always loved storms; she enjoyed the rush of raw power and the way it felt against her skin.

But then a different energy altogether smoked under the door and into the room. Raven silently recited a protection spell and then opened her senses to identify it.

Shade mumbled in her sleep, and her body twitched several times.

Raven couldn't see it yet, but felt the presence move from left to right, closer to the bed. She rose and stood protectively over Shade. "Get out," she hissed; the command was quiet, yet still forceful. "Leave her."

Raven rubbed her hands together and gathered energy from the storm to throw as a weapon. When her palms felt as if they were on fire from the friction, she raised her arms to encompass the entire room and let it fly from her hands. After the burst, the entity slipped back into the hallway. She said a silent prayer of thanks to her brother who had taught her that move.

Shade stopped moving, and her breath evened out.

Bring it on, Raven thought defiantly. She felt bigger, stronger, and completely confident she could protect Shade while she slept. But she couldn't figure out what was waiting in the hallway. Had Shade brought the demon goddess back with her? Or was it something else? Regardless, it was after Shade, and she'd be damned if she would let it get anywhere near her, especially after all they'd done to bring her back.

Raven charmed herself with a keep-awake spell. She'd gotten so good at it the last several weeks, she didn't even need the words anymore. She just brought up the emotion she'd felt when reciting it, and it kicked in automatically.

She really needed to have a discussion with her mother about that. Raven was getting magically stronger each day, in little ways, and in big ones. It was nearly too easy.

It was almost scary.

Her heart rate slowed to where it had been before the intrusion, and she officially began her vigil for the night.

"Sweet dreams, Shade," she whispered. "I'm here."

❖

Shade sat on the creek bank. Between the hypnotizing sound of the flowing water, the sun peeking through the trees and warming her, and the silence, she felt calm. She turned her face toward the sun and felt a moment of completeness. The heat made her sleepy, and she lay down in the grass, watching the clouds pass overhead.

She wasn't aware of time; she only knew she was content and relaxed. It was a foreign feeling, but she didn't question it. For a few seconds, she felt pure grace and gratitude that she was alive, and the beauty of the earth filled her soul. Shade smiled at the wonder of it.

The birds sang, and the water burbled in her perfect, idyllic dreamscape.

A dark cloud covered the sun, and lightning struck a tree next to her, causing it to fall to its side mere inches from her head. She tried to roll away from it but found she couldn't move. Thunder crashed overhead, and she felt the force of it shake the ground beneath her.

She had a moment of panic before a solar flash from the sun forced the dark cloud to move on, returning her to peace.

She smiled and settled back into the grassy bank and watched a raven soar in the sky above her.

❖

Shade heard someone crying softly and felt Tiffany's energy surrounding her with a healing energy, but one laced with deep sorrow. She was lying partially on the bed, on her side with her forehead close to Shade's. At some point during the night, the nurses had shifted Shade onto her side, probably to alleviate the bedsores.

Shade felt a cold breeze on her backside. She made a clumsy attempt to pat Tiffany, but her limbs weren't obeying her just yet. The drugs made her sluggish, and there appeared to be a delay between thinking about moving, and actually being able to.

Her throat was parched, but she managed a sound she hoped was soothing because it was the only thing she was capable of at the moment.

Tiffany startled. "Oh, you're awake."

"S'okay. Thirsty. My ass is in the wind, Tiff."

Tiffany giggled and carefully lifted herself off the bed before covering Shade's backside. "Sorry."

Tiffany fed her some ice chips from the Styrofoam cup on her stand, and Shade noticed she wouldn't quite look her in the eye.

"Whaswrong?"

Tiffany's voice hitched. "I'm so sorry."

"Forwha? Wait. Christ, gimme a minute here."

Tiffany laid her head on Shade's shoulder and cried harder, making it impossible for Shade to understand her, but Tiffany's words were clear in Shade's mind. *It's all my fault.*

"Stop, please," Shade said and stroked Tiffany's hair clumsily. "I can't stand to see you hurting, and I'm fine."

Tiffany lifted her head and looked at her with swollen eyes and a red nose. Her hair was a mess, and she looked as if she'd been at it for hours. Tiffany would never be a pretty crier, Shade thought, but it was still endearing.

"I thought I killed you," Tiffany said.

"Not you." Shade cleared her throat. "Not your fault. And if I know you, Sunny, Aura, and you did far more to heal me than the doctors ever could."

"True," Tiffany said. "But when you were stuck in the coma, I was so scared for you. We couldn't reach you, and it nearly destroyed me. We came every day to see you."

Shade smiled. "I know that, Tiff. It's what you do."

"Raven took the night shift, and Sunny and I took shifts during the day."

Shade wanted to see how the events unfolded from outside her perspective, so she held Tiffany's hand and slipped around her mental blocks to watch.

"No! Shade, stop it!" Tiffany snatched her hand back.

But Shade had her memory now. She saw herself waving good-bye and remembered how she'd made a bargain with the devil, Mark, to save her family.

After a blinding light, Shade heard Tiffany's front window shatter, then several car alarms went off. Tiffany screamed and ran outside, and Shade felt the horror she'd experienced. There had been black smoke, thick and nearly impossible to see through, but Tiffany unerringly made her way to where Shade lay across the street, broken and twisted.

When she heard Tiffany continue to scream, she felt her heart break, then break again while she waited for the ambulance and gave Shade all of her energy until they got to the scene.

Shade had no doubt Tiffany saved her life. If it weren't for her extraordinary gift of healing, Shade would have died on that lawn.

"Where did his evil spirit go then? Did you see him on the other side?"

"No. That's a prize worth having," Shade said. "His lives were over, we broke the chain of curses, I made the sacrifice, and he's probably sitting at Satan's right side or whatever. Not your fault, baby."

"Is," Tiffany said and lifted her chin higher.

"Not." Shade knew her well enough to know that was Tiffany's stubborn, I'm not going to consider what you're saying look, but tried anyway. "It was that fucking lunatic Mark's, fault."

"He was my problem, my nightmare—not yours."

"He threatened to take Angel, or you."

Tiffany's eyes widened at the implication. "He was dead, Shade. Very powerful, yes—but enough to plant a bomb?"

Shade shook her head. "No, and I hadn't counted on that. I knew I was the best choice to fight him on the astral, but not only was he not there, he must have still had an accomplice on this side. Someone he could control."

"Beenie-bitch." Tiffany gestured angrily. "She came here, and we caught her, but she got away, and..." Tiffany's face turned red, and she sputtered. "And..."

"It's okay. Calm down, sweetie. Let's not talk about this right now."

"Excuse me, that just reminded me, I have to call Jordan and ask if she learned anything new about the case."

"She's not a cop anymore, Tiff."

"I know, but that's hard to remember because she still has good contacts." Tiffany's phone rang in her pocket, and she checked the caller ID. "It's Kat. I have to take this. Stay here. I'll be right back."

Shade smiled. "Not going anywhere," she said then chuckled.

Her heart swelled with love and affection. She'd do it all over again for Tiffany, and Angel, if it came right down to it.

No, she hadn't seen her assailant coming, and she never realized she had a savior until Raven flew, literally, into her personal nightmare.

Shade heard a snap of a clipboard in the nurse's station across from her door, and she went straight into the memory.

That damn click in her head, followed by the flash of fire, and then nothing.

A hollow, constrictive tightening in her chest closed her lungs as her heart rate picked up. She was hyperventilating, and she thought she might be having a heart attack. The clip of memory played in a loop, over and over again, and she felt the cold of the cave as if she were still there.

The button, where was the button? Her right hand found and pushed it several times in succession. She knew it wouldn't give her more, but she wanted to end this right now. *C'mon, dammit.*

The relief was instant and the band around her chest dissipated. One thought persisted, making her ache inside. She'd wanted to die. She'd even taken her dead father's hand and stepped into the light with him. She'd been ready.

But even the afterlife hadn't wanted her.

Thank God for the red button. At least Shade had that.

CHAPTER TEN

"Well," the doctor said. "I can't believe we're not keeping you here any longer." He looked at the chart. It clearly didn't explain why Shade had healed so fast from such a devastating injury. "You're a very lucky woman."

Was she? Lucky? Shade wasn't sure. She just might not have been worthy of the light.

She wanted to kick herself for the thought. She'd been shown nothing but love this past week. The flowers she'd received were enough to start her own florist shop, if she were so inclined. The thought amused her. The nurses had been awesome, and she'd grown attached to Mary, who had the night shift.

She continued to stare at the perplexed doctor and smiled absently. She was still pondering the bizarre fact she hadn't seen one dead person since she woke.

Not one.

In a place where people passed away daily, none had come to bother her.

It wasn't just unusual. It was weird, alien. Unsettling.

She could still hear stray thoughts, define different energies, and raw, random emotions flew around all over the place, including the relief and gratitude from families who received good news about their loved ones, and the ones that didn't. Hope, dread, grief, and relief were evident all around her. The boredom of the nurses tending patients that didn't interact, although she was able to sense there were a few nurses who preferred not to deal with attitudes, and chose to work in this quiet ward.

The emotions she felt varied from light, almost white gray, to the dark charcoal shades of the more devastating ones.

It was driving her crazy. She hadn't felt one iota of black energy. Zip, zilch, nada.

Instead of being relieved, it made Shade anxious, and she felt as if she were waiting for the other shoe to drop. A piece of her she'd long ago accepted, and even embraced, was missing.

Had she lost her ability? Or conquered a curse? Realistically, she knew she'd never be consumed by the Dark completely because she had Sunny and Tiffany to keep her balanced, when she couldn't do it herself.

Then she could share the joy they felt when they helped a lost soul pass into the light. Shade's job was to help when a spirit was trapped by something against their will.

What was she going to do for a living if she lost her clients? Sisters of Spirits would lose the balance they'd carefully cultivated through the years. An all-inclusive paranormal group needed someone to fight the dark, someone who could take it and not be consumed by it. That had always been her. So what would she be now?

"That's it then." The doctor snapped the file shut and shrugged, still looking mystified. "Take care." He left quickly.

Shade hadn't heard half of what he said. Not that it mattered. She had Aura and Tiffany to help her. For some reason, being out of the coma jump-started some amazing results. Their healing session worked miracles, and it was the sole reason she was walking out of here, instead of facing the possibility of life in a wheelchair. Well, with a little help, she thought, as she looked at the walker. Whether she'd be able to walk without it in the future remained to be seen.

Raven was due to pick her up in an hour. Shade had little recollection of what they'd talked about when she'd been between morphine doses, but she knew she'd felt comforted when Raven was beside her.

Shade didn't have the guts to process anything right now, especially how she felt about Raven. Now that she thought about it, she couldn't remember if she asked Raven about the attack on her by Phaedra. She hadn't even checked to make sure Raven was okay.

"You're such a bitch," she said to the room. She stood carefully at the side of the bed and dropped her sweatpants on the floor. Damn it.

Shade tried to turn and nearly lost her balance, but managed to grip the sheets so she didn't fall. "Hey. You're not supposed to be here for another hour."

Raven crouched gracefully next to her. "Here, let me help you. Lift your foot."

Shade let her put the legs of her pants around her ankles and stood still while she lifted them. When they were eye to eye, her stomach flipped. *God, she's gorgeous.* "It's all good," Raven whispered. "I've got you."

She helped Shade sit back on the edge of the bed, and then she was faced with Raven's breasts. She wanted to lay her head and rest on them so badly, but didn't.

Now, more than ever, she had to let her go. She was lost, and she wouldn't take Raven into Limbo with her.

❖

Raven pulled into Shade's driveway, parked, and then looked at her. Shade's stubborn expression hadn't changed since she'd gotten in the car. "You realize you've disappointed your friends and family, right?"

"What? It's wrong for me to want space? I'm tired."

"But they wanted to see you. Tiffany and Angel planned on decorating your house."

"Aw, I miss Angel," Shade said. "But still."

Raven wanted to shake her. Shade was the only person she knew who could be more stubborn than she was. And that was saying something. She sensed Shade's agitation. She wanted to get to her prescriptions, because the nurses had taken her morphine drip away hours ago. "These people died a little each day you were in a coma. To shut them out is unfair and inconsiderate."

"But I don't feel good," Shade said. "Living through an explosion will do that to a person."

"Are you whining, Shade?" She noticed a tiny pout on her face. "Oh, my God, you are! I never thought I'd see the day."

"You don't see anything." Shade turned away.

"Now you're just snapping at me to be mean," Raven said. She got out of the car, took the walker out of the trunk, and went around to Shade's door to help her out.

Shade waved her off. "I got it. Back up."

"Mean and stubborn." Raven sidestepped, out of Shade's way, but near enough to catch her if she slipped. It hurt to watch her suffer while she struggled up the walkway, but Shade managed it, slowly and carefully, while Raven followed close behind.

"Shit!" Shade yelled.

"What—what's wrong?" Raven hurried to the door.

"My keys were in the goddamn van."

Raven put a hand on her shoulder. She couldn't imagine how Shade felt, being constantly reminded of the attack both physically and now, by something as simple as a house key. "It's okay," she said. "Sunny told me where to find one." Raven ducked behind the bushes alongside the house and picked up the rock under the hose with the key hidden inside.

"Clever, but predictable," Shade said.

Great, Raven thought, she was going to keep her cranky attitude. Well, she would just have to keep meeting her snotty behavior with cheer.

Until she wouldn't anymore.

Raven wasn't always sure when she would lose her temper. And by then it was usually too late. Shade opened the door, and Raven followed her in to make sure she reached the big recliner. She was in obvious discomfort, but never made a sound while she settled in.

"I'll be right back. I have stuff to get out of the car."

"Not going anywhere," Shade said.

Raven hated the way her words dripped with sarcasm.

Fine, thought Raven, be that way. She felt her own temper rising, but she refused to give in to her smartass comments. She was here to show Shade that she needed Raven. But if Shade didn't admit to needing anyone, even for a moment, Raven didn't know what else to do. Shade just might find herself alone. Which meant Raven would be alone too, a thought she couldn't stand.

Raven realized she'd had on rose-colored glasses when she thought of how it would be when she brought Shade home. In her head, she'd pictured it differently, and now she felt stupid. What had she been thinking? She was going to move in and play Suzy Homemaker? That Shade would be grateful and confess her never ending love?

No. She was Raven Morales, a kickass witch, and an independent woman. As much as she thought she loved Shade, she would never be a doormat.

It was time to set boundaries, ones that Raven would have to back up. Which meant if Shade crossed them, there would have to be consequences, and she'd have to walk out. Raven respected herself, and Shade would have to as well.

They hadn't yet spoken about the cave or Raven's injuries. They'd hardly been alone in the last week, and when they were, Shade was high, drifting in and out of consciousness.

Now that Shade was home, she knew the time would come that they would talk about what happened. She was nervous, but ready. Raven grabbed her overnight bag from the trunk, along with Shade's medication. With all of the flowers and balloons, Raven realized she'd have to make at least two more trips.

She dropped her bag inside the door, the medications on the dining table, and went back out to retrieve more, leaving the front door open behind her.

By the time she'd returned juggling the cards and gifts, Shade was already at the table ripping the bags open to find her pain pills. "I would have got those for you," Raven said. "It would have only taken a few more minutes."

Shade looked a little frantic, and Raven softened her voice.

Sit down. I'll get you some water."

Shade shuffled out of the kitchen, back to the living room. Raven crossed to the refrigerator and realized she hadn't thought to go shopping. *Damn it. Sunny or Tiffany would have.* As soon as she closed the door and turned to get water out of the tap, she heard a squeal, and the sound of small feet running into the living room. She looked around the short wall and watched as Angel made a beeline to Shade.

"Shay!"

Raven started to call out for her to be gentle, or for Shade to brace herself, but Angel stopped just short of leaping into Shade's lap and leaned over the side of the chair instead. The joy on Shade's face warmed her heart and removed most of her agitation.

Tiffany and Kat came in the open front door and into the kitchen loaded down with grocery bags. Raven wanted to laugh. *Of course.*

It felt nice, everyone was in tune with one another, where there was a space to be filled, or if somebody was overloaded with something else, someone in their group always jumped in to pick up the slack. She'd noticed it since she began working at SOS. Everyone was connected. "Thanks," Raven said to Tiffany, and began helping put them away.

"Of course, we knew Shade wouldn't have anything, and if she did, there was only a one in a million chance it would be healthy for her."

Raven laughed. "Right?" She opened the flat of water they'd carried in, took a bottle out, and handed it to Shade. She noted the way her hands shook while she opened the cap, and reached for it so she wouldn't have to try to close it in front of Angel. She knew Shade would despise looking weak in front of anyone.

"Thanks," Shade said and looked up at Raven. "I'm sorry I snapped at you."

"An apology?" Raven put a hand over her heart and raised her eyebrows slowly.

"Whatever," Shade said.

Raven knew it was a front, a way to push her away, but she saw the smirk before Shade looked away.

Angel sat on the wide arm of the recliner and chattered at Shade. Raven had young nieces and nephews, and she had the skill it took to catch every other word necessary to decipher their meaning.

"We're all glad she's home," Raven said with a smile.

The front door opened, and Sunny came in with Jordan and Aura in the rear.

"An all-star family reunion," Shade muttered. "I thought I told everyone to not come."

"And aren't you glad no one listened?" Raven asked softly.

Tiffany and Kat were already seated, and Jordan was hanging up her coat. Sunny was walking toward the living room when Raven watched her stop abruptly.

Angel was humming a beautiful melody Raven had never heard. It was clear, but didn't sound at all from this earth. She heard traces of harps and vocal harmonies. "What's happening?" she whispered.

Tiffany's eyes pooled with tears. "She's healing her."

There was an otherworldly energy present in the room. The hair on the back of her neck rose, and Raven's scalp tingled with the sweet, pure resonance of its power. The sound rose until Raven felt the floor vibrate.

The song ended when Angel smiled brightly, and then she broke into giggles. "Almost better," she said. "The pretty lady says you have to keep some of it, 'cuz it's your path."

"Who is the pretty lady?" Raven asked.

"Airimid," Kat answered. "The—"

"Keeper of the Spring," Raven finished for her. "One who can regenerate life. I know about her." Raven looked around the room at everyone's expression of wonder. They had just been in the presence of a Goddess, through Angel. She had just witnessed something few people ever did, and she felt completely blessed. There wasn't anyone in the room whose eyes weren't wet.

Shade included.

The group was quiet for several minutes. Raven assumed it was because no one knew what to say. How do you follow that? She was riding it like a perfect wave, coasting within the energy, while the shore of reality was nowhere in sight.

The lights in the house flickered and went off. And still, no one moved. When they came back on, it seemed as if it were a cue to release them from their fugue.

❖

"Where's everyone going?" Shade asked. "You just got here." She felt awesome. Angel's healing song had taken away the worst of her pain, but she still had an ache, a medium level buzz at the base of her spine.

She was exhausted, and her mind wasn't clear enough to think about what Angel had told her, that she couldn't take all of it because of Shade's path. She added it to the growing list of things she needed to sort out in her mind. At least she wasn't having shooting pains down her leg and into her shoulder blades, and that she wouldn't question at all.

"It's Angel's bedtime," Tiffany said. "After that, I want to make sure she gets good rest."

"Not tired." Angel pouted.

Kat picked her up, easily placing her on a hip, and soothed her. "By the time you take your bath and feed your cat, you will be."

Angel grinned. "Nope. Kat and Mommy will be, not me."

"But," Kat whispered loudly. "You have to be in bed to hear more about Tanna and her adventures."

"Past-Mommy!" Angel clapped her hands and then wriggled until Kat set her on the floor. She climbed back on the armrest and kissed Shade's cheek. "Sorry, Shay. I have to go now."

Shade held her close and wondered if she could ever love anyone more than Angel, who'd come from such an evil man, yet only carried her mother's sweet nature, not to mention massively amplified psychic abilities.

If she were to have a daughter, would she be able to escape the dark abilities Shade had?

Where did that fucking come from? She visualized and dove headfirst into some snow at the Arctic Circle to snap out of it. A thousand more questions surfaced, and she shoved them away. "Good night, baby," she said. "I'll see you soon, okay?"

Angel nodded and climbed down to take Kat's hand while Tiffany hugged Shade.

Sunny was next in line, and while Shade patted her back, she saw Jordan shaking her head.

"I'm not going to hug you," Jordan said with a slight grin. "Get over it." When Sunny stood, Jordan put her arm around her shoulders.

Shade waited for the tug of resentment that usually followed by such an action, but it never came. She supposed she could force a smartass comment, but she didn't actually want to. Instead, she held her hand out for a fist bump.

Jordan, being the easiest to read in the group, filled the air with her confused energy, but finished the action. Shade thought it might be a little harder than was necessary—but also knew she deserved it, since she'd been hard on Jordan from the moment she'd stepped into a relationship with Sunny.

The smile of gratitude from Sunny made Shade feel good about it. She waved to her sisters as they walked out her front door. It was a weird feeling. She'd never had all of them to the house at one time.

It had always been easier to meet up at Sunny's house, before they purchased the building downtown for Jordan's teen outreach program, and moved the SOS offices there. The hug she received from Aura felt like a true homecoming, a circle of maternal love warmed her soul. She let herself relax into Aura's soft embrace and sighed.

"I'll be back to see you soon," Aura said. "You take care tonight, okay?"

"Mmm hmm." Shade reluctantly let her go. Aura had always been more than Sunny's mom, she was Shade's chosen mother. One far more precious than the creature she'd dealt with while she was in a coma.

Shade watched Raven close the door behind Aura, and she was unsure what she was feeling. It was an odd mix of pride, gratitude, and longing, with a trace of possessiveness. She should probably blame the drugs. Raven bent over by the door to pick something up, and her silky pants outlined her curvy ass and framed the triangle between her thighs. Shade felt a familiar tug, but knew she could never follow through with it tonight. Though knowing it didn't stop her mouth from watering as she recalled the way Raven tasted.

"Are you staring at my ass?" Raven turned to face her, her bag on her shoulder.

"Um..." Shade stalled. "No?"

Raven laughed. "Yes, you were."

"I plead the Fifth. What are you doing?"

"I'm staying here." Raven crossed the living room and then walked down the hallway, out of Shade's sight.

"Really?" Shade asked. She hadn't thought that far ahead. She was used to living alone, and taking care of herself, without complications. But at the moment, she felt far from capable of it. She just thought she'd figure it out, somehow.

Raven was definitely a complication. At least, Shade had thought that a few weeks ago, right? It was a weird feeling to lose time. Even though her trip through hell felt like forever, once she'd wakened, events here, on this side, felt as if they happened yesterday. Not weeks ago. "Raven? I don't think I can sleep with you."

"Don't flatter yourself," Raven yelled from the back of the house. "I'm staying in the guest room."

Ah, well then. Shade was exhausted, and despite the fact she didn't feel any level of the physical pain she'd had when she got home, she reached for the orange bottle anyway. She didn't want to argue with herself tonight whether or not it was a nasty habit—*these* pills were prescribed to her.

Nope, she thought. Nothing wrong with these, baby. They were guilt-free.

❖

Raven finished putting away the clothes she'd brought with her and then stopped in the bathroom to put her toiletries on the counter. She'd given both rooms an intense cleansing the day before, when she learned Shade was finally coming home.

Home.

The word hitched in her chest. It seemed to Raven she was somewhere in-between. The last several weeks had been so intense, she didn't feel as if she belonged at home, where she'd been a little girl—but Shade's house didn't quite fit either.

She'd promised herself she wouldn't chase Shade, though she was certain Shade had lied to her about her feelings for Raven. It wasn't enough. She wasn't going to settle for half of anything.

Raven refused to have a relationship she had to decipher on a daily basis. She wanted an honest one. It was exhausting to have to read the undercurrents of Shade's sarcastic remarks and not react to them. She absolutely refused to sacrifice her integrity or her self-confidence—no matter how she felt about Shade, or how long she'd dreamed of being with her.

Raven was going to try to keep her feelings quiet for the time being. She was only here to take care of Shade after her lengthy hospital stay. Then, she'd see what was what. But not until after they had some honest communication and conversations about what had happened in that cave. Raven didn't want Shade to know about the wounds she carried forward from that night. It would only give her another excuse to push her away. She didn't want the scars to be an issue.

She had chosen to travel there. Shade didn't get to tell her what to do, or for what reason. Raven didn't need her permission for anything, actually.

Shade would have to deal with it.

Or not.

No matter how badly Raven wanted the former choice, she was prepared to walk away when Shade was well enough, even if it cost her heart to do so.

Her cell phone rang in the guest room, and she hurried to answer it before the ringer woke Shade. "Hello?"

"Did you get her all settled?"

"Yes, Mama. Thank you."

"David said he was sorry he missed you at his going away party."

Her uncle David left each year at this time, so one missed party wasn't the end of the world. "It's not as if he's not coming back in the fall," Raven said.

"How do you know?"

Her mom had a habit of making routine events sound mysterious. Then again, with her family, maybe her mother knew something she didn't. She decided not to press the subject further. Her mother and the rest of her family had been gracious, none of them had pushed her for details about what happened to her in the ritual, so she would return the favor. "I'm sorry I missed it, too," Raven said. "It couldn't be helped." Her mother was right. She'd been consumed with Shade, splitting her time between SOS and the hospital.

"He asked if you would stop in this week to water all of his plants at the lake house, and spend some time there if you want."

"Isn't that Hawk's job?" Raven hardly ever got the privilege of taking care of the lake house. Her older brother and sisters usually took turns. Being the youngest, she was last in line, and now that she thought about it, her mother had never asked her to do it before.

"Sí, but your uncle asked for you specifically this time."

Raven considered it. She wasn't sure why, but she understood the importance of the message. She was being trusted with something special, and it was perhaps an acknowledgement of how much she'd grown in the past few months. She swallowed a tight ball of emotion before she could respond. "Of course, I'll do it. Thank you, Mama. I love you."

"I love you too, mija. Good night, and call me if you need anything."

"*Bueno.* Good night."

Wow. This would be a wonderful opportunity to get Shade out of the house and spend a day in the sun. Maybe if she relaxed, Raven could get her talking. This was an unexpected, but very cool, opportunity. She'd make it a surprise. Raven went back to the living room to check on her.

Shade still appeared to be sleeping in the recliner, and Raven debated whether she should leave her there, but her neck was at an awkward angle. She was too heavy for her to carry, though. Shade would have to be lucid enough to help her. "Psst."

"Huh."

"Are you awake?"

"Uh."

"I'll take that as a yes. Let's get you to the bedroom, okay?"

"'Kay."

The trip down the hall with Shade using the walker was awkward, but Raven knew it would get easier with practice. She managed to get her into bed, tuck her in, and climb into her own bed in the guest room within twenty minutes.

Not bad, she thought. Raven was prepared for the usual mind movies that kept her awake, but instead drifted into the wonderful place between wakefulness and falling asleep, floating comfortably until she drifted off.

CHAPTER ELEVEN

"Get up!"

Shade mumbled and pulled the pillow over her eyes. "It's only eight thirty," she said. "My day doesn't start until at least eleven."

The pillow was ripped from her face, and Shade saw Raven looking down at her. She was so near, Shade startled and hit her head on the wall. "Ow."

"Aw, poor baby," Raven said. "Poor, poor baby."

Shade knew she wasn't sincere; it was pure sarcasm and glee. And exactly what she would have said if the situation were reversed. She held back the chuckle in her throat.

Because that would come too close to the line, leading Raven into...what? Raven had already witnessed Shade's greatest humiliation.

The sheet flew off her legs. "Stop it!" Shade tried to pull the blankets back up. She was embarrassed at how puny her legs looked, how sick she appeared. But Raven had already moved to the foot of the bed and dropped the blankets on the floor where she stood with her hands on her hips glaring at her. Shade blinked a few times to clear the sleep from her eyes so she could stare her down.

Oh. My. Gawd. School girl fantasy, much?

Raven's bare, tanned thighs rose up from behind the footboard, and Shade took her outfit in. Well-worn genuine jean cutoffs, so short the tips of the pockets peeked out from underneath the white fringe. They hugged low on her hips, and Shade considered herself privileged to see another expanse of smooth skin at Raven's midriff. A crystal in her belly button ring caught a ray of sunlight and sparkled. Above that, Raven's sleeveless shirt was tied up underneath her breasts.

The silky material perfectly defined their generous shape and, although not visible, Shade knew exactly where her nipples were.

A high ponytail brushed the tip of Raven's bare shoulder, and the shiny red lipstick she was wearing was the icing on a cake. With the addition of subtle smoky eye makeup, Raven had taken what was already lush and made it irresistible.

Shade's eyes burned, and she realized she hadn't blinked for several moments.

She wasn't only struck by the sight of her, she was floored, and that felt a little dangerous. "Stop teasing the lesbian, wench," she said.

Raven looked surprised, which puzzled her. Shade was convinced Raven knew the power she held. How could she not? She was pretty sure Raven owned a mirror.

Her beauty made Shade painfully aware of how she must appear. She hadn't been insecure about her own looks since she was a teenager and began to make the girls sigh, and chase her. Shade with her badass attitude, the image she'd created.

She'd only wanted Sunny, but that hadn't stopped her from taking what was offered on a regular basis.

Raven's voice interrupted her thoughts. "If I asked you, please, would you get up?"

"What for?" Shade asked.

"It's a surprise," Raven said quietly. "And you're spoiling it." Raven turned to the door, her shoulders slumped. "Never mind. I'll be in the kitchen."

Shade felt horrible about the disappointment on Raven's features, but she also felt uneasy about wanting to make it better. This rollercoaster ride was getting old. She would have to get off sooner or later or it would kill her.

Shade carefully got out of bed and silently thanked Angel because the action only produced a fraction of the pain she'd felt the day before.

It was enough of a difference to make Shade scorn the walker and reach for the cane instead. Aura must have made it for her. It was beautiful, carved out of wood, and topped with a dragon and a crystal. It was exactly something her chosen mother would do for her.

She was halfway to her bathroom when she sensed Raven in the hallway watching her progress. Shade smiled to herself and kept walking.

When she was in the shower, she recalled the dream she'd had during the night. She was back in that cursed cave, but Shade's living room furniture was in it, and Phaedra was sitting in Shade's recliner.

"Some setup you have here," Phaedra said.

"Go away," Shade yelled. "And get out of my fucking chair."

Phaedra made a tsking sound. "Not so fast."

"What do you want?" Shade asked. "Go back to hell where you belong."

"Oh, that hurt. I thought we were friends." Two fat tears slid down Phaedra's cheeks.

"Don't turn on the waterworks," Shade said. "Your alligator tears don't faze me."

Phaedra laughed. "Okay."

"Tell me what you want and what it will take to get you to leave me alone."

"Come back with me."

"Um, let me think about it—no."

"How long are you going to play house and pretend you deserve this?" Phaedra looked at her nails. "How long do you think Raven will stay with you? A year, two maybe? She's very young. How much longer until she realizes she has the shitty short end of the stick and leaves you?"

Shade's stomach twisted in knots. "Why are you doing this to me?"

"Just keeping it real, Lacey. You're a novelty, a childhood crush. What's going to happen when you fall off that pedestal? And you know you will. When do you think she'll get tired of the

depression, and the pity parties you throw for yourself on a regular basis? Mmm? And what do you think she'll say about the pills, and your addiction? What then?"

Phaedra sounded exactly like Shade's conscience before the accident. There might be something to that, but the idea scared her to death. As much as she wanted to hate herself, she didn't want to disappoint Raven any more than she already had. Shade let the hot water run in her face, and washed the doubts and accusations Phaedra had thrown at her down the drain.

Raven had piqued her curiosity, and although she didn't want to admit it, Shade was excited to know what the surprise was. It had been a long time since someone had wanted to do something to surprise her. In a good way, anyway.

❖

"Where are we going?" Shade asked.

Raven glanced at her while she drove. "For the umpteenth time, you'll know when we get there. And stop whining."

The look of surprise on Shade's face, and the way her shoulders squared when she turned to look out the window, indicated to Raven she was pouting, and she hid her laugh behind a discrete cough.

After navigating the long back roads behind Silverdale, Raven drove past the sign for Wildcat Lake's public beach and took the road toward the private residences lining the shore.

Ten minutes later, she pulled into a long, steep driveway and parked by the side of a three-story house.

"Here," Raven said. "This is where we're going." She got out of the car, ignoring Shade's protests and questions, and went to the trunk. She pulled out a collapsible wheelchair, opened it, and returned to the passenger side.

"I'm not using that!" Shade said. "Fuck no."

"Please," Raven said while she held on to her patience for dear life. "It will be easier for both of us. Could you please stop arguing and just trust me."

Shade looked as if she might protest, but then surprised Raven by sitting down. Raven leaned over to adjust the brakes and felt hot breath fan across her cleavage. "You staring at my tits now?"

Shade muttered something Raven couldn't quite make out, and she stood. "What was that?"

"I said," Shade's jaw tightened, "I can't help it when you stick them in my face."

Raven smiled. "Okay, I'll give you that one. See how easy it can be when you don't argue?" She pushed the chair down the remaining walkway, past the hedge barrier and heard Shade's intake of breath.

Spread out below them was the lake, its surface smooth as glass. The slight breeze brought the scent of flowers and trees, and laced it with morning sunshine, promising a beautiful day.

Raven loved it here and came as often as she could, or the weather would allow. She was glad to be able to share it, particularly with Shade. "It's stunning, isn't it?"

"It is," Shade said. "Who lives here?"

"My tio, Dave."

"Your mom's brother?"

"No," Raven said. "My last living relative on my father's side." She muscled the wheelchair over the gap between the path and the patio, circled the pool, and stopped at the table overlooking the lake. "Here we go. The sun won't come into this area until later."

"It's fine," Shade said. "Beautiful."

"I know, right?" Raven locked the brakes. "It's my favorite place in the world. I'll be back. I have to unload the car."

Shade nodded and continued to stare at the water. The breeze ruffled her hair, and Raven watched her inhale the wonderful scent of early summer. Raven ran back up the path to get the baskets and bags of food.

While Shade had mostly slept during the last two days, Raven had planned the picnic. Sunny, Tiffany, Aura, and surprisingly, Raven's mother, had all contributed their own dishes. She knew that Shade considered herself a night person, but they all agreed the excursion would be healthy for her. The accident and long stay in the hospital seemed to cling to Shade, and surrounded her with the air of illness. Raven didn't have high expectations for the day, but considered it a good start.

Maybe she could get Shade to smile.

Maybe.

Raven hauled in the goodies, spread them out on the counter, and made platters to put in the refrigerator, to serve when lunchtime came around.

She glanced out the sliding doors. Shade was still sitting at the table, appearing calm. Raven felt some of the stress of the last several weeks slide off her shoulders, as she felt able to put more of the trauma they'd been through to rest.

Today, she just wanted to have a carefree day with Shade. Something resembling a date.

The sound of the sliding door opening had Shade turning to look at Raven.

"Sorry it took so long," Raven said and handed her a bottle of cold water. "There was more food than I thought."

"A picnic by the lake?"

Raven smiled and nodded. "Do you like it?"

"*This* is my surprise?" Shade's expression was unreadable.

Raven had a put a lot of effort into this day, yet now, with one comment, she felt unsure. "Yes."

"It's amazing," Shade said softly. "Thank you."

Raven was pleasantly relieved and glad she hadn't snapped that Shade was being ungrateful. Score one for her, she thought. "You've been cooped up for too long."

Shade nodded. "Feels like forever."

"It does, doesn't it?" Raven asked. "I can't believe my birthday was less than three months ago. It feels like ten years."

"I'm sorry."

"No," Raven said. "I wasn't looking for an apology—and it's not necessary in any case."

"But—"

"Look," Raven interrupted. "Anything I've gone through, I chose to do. You don't *get* to take responsibility for my choices, got it?"

The muscles along Shade's jaw twitched and jumped. Raven knew she was holding back.

Raven lowered her voice. "Can't we just have a real conversation, like other people?"

"Can we?" Shade looked wistful. "I don't know if I remember how to."

"But you can," Raven said. "Let's try, okay?"

"All right, we'll see." Shade opened her bottle and took a long drink, but she never took her eyes from Raven's.

It was a little unnerving, the hungry intensity of Shade's gaze, but it also caused the muscles in Raven's belly to flutter. It made her feel naked, both emotionally and physically.

Neither one wanted to be the one who gave in first, so the stare continued. It had become sort of a ritual between them. Finally, Raven realized she should just let it go. It wasn't important who won this battle, just that they get through it. She looked down at the table and drummed her fingers along the edge. "So, do you want to talk about..."

"Not particularly," Shade said. "I haven't worked it all out in my head yet."

"How awkward is this?" Raven asked. "We've been buck naked, fucked each other silly, and we can't find something easy to talk about?"

Shade grinned. "Kind of backward, huh?"

"Absolutely." Raven felt better and asked the next question on her list. "Did you actually not remember being with me?"

Shade put her elbow on the table and leaned closer, fixing her dark eyes on Raven's again before she licked her upper lip. "No, I lied."

"Stop that," Raven said. "I can't think when you look at me like that."

"Like what?"

"Don't you play stupid with me. You know exactly what *that* look does."

"Touché," Shade said and tipped her water bottle in a toast. "As do you with that outfit you're wearing. But you and I both know this isn't about sex."

Shade had her there, thought Raven. She didn't know what to say, so she looked down again.

"Raven," Shade said. "*Why?*"

She could sense the genuineness behind Shade's question, the almost desperate need to know something, anything to help her understand. But this was the subject that meant the most to Raven. Her feelings had been building for years and there was no denying them. Nor did she want to, really. In her heart, she'd loved Shade for over a decade; it was beyond difficult knowing that Shade didn't hold the same feelings for her. Her throat started to close, the lump preceding the tears that Raven knew were coming. She had to get away first. "I'll go get some food."

❖

Shade watched as Raven entered the house, her shoulders obviously tense. See, Shade thought, she didn't even need to *try* to piss her off. All she had to do was show up.

Her mind returned to the time she was Raven's age, and it made her feel ancient in comparison. It was during the time when Shade was head over heels in love with Sunny. Twenty-one seemed a thousand years away.

Sunny, who'd been all light and sweetness, until she became lovers with Shade. Then she'd changed, became jumpy and nervous all the time. Dark circles ringed her eyes, and Sunny had worn Shade's feelings like an old army coat that was too big for her.

Shade had been so caught up in her fantasy, reveling in the victory of actually winning Sunny after she'd longed for her for years. She hadn't seen the signs. Even after she'd left her, Shade's fantasy hadn't changed. She'd refused to see the reality of the situation, and blamed Sunny for something that wasn't her fault.

Despite that, Sunny still loved her. Shade considered herself fortunate for that, and conceded that the glow Sunny wore these days was due to Jordan.

Shade made a vow to be nicer to her and retrieved two pills from the bottle of painkillers in the side pocket of her cargo pants.

She thought about it for a moment, then put one back. She didn't want to hide from all the memories today.

Raven's in the same position I was with Sunny. Shade knew exactly how that felt, and yet, she'd been horrible, and hurtful, to her.

Raven had kicked her ass before the accident, and Shade was still secretly impressed. But when was the last time Shade had considered someone *else's* feelings?

Ever?

It had always been about Shade's wounds, Shade's past, and the resentments she held against the people who'd hurt her.

Shade considered all of it justified resentment—against her mother, the man who raped her, the doctors that kept her locked up, and the list went on.

Phaedra had been right. The girl who had been Lacey was still helpless and still cried in her prison. Didn't that make her a victim? Holy shit, that was a lot to take in, and she wasn't certain she could fix her if she tried.

Badass Shade, who wasn't afraid of anything, was terrified to let Lacey out. Maybe she should take another painkiller.

Before she could reach for the bottle again, a plate was set in front of her. Shade glanced up into Raven's face. She attempted to read her, but Raven's blocks were secure. "You're getting excellent with that."

"Gracias, I've been working on it. Tiffany is teaching me."

"She's the best at it, well, I used to be the best, but hey, go Tiff." Shade looked down at her plate of fried chicken, potato salad, and another salad she couldn't readily identify because the greens had violets and other flowers in it.

"My tia's specialty. It's a mix of relaxing and happy stuff."

"Oh," Shade said. "That helps."

Raven smiled. "It's good. We just call it Tia's happy salad. There's more food in the house for later. My mother made the fried chicken, Tiffany made the potato salad, and Aura and Sunny made the desserts."

"It looks great. What did you make?" Shade asked.

"I volunteered to put up with your ass for the day." Raven set down the silverware and napkins.

"Wow, really?" Shade said. That remark stung a little, and she sought Raven's eyes again.

"I'm only joking." Raven sat in the chair to Shade's left. "It isn't hard to spend a day by the lake is it?"

"No." Shade ate the small purple flower. "It's good."

"I know." Raven nibbled on a chicken thigh. Shade was fascinated with her lips.

Raven oozed sexuality, even when she was mad and spitting with temper, Shade found her incredibly hot. The juxtaposition of her attraction and the need to push her away for her own protection was strenuous.

"I don't need your protection," Raven said.

"You can read *me?*" Shade asked. "That's so not fair." Christ, she felt like a failure. Nothing was coming back yet, and even her blocks were still down.

"Just since you've been home, and you can't? I didn't know that." Raven set her fork down. "Can we please just enjoy the day? We don't have to save anyone alive or dead. We don't even have to fix the world's problems. Today, we are enjoying the view, eating good food that our friends and family prepared, and..."

"And what?" Shade asked.

"Getting some sun on your pasty *gringa* skin. You're so white, you're almost transparent."

Shade laughed. "I could tan for an entire summer and not get the beautiful color you have."

"When was the last time you didn't live like a vampire?"

Shade thought about it and couldn't remember. "I don't know."

"How does your back feel?"

"Okay." Actually, Shade wasn't in any pain at all. The thing causing her the most discomfort was how exposed she felt. Usually, that was something she shut down, so she'd never known what walking through to the other side being vulnerable could bring. It was new territory, but Shade felt she might be a tiny bit willing to find out. Somehow, the time felt right.

Raven wiped her hands on one of the bright orange fabric napkins her mother had packed into the basket. The light breeze caught a tendril of her hair that had escaped her ponytail, and blew it across her face.

Shade took a deep breath. "Raven, please tell me why you chose *me*."

Raven's expression was unreadable, but her eyes were deep with emotion. "I don't think you're ready to hear my answer," she said. "In any case, I don't think I want to share it just yet." She picked up their dishes to take them into the house.

Shade had nothing but more questions. When she finally wanted to explore Raven's feelings, she shut her out. It made her sad to think she might have lost her opportunity to get to know her better.

And realistically, she had no redeeming qualities to offer her. She'd slept with hundreds of women, taken too many drugs to name, and dead people popped into her life at all hours of the day and night. Well, they used to, anyway. Shade felt a true and deep regret for some of the choices she'd made over the years. Choices she'd thought would make her feel better, but in reality, only reinforced the bars around Lacey's prison.

She'd yet to see one dead person since she woke from her coma. Maybe she'd been given a reprieve by the Universe, kind of like maternity leave. You die, and you get a break to deal with it when you get back.

Shade hit an emotional wall. It was too much for one day. The sun had moved position in the sky, warming her body to the bone. The heat was welcome, and she rested her head on the back of the chair before she drifted off.

❖

Raven washed the dishes as she watched Shade nod off outside. She'd come to the decision earlier, when Shade had asked *why* the first time, she was going to keep that answer close to herself for a while. The first time she'd shared her crush with Shade, she'd basically laughed her out of the room and mocked her. Raven knew deep down that Shade had been lying to her about how she felt, but she wasn't going to give her another chance to do so. Not anytime soon, anyway. She was content to help Shade recover and be her friend if she needed her, but she wasn't going to serve her heart up on a silver platter just yet.

Shade had some issues she needed to work on first. Anytime Raven touched on the memory of her time in the cave, her scars itched and burned. Raven wasn't going to be the first to bring it up in a conversation because she had a feeling Shade would use it as another excuse to push her away, for Raven's *own good.*

Raven had grown to hate those words. As far as she was concerned, she was a grown woman, and nobody, not even her mother, had a right to tell her what to do. Raven was old enough to decide and define what was right for her.

She supposed she should wheel Shade out of the sun before she burned. A little color would do her good, some natural vitamin D, but not enough to burn her.

She hung up the dishtowel and returned to the patio. She was going to release the wheelchair brake, but instead, sat down and just stared at Shade.

She looked ten times better than she had while in the coma, but not even close to resembling herself before the accident. And that was when she was strung out on alcohol and drugs. Raven's resolve weakened. She could love her enough to fix her. All Shade needed was someone to love her, and she would be happy.

Raven could do that.

If only Shade would get out of her way.

Raven shook her head. She knew better. You couldn't fix someone who didn't want help, you couldn't love someone enough to cover both people in the relationship. You shouldn't involve yourself in a couple where only one person did all the compromising.

It never worked. Or, if it did, it was temporary; a Band-Aid that eventually rotted and fell off.

Can't, doesn't, shouldn't, wouldn't, never.

More words she hated.

Yes, anything was possible—but only if you drew that energy to you. Shade was going to have to work for it this time. That's all there was to it. She'd learned her lesson about casting love spells, so that was out of the question.

Raven sighed and reached down to release the brake. Shade didn't stir, so Raven kissed her forehead softly, loving the feel of her soft skin against her lips.

She wheeled her to the shady side of the patio, right next to the pool, and Shade woke up when they hit an uneven brick. "Where we going?"

"Into the shade. You're turning pink. You'll be more comfortable in the chaise than the chair."

"Okay." Shade stood, a little shaky at first, but made her way over to the recliner to sit, then stretched out. "This is good." She closed her eyes again.

Raven had been expecting a fight, or an argument, after she told her what to do, and was astonished Shade was so compliant. It made her nervous for some reason, as if Shade was saving it all up to explode later.

Raven adjusted the umbrella to maximize its coverage over her, then spread her towel a few feet away, in the sun, and lay on her stomach, watching Shade.

The birds were active in the foliage, and several wind chimes rang in the small breeze. Raven closed her eyes to listen to their songs and let the sun heal her turmoil. She was aware she was dozing, and loved it. From somewhere in that wonderful space came the thought that maybe Shade was simply trusting her. Raven smiled to herself and then let sleep take her completely.

Chapter Twelve

S hade felt horribly guilty on the ride home. "Sorry I slept most of the day. It was a wonderful surprise. The food was awesome."

"It's okay, and you're welcome. Sleep is healing. You need it. Besides, I took a long nap as well."

"I can't believe how tired I am all the time." The painkillers no longer energized Shade; they made her sleepy. Maybe, she thought sarcastically, because they were actually *for* the pain. She wasn't going to lie to herself and say she didn't want more; she was being honest about that. But at least now she knew the reason. Perhaps that's why she had to die in order to find out why she needed the drugs so bad. The Universe knew how stubborn she was. Her protective illusions had been shattered, her barriers had fallen and laid bare her emotions. It left her feeling raw, but strangely optimistic. It was such an odd oxymoron.

Raven pulled her car into the empty garage, and Shade was reminded she needed new transportation. It was weird to feel a warm sense of homecoming. Home was usually the last place she wanted to be.

Was it Raven's presence that changed that? God, she was so damn tired of thinking and analyzing, second-guessing every thought that came up. She realized it was another reason she'd drowned her emotions. Dealing with so much crap on a daily basis was wearing her out. Her mind was never fucking quiet.

When they were inside, Shade shuffled down the hall to her room, and snuck in two more painkillers. In twenty minutes, she would feel comfortable, and hopefully, she could shut up the voices in her head.

She sat on her bed, heard Raven putting stuff away in the kitchen, and thought about going to help her, but Raven was done and standing in the doorway before she got up. Shade didn't want Raven to help her into bed—much. The reasons why she shouldn't be with Raven were being met with opposing suggestions why she should. Shade was stuck somewhere between hope and terror.

Raven crossed to her side, and Shade slapped at her hands when she began to unbutton her shirt. "Jesus! I can do that."

"You let the nurses dress you," Raven said calmly.

I wasn't attracted to them. "That's different."

Shade's closet was in the back of the master bath, and Raven stalked in that direction. "Fine, tell me what you want, then."

"In the dresser, third drawer, there are boxers and T-shirts." At least that's where she remembered them being put before the accident, when she'd done her house-cleaning spree. "Thanks." Shade sat on the edge of the bed and waited. Usually, she slept naked, and didn't care what she wore, but she wanted to be covered in front of Raven.

"Did you know there's a woman in the tub who needs help?" Raven asked loudly from the other room.

Shit, Shade thought. If Raven was seeing the same woman she had, she was bloody enough to beat the band, and her appearance was horrific. Shade hadn't known Raven could see the newly dead. *Why didn't I know that?*

Raven appeared, handed Shade her clothes, and then turned to leave the bedroom.

Shade felt a little panicky. "Where are you going?" Why wasn't Raven affected? Oh shit, she must be leaving. She hadn't realized how much she'd wanted her to stay until she was going away.

"Put your clothes on. I have to get something from my room."

"For what?"

"Since you're a little indisposed, I'm going to help her." Raven glanced over her shoulder. "And by the way, she's says you're very mean."

Fuck me. Shade sat very still on the bed, willing her to come back in, hoping Raven hadn't used an excuse to run out the front door.

Instead, Raven walked back in, crossed the room, and entered the bathroom again.

"Do you want any help?" Shade called out.

"Got it, thanks." Raven closed the door behind her.

Shade managed to get under the covers and leaned against the headboard. She heard Raven's muffled voice but couldn't make out what she was saying. She couldn't hear the spirit either. She bit her fingernails and worried until Raven came back out.

"Okay," Shade said. "I have to ask you something."

"Shoot," Raven said. Perspiration dotted her face, and she gleamed with power.

"Come here," Shade said, gesturing to the other side of the bed. The sight of Raven was incredibly hot, and she wanted to touch her.

Shade patted the bed again, testing her.

Raven didn't balk and gracefully crawled up beside her to rest against the headboard. Shade could tell she wasn't afraid of what she'd seen.

"How did she appear to you?" Shade asked.

"Um, dead?"

"I'm serious, Raven. This is important."

"Okay. I was coming out of the closet, and she was there in the bathtub. She was covered in dried blood and had several broken bones. She told me her name and that she'd been in a car accident."

Shade swallowed. That's exactly as she'd seen her, before she'd told her to leave so callously. "She didn't scare you, or hurt you in any way?"

Raven shook her head. "Why should she? I put together a little spell and convinced her she was dead before I shooed her on into the light. She just wanted someone to hold her hand because she was alone and scared."

The relief that washed over Shade was a cleansing of sorts. She'd been dealing with the dead and taking the role of protector for so long, she didn't know anyone else who could have dealt with the spirit's terrible visage and not at least cringed. Raven seemed stronger for it, and not at all disgusted or scared. "Good, that's good."

Raven tilted her head. "You thought I would run."

"Truthfully, yes."

Raven smiled. "That was nothing. Raul, my mother's second cousin? He blew his own head off, and he comes to see us at least once a year."

Shade laughed until she couldn't catch her breath, and she lay gasping for air.

Raven handed her the water on the bedside table and then rubbed her back in small circles. "My dad committed suicide too, but he never comes to see us."

What? Had she heard her right? She stopped laughing. "I didn't know that." Shade awkwardly turned to face her. "I'm sorry."

Raven looked sad. "I was very young when he overdosed, and I hardly remember him."

"Mine too." Shade nodded and thought back. "Died when I was young, I mean. But I think my mother had him murdered."

Raven's eyes widened. "Really? How do you know that?"

"Do you want the long version or the short one?" Shade asked. She hadn't shared this story with anyone outside her circle, and they hadn't talked of it in years. But she felt like she needed Raven to know the story.

"I'm here, tell me." Raven slid down into the pillows until her body was even with Shade's, and only a foot and a half away. "We've got nothing but time."

Shade wondered where to start. Raven had already seen what happened on that rainy night, courtesy of Phaedra. She looked into Raven's eyes and didn't see anything but compassion and a willingness to listen. She wished she could read her, but she was going to have to settle instead for gauging her general aura. "One rule," she said.

"Rules?" Raven asked. "Telling me a story has rules? I don't know if I should be offended or not."

"Not," Shade said. "I'm just going to ask you not to psychically probe, okay? Let me tell it myself."

"That sounds totally fair. I agree."

Shade found it hard to tear her gaze off her face, but knew she had to in order to continue. "Okay." She took a few deep breaths. "The first dead person I ever saw was my father."

She let that hang in the air between them for a few moments while she gathered the rest of her thoughts. "It was that night. After."

"You don't have to go there," Raven said softly. "It must be horribly painful."

"I didn't remember much about him. I used to ask my mother, but she'd always just tell me he was a loser. Some no good, worthless, son of a bitch biker she'd picked up in a bar one night that'd walked out and left her pregnant with me."

"Funny thing about that is when we were in the cave? My father came again, and I remembered he loved me. I thought he'd come to take me away. I took his hand, and I thought it was over." Her father's hand had felt as real as her own did. She was sure she died. "But I woke up."

"I'm glad you did," Raven said.

Shade still thought it was another kind of a rejection. As if she were found not worthy, but she didn't mention that. "I'm not so sure I am." She felt Raven tense up next to her before her temper exploded.

"What an incredibly selfish and ungrateful thing to say," Raven said. "It would have destroyed the people who love you. Did you know you weren't ever left alone in the hospital? We all took turns by your side, watched over you, gave you our energy, and prayed in each of our own ways?" Raven sat up and continued her tirade in Spanish, her hands gesturing wildly.

Shade didn't know what she was saying but was stunned silent by her sharp words and tone. Hadn't Sunny just called her selfish as well? She'd never viewed herself that way before the coma.

She'd really, truly thought herself to be the one who made sacrifices for others.

Raven pushed at Shade's arm. "Are you listening?" she asked. "I *bled* for you. And you say you wanted to die? I'm so pissed at you."

"What?" That got her attention. "What did you say?"

Raven unbuttoned her shirt and opened one side. Three uneven jagged scars started on her shoulder, traveled across her left breast, and ended at her ribcage.

Shade was horrified. How could she forget Raven's cry of pain? She'd been so caught up in reliving the trauma, she hadn't even asked about it. "Aw, no, honey. *Nooo.*" Shade pulled Raven to her and placed her hand over her mauled breast. Raven fought a little, but Shade held her tightly until she quit, ignoring the lightning strikes in her back. "I'm so sorry. So sorry, Raven."

Here was the reality of her situation, and the reason why she didn't let anyone in.

They always, always got hurt.

❖

Raven had attempted to gently disengage herself from Shade's side, but each time she was forcefully pulled back into the embrace, even though Shade appeared to be sound asleep. Raven didn't want to struggle. She could take a short nap, then move to the guest room later.

Her eyes opened at three a.m. The witching hour. When she was little, she'd called it, the deadening. It had made sense to her then, when spirits would show up full of pain, and she would soften it, numb it, and take it away if she could, before she sent them on.

With her gift, she was able to transform the spirit's appearance before they crossed over. And if they needed help or directions, she had her raven-form to assist.

Shade's breathing was deep and even as she slept. Raven warred with the rule she'd set earlier. The one about not peeking. Did that apply when she wasn't awake? What if she ignored it and read Shade's thoughts, *for her own good*?

Raven smirked and played with semantics. Shade had never finished her story, she'd freaked out about Raven's wounds instead.

Shade would now have the most powerful weapon in her arsenal, the weapon to try to convince Raven to leave, to not get involved.

She resisted the urge to chuckle. As if anything could make her go if she chose to stay. Shade wouldn't stand a chance against her charm. But she didn't want to be with her by seduction. She wanted Shade to choose her as well. As if it were her idea all along.

Raven consciously relaxed her neck, then her shoulders, and let the progression continue down, throughout each area of her body, until she finished with her feet. The process left her feeling tranquil.

The day spent in the sun had done wonders helping her muscles feel loose. As she relaxed further against Shade, Raven felt her grip loosen slightly, and then she reached for the words to build a chant.

She took three long breaths, holding the last one for as long as she could before exhaling.

With these words, my intentions be, to enter Shade's dreams, and observe as me. No harm I mean to her or I. A trip for love my goal to fly. As I will it, so shall it be.

As Raven repeated the rhyme two more times, her feet tingled first, then the sensation traveled up her calves to her thighs, and continued onward to the top of her scalp, until her entire body felt lighter. Raven was aware her body temperature was rising, and she transferred some of the warmth into Shade.

In order for the inner meditation hypnosis to work, she had to combine their lifelines on the astral plane. She reached for Shade's ribbon of energy, the murky, muddy color concerned her, so she used caution while she braided their essence together, taking care with the traces of the strands that appeared fragile and burnt. She finished weaving the weakest areas with her own stronger and healthier lines of green and blue.

They took flight.

This trip was easier than the last two. Like her mother had promised, because Raven had forged a path previously through Shade's mind, it remained one she could see and follow.

Raven swallowed her apprehension and ignored what happened last time she traveled here. Fear was not allowed, she had a purpose, and to be afraid could derail her plans.

"Shade?" Raven called to her telepathically.

"Yes. Where are you? How did you—"

"No," Raven thought firmly. *"You can ask questions later. First, we have to go and find Lacey. Go back to her, Shade."*

"No! Lacey is dead". Shade's tone was younger, combative, and petulant. It was also the weakest point in her energy trail.

Raven drew the brittle line tighter, weaving in more of her own to give Shade strength. *"Lacey is not dead, honey. We need to find her. I want to help her."*

"No one ever helped Lacey." Shade's voice was younger still, and the despair Raven could hear in it broke her heart. As much as she fought with her mother, and siblings, she had never, ever, in her life felt unloved or unwanted. The wounds were far deeper than she could have ever imagined, because she'd hadn't experienced them. The emotion was foreign to her, and even second-hand, it curled in her stomach and made her queasy.

"Shade? Was there ever a time when you felt happy?"

"I can't remember. No, wait. My mother had a nice boyfriend one time. His name was Larry. He played in a bar band and gave me one of his old guitars."

Raven was relieved to feel Shade's smile. This was an excellent place to start. Shade's energy pulled even closer, and this time, Raven felt stronger. *"Did you learn how to play?"*

"Yes. I taught myself. I would practice whenever she wasn't home."

Raven wasn't touching the subject of her mother yet. She wasn't able to get past the monstrosity of her actions, so better for now to leave that out of their traveling. *"Can you show me?"*

A scene formed behind her eyes. A young girl sat on the edge of a small bed with no sheets, with a worn black guitar in her lap. Raven couldn't see her face, because a shock of unkempt dark hair covered everything except her mouth, and Lacey was biting her lower lip while she concentrated on stretching her fingers to play the chords. Her other hand picked at the strings, and Raven easily recognized the haunting intro to "Stairway to Heaven." She was duly impressed. She had so much talent for such a young girl, and Raven felt the notes as if they were Lacey's emotions flowing through the music and straight into her soul.

It was a breathtaking moment.

Without warning, Raven was forcefully drawn forward in time to see Lacey climbing in the car again. *"We don't have to go there."*

Shade didn't answer. Instead, she placed a steady image into Raven's mind. She saw the battered case in the backseat covered in rags. No, not rags—Lacey's torn clothes. She heard the drumming of rain on the metal roof, and a scream. *"No, Shade. Not here, please. We can't stop this. We have to go forward."*

In a flash of bright orange, Raven realized Shade had taken over this trip. They flew toward a porch, through a busted door, to the end of a hallway where they stopped in front of a door. The frame was crooked, and light poured into the dark and dingy hall from underneath the crack.

People laughed and talked in a room somewhere behind her, but under that noise, she heard a small splash and quiet sobs that held such anguish and sorrow, she didn't know if she could go in and face it.

Her illusion flicked on and off with sharp, snapping sounds. The unexpected dead spot took her by surprise, and before she could fix it, she was sucked under the door and into the bathroom. Raven was no longer an observer. Now she was trapped in Shade's mind and staring out of Lacey's swollen eyes.

CHAPTER THIRTEEN

It seemed to Shade that one second she was aware of being in a semi-hypnotic state, and the next she was back in her eight-year-old body. Through the shock and trauma, she realized she was speaking with her dead father.

She was conscious of a rhythmic beating sound. She could remember at the time she'd been a child, and she'd thought it had been her own beating heart. It was an eerie déjà vu, and it chilled her.

Whoosh-whoosh.

The rhythm grew louder, more urgent, and then she heard her name.

Shade!

Raven. Shade had drawn her straight into her personal nightmare. *Fucking great.*

She reached for Raven in her mind to soothe her, and listened to Lacey's conversation with her father's ghost. At any moment, her father was going to tell her he wasn't an angel come to take her to heaven.

Shade felt as if her father looked deep into Lacey's soul and saw her hiding.

Baby, the only way out is through.

The shock rushed through Shade's body, blending with Lacey's astonishment over seeing a dead man, and she was left dizzy from the impact.

Raven was quiet in the background of Shade's thoughts.

The moment hung suspended in time, and it was clear as newly spun glass.

This was the minute Lacey retreated and Shade was born. It was a child's solution for dealing with the impact of the agonizing rip to her soul.

Her father smiled at her, ran a gentle hand over Lacey's hair, and whispered he'd be back when Shade needed him the most.

He stood straight in the small room, looking as if he were waiting or expecting something. Shade was pulled out of Lacey amidst a kaleidoscope of colors and stood in front of him. She quickly glanced back at Lacey, who was still in the tub, but her eyes were closed, and beneath the bruises, she looked almost peaceful.

Shade startled when Raven took her hand and stepped up next to her. She watched her extend her other hand toward her father and lay it on his shoulder. The pull of energy Raven was using caused the visible gunshot to close, and his shattered ribs knit themselves back together.

"Thank you. Again."

"Again?" What was going on now? *"What are you saying?"*

Her father kissed Raven on the cheek, then Shade. "She'll explain later." He turned toward the outside wall. *"And, Shade? Before I go, I want to ask a favor, okay?"*

"Huh?" Shade was beyond confused. She poked her finger at him and met solid flesh. Everything felt so real, yet she knew it wasn't. She let down her guard anyway, lifted her arms, and hugged her father close.

"Take care of my little girl, please." The whisper in her ear brought back all the love she'd felt from him when she was in the coma. The emotion was still there, and now Shade realized it wouldn't leave her. She could access the feeling when she wanted to.

He held her for a minute, and then drew back to smile at her. She realized he was younger than she was now when he died. He was quite handsome.

"What?" Her father laughed. *"You thought you got your superior looks from* her?*"*

"Nah." Shade winked at him. She felt considerably lighter. *"Clearly, it was you who gave me the sexy gene."*

"I have to go now, kid. See you around."

"Later, Dad."

Shade watched him fade gradually until she was simply staring at a moldy wall in her old, childhood home.

Shade turned back to find Raven crying. *"We have to take care of her. We can't leave her—you—like this."*

"I know." Shade picked up the rag masquerading as a washcloth and gently wiped Lacey's face while she thought of the questions to ask Raven.

Before she spoke, Raven started talking. *"I didn't know the details, or remember them anyway. I just knew when I met you for the first time, you were mine. I only had the feelings, not the story. This was buried somewhere in my consciousness, knowing I was connected to you."*

The moment felt surreal, and Shade felt both lost and safe. *"I remember hearing birds flying in my mind at different times in my life. That sound started here, on this night. I never knew what they meant. I couldn't have known you then; you hadn't even been born yet. God, it's too much to comprehend. I don't even know if I can."*

"There's time for that later," Raven said. *"Right now, we're going to help her."*

"It hurts to look." Faced with the most traumatic event in her life, and the otherworldly circumstances, she didn't see any reason to be anything less than honest with Raven.

Apparently, they'd done this once before. It was mind boggling.

"She needs us right now."

Shade heard a crash outside the bathroom door, and she was nearly overcome with dread and rage for the woman she knew was standing outside it.

"No, Shade. This is about her, and we have to do this with love." Raven pushed the emotion toward her, and Shade had to choose. She could continue with fury, or accept the love. She couldn't have both because one couldn't live with the other.

"Choose." Raven's eyes pleaded with her as she held out her hand.

"Choose, necromancer," Phaedra screamed in her mind. With a vicious start, Shade realized Phaedra *was* only in her mind, also born in this bathroom twenty-five years ago.

The enormity of the situation flooded through her, and brought with it the realization that the *last* time she made this choice, she had chosen wrath over love.

Her life flashed in images, every slight, fight, bad choice, and horrific consequence she'd faced over the years came back to this second.

This choice.

Phaedra laughed and held out her hand. She had a smug look on her face, appearing to have no doubt in her mind Shade would take it again.

"Fuck that."

Shade lunged sideways to put her arm around Raven and protect Lacey from what she could, had, become.

When she made contact, a ribbon of blue and green energy wrapped around them, and they were pulled back into the night.

Shade felt only the slightest impact when they stopped. She found herself on a deserted white sand beach. Raven's soft voice whispered in her ear, and she knew she wasn't alone.

"Close your eyes and listen to the waves. The sand is warm between your toes, and the sun feels amazing on your face. Do you feel it?"

Shade paused. *"Yes."*

"Good," Raven continued. *"The water draws you closer, and with each step, that memory, that life, gets left behind. You have no worries, no stress, and a light breeze blows through your hair. You feel like smiling as you walk along the shore's edge. The water tickles your feet as it races back to the sea. Can you feel it?"*

Shade inhaled deeply. *"Yes, and I can smell the salt in the air."* The repetitive sound of the waves was hypnotic and soothing. Shade felt wonderful.

"Excellent. Now, in the distance you see a small girl sitting alone in the sand. As you approach, you can see she's crying. Compassion fills your heart for this little child, and you sit next to her in the sand to hold her tiny hand. You recognize her. She is you. Only you can give her the love she was denied."

Shade was deep inside the meditation, but in the background she was also aware of her physical body, and the way her eyes filled with burning tears for the child she'd been.

"You wrap your arms around her, and rock with her in the warm, white sugar sand, and the waves roll gently in front of you. She is you—and you have the power to heal her."

Sharp pains in her chest nearly took Shade back to the waking world, but she fought to stay on the beach with Lacey. She would gladly take her pain away, but now she felt it in stereo, in both her dream self, and her body on the bed so far away. She took the dual agony into herself and let her adult heart break in two for both of them.

"Shade. There's more, honey. Stay with me now." Raven brought her back to the sand.

"Listen, you are her. Small arms hug you back. She has the power to heal you. Hold her close, smell her hair, the skin on the back of her neck. This is the scent of love and compassion."

"She is you, and you are her. Wipe her tears as she wipes yours. Promise to honor her, and tell her that she is free now."

"She is loved. You are loved."

"The sun is setting, and you both feel serene and peaceful. This is where you will find each other when there is a need. Now, hold her tightly and tell her again how very much she is loved, and hear her tell you. You feel her growing smaller, lighter, and smaller still— until you can hold her in the palm of your hand. Do you see her? She is smiling and full of happy joy."

Shade couldn't answer, even telepathically; her throat was closed with emotion. She could see, really see, Lacey in her hand.

"Carefully, and oh so tenderly, place your palm over your heart, and place Lacey inside it. Can you hear her laugh gently as she safely curls up to rest?"

"She will never leave you. She is yours to love. You are never alone—she lives in your heart. She is you, you are her, and together—you are one."

"Whole."

❖

Raven was jolted awake, and she wasn't sure where she was. She was on her side, and the clock read 4:44. Oh, she thought, okay. Their journey returned to her in pieces, and now she was back in bed. She felt Shade's absence. The warmth of her body and the tight grip she'd been in was missing.

She was exhausted, but she wanted to find her. Good Lord, that was intense. But at least they both had answers to questions that had haunted each of them.

She tried to lift the sheet draped over her and found she couldn't move her arms. She tried to call out for Shade, but her mouth wouldn't open, and no sound came from her throat.

The bed shifted and Shade curled up against Raven's back. "Little breath," she whispered. "That's it."

Raven felt a small amount of air enter her dry lungs.

"Another one. Don't panic. It's okay. I'm here." Shade rubbed between her shoulder blades in a tight, circular motion, and Raven felt the tightness in her lungs recede.

She repeated the process until gradually, she could take a full breath.

"Better?" Shade asked.

Raven nodded. Shade's breath tickled along the outside of her ear, and Raven felt goose bumps rise along her neck in its wake. Tears burned the corner of her eyes, and she realized it had been a long time since she'd been held, and it felt wonderful.

She'd been strong and steady since the bombing, and the pressure she kept herself under eased up just a tiny bit as she let Shade comfort her.

"We were gone a long time," Shade said. "Do you need to throw up?"

"No," Raven said. That was why her body had seized up, why she couldn't breathe when she woke. That much time spent in the astral territory was hard on the physical body. Shade played with her hair, and she smiled to herself. "I am thirsty though, and too tired to go and get something."

"Already got it," Shade said. "I knew we'd need it."

Raven squealed when the cold bottle was pressed against her neck. She grabbed it and turned over, scooting up to sit against the headboard.

Shade laughed. "You should see the look on your face!"

Raven glared at her, but inside, she was happy to hear the amusement, the laughter that rolled up from her belly. It was genuine and real, and Raven would do it all over again to hear it.

"Seriously," Shade said. "Where the hell did you learn how to do that?" She turned on her side to face Raven and rested her head in her hand.

Raven leaned back and took another long drink. "The first time I did was an accident. I fell asleep in the chair next to your bed, and it just happened. That was when I pulled you out of the river."

"Holy sh—"

Raven interrupted. "When I was little, I apprenticed with my tia Delores. Her gift is dream walking and she uses the inner-child script to heal women who have been traumatized as children." She nostalgically remembered the smells and sounds of her tia's kitchen. "Most times, the women were joyful afterward. If not, they were sent to my tia Reina, who could tell whether or not a dark spirit was involved."

"How many aunts, uncles, and cousins, do you have?" Shade asked.

Raven smiled. "We are legion." She considered everything she'd learned up to this point had been to help Shade, and Lacey, the girl she'd once been.

"Maybe it was an accident. The first time, I mean."

"Your father clearly said we'd done this before." Questions bombarded her until Raven gave up. "It's like I can completely grasp the concept that time is circular for a few seconds, and can travel any direction we choose…"

"Then it slips away and you feel more confused?" Shade finished her sentence.

"Exactly," Raven said and slid down the bed to mirror her pose. Shade's eyes were deep with emotion, lacking any of her previous wariness.

"Raven?"

"What?"

"How come I didn't know you could see the dead?"

"Really? You don't remember?"

"Am I supposed to?"

"Maybe not. You were pretty loaded that night."

"I'm sorry," Shade said and covered her eyes.

Raven removed her hand and held it down between them on the bed. "When I came over on the second night, not the first—I was pretty tipsy that night, too. Anyway, I asked you who it was lurking in the corner."

"Oh, God," Shade said. "Travis, the dead drug dealer."

"But I haven't seen him since. Did you help him cross over after that night?"

Shade blinked. "Um, no. I think I completely obliterated him."

"Come again?" Raven didn't want to think of the possible backlash from that stunt.

"He was watching us, and made smartass comments about you, none of which I'll repeat." A hard glint appeared in Shade's eyes.

"You were jealous?"

"Yeah, well." Shade turned onto her back. "He pissed me off."

It was a horrible thing to do, yet Raven couldn't help but be flattered a little bit. She didn't know what else to say, and right now, she was tired. She blinked, her eyes stayed closed, and the silence stretched.

She didn't know how much time had passed, but she heard the drawer of the nightstand open, the sound of pills in a bottle, and the drawer closed.

She didn't have the strength to ask about it, but she knew that Shade had been overmedicating because Raven had counted what was left of the prescription earlier.. Couldn't she relax for one freaking night without worry? Was that too much to ask? It was yet another conversation they had to have. When she could drum up the energy to do so.

Her mother's warning continued to ring in her mind as well.

"Never tangle with a necromancer, mija. They walk a hard life with one foot here, in this world, and the other in the land of the dead. Nothing but darkness surrounds them. Heartache is a way of life, and no one ever loves them enough to stay."

Right this minute, Raven was scared that she might be right. It wasn't that she didn't love her, but that loving her was draining. She didn't feel as if she had anything left to give, and there always seemed to be another hurdle.

❖

Shade watched Raven fall asleep. Sometime in the interim of their astral trip and their return, Shade had regained the ability to read her thoughts. When she heard Raven's last words before she fell asleep, she wanted to justify leaving again, she really did. She hated being the one people thought of as broken.

The first to wake up, she'd felt super energized and used the momentum to fetch the water Raven would need. She wanted to be able to help her over the lag being gone so long produced.

The psychic weight of depression was gone. She had no measuring stick, no point of reference of what normality should feel like. Somehow, she felt *more* of what she'd been. Had her childhood trauma kept a part of her soul trapped in that bathtub? Was that why she felt more present? What was life going to feel like without the burdens she'd held for so long? Would she be able to live and love like a normal person? Could she accept Raven into her life without worrying about her safety?

She'd been excited to find the answers—until she heard Raven's thought that loving her was hard work.

Shade knew it was true.

But *goddamn* it, she didn't want to give up either. Couldn't she just grasp the fucking brass ring for once?

Gray light showed between the gap in the drapes, and a brand new day loomed in front of her. One she had no idea of how to deal with except with help from a substance of one kind or another. She was more scared of facing life clean than she was of the demons in the tunnel. Before she closed her eyes, she made herself a promise.

Things were going to change.

CHAPTER FOURTEEN

The fresh smell of coffee lured her to wakefulness. Shade stretched and yelped when her back seized. It felt as if a thousand years had passed. She'd had some freaky dreams last night, but they were blurry. Shade made her way to the bathroom to splash water on her face and then started to the kitchen. Halfway there, she returned to the bathroom, and swallowed three times her prescribed morning pain dose. She had pills stashed all over the house, but her supply was running too low for comfort. She was going to have to find more, and soon.

Or suffer the consequences of withdrawals.

She promised herself she would finish the prescription, and then quit.

Shade tried not to remember how many times she'd said the same before as she made her way to the front of the house.

Raven stood with her back to the hall, her damp hair braided in a long twist down the back of a plain white T-shirt. The black jogging shorts she was wearing hit her mid-thigh, and she was barefoot. She looked...delicious.

Shade's stomach growled and she cleared her throat.

"Something on your mind?" Raven asked.

Absolutely, Shade thought. There was something on her mind, and it had nothing to do with food. It involved picking Raven up, putting her on the counter, wrapping those long, tan legs around her waist, and doing battle with their tongues. That's what was on her mind. "Um, no, nothing."

She didn't want to think about the paranormal, metaphysical, or any of the time traveling they'd done last night. Shade desperately wanted something normal and simple, even if she had to make it up as she went along.

Raven turned and gave her one of those sexy smirks—the one Shade had in her own arsenal, and it had the same effect on her as on the women she'd used it on. Before Shade could smile back, the old internal tape of doom began playing.

Run. Get out while you still can, and no one gets hurt.

Raven's eyebrows shot up. "Your wheels turning?"

"No mind reading. Let's just have regular conversation," Shade said out loud while she told the voice in her head to shut the fuck up.

"Okay," Raven said. "I'll try and ignore the fact you're screaming at yourself, and let you go first."

Shade was rusty, but raised her mind blocks before continuing. *Smartass.*

Raven gave no indication she'd heard the thought, and Shade felt better. "I've never seen anyone cook in here before. Well, other than frozen pizza or microwave stuff."

God, that was lame. Can't you do better?

The spirit of a woman appeared, and manifested through the wall like smoke.

Apparently, she could see the dead again, but before she could react, Raven turned with a spatula in her hand and waved it in the air while she reprimanded the ghost.

"We're closed right now. You're going to have to wait until after we eat."

To Shade's utter surprise, the spirit left the way she'd floated in. "Wow," she said. "I never considered that."

"What? Asking them to leave?"

"No, I tell spirits that all the time, but I never considered asking them to take a number."

"Just one of my many talents." Raven smiled and returned her attention back to the stove.

The words brought a pleasant wave of memory, and Shade stirred in her seat.

Raven was talented in many areas and she complicated everything Shade was used to. She'd only had to look around to see a spotless house, glance down to notice her clothes were wrinkle free and smelled of fabric softener. Raven had polished Shade's environment similar to the way she'd helped her clean her emotions. It was terrifying and intoxicating.

The dead flowers on the table had been replaced with fresh lilacs sometime this morning before Shade got up. She didn't even know if they came from her own backyard. Plug-in thingies were in different outlets around her home, filling it with a clean linen scent. Raven was beautiful and strong. Shade had never seen her flinch away from confrontation; she met it head on with style, and had put Shade in her place more than once. Raven had slipped around all her barriers, and into her heart.

Shade was scared out of her mind. Raven was a dream girl, and certainly not the one she'd ever thought she'd end up with, because fantasy girls like that stayed in your mind, not in your bed.

Shade didn't have any redeeming qualities to offer in return.

She felt the effects of her medicine coming on. She welcomed the happy lift, the detour from the path her thoughts had taken.

Shade shook off the inner dialogue and hoped she didn't look as high as she felt when Raven set a plate in front of her. "Looks good. What is it?"

"Frittata," Raven said and sat across from her.

"What's in it?"

"Bacon, eggs, fresh spinach, onions. A little spice of this, and a little flavor of that."

Shade took a bite. "Delicious." And it was, but Shade had another hunger as well. "No lust spells?"

Raven shook her head. "Nope. Why, do you need one?"

"I was just teasing," Shade said.

"Of course you were." Raven smiled. "Are you feeling—hot?"

Oh yeah. Shade wanted to fan herself, but continued to eat, though concentration was difficult as she watched Raven's lips wrap around the fork with each bite she took. More out of habit than anything else, she probed a bit to see what Raven was feeling.

"I feel you," Raven said. "And don't. It was your rule, remember."

"I'm sorry. Being normal is difficult. Can you read me right now?"

Shade felt a tiny push, but her shield held.

"No, seems you're doing better." Raven dabbed her mouth with her napkin.

"This is all so fucking civilized, I feel out of place."

"Why?" Raven asked.

"I'm not used to it."

"What? Eating at the table? Having brunch? What? It's like pulling teeth to get you to explain something."

Shade felt her defensive walls come up, but made an effort to slide them back down. She looked at her plate. "Having someone take care of me."

"See?" Raven asked. "How hard was that?"

More difficult than you will ever know. Shade took several more bites to avoid saying anything else. The dark cloud she carried around began to reappear, to feed her anger and self-hatred. Raven was too good for this shit. Shade couldn't shake the feeling of being an imposter.

"It's not like you're taking advantage of me," Raven said. "I enjoy doing things for you."

"Enjoy taking care of a dark, fucked up invalid? What's *wrong* with you?" Shade was convinced there had to be something about Raven she didn't know about, otherwise why was she here? To make Shade feel even worse about herself on a daily basis? It was easy being bad but damn hard work to be good and fit in. Hence, the drugs.

Raven looked as if she'd been slapped. Two bright spots of red appeared high on her cheeks.

Uh oh. Shade had a memory flash of Raven's temper before her accident. "Wait a minute, please. Let me phrase it in a different way. You're young and have a busy life. I'm sure you have a pack of friends that miss you. You also have a job at SOS, and work in your family's store. Why on earth would you choose to be *here*?"

"Oh no, you don't," Raven said. "I see that look. You will not—I repeat not—give me any more flimsy excuses on why I don't belong here."

The venom in her tone stalled Shade's next argument.

"And I'm tired of the whole, 'you're too young' thing." Raven's tirade picked up momentum and volume. Shade put her fork down and shut up. She wasn't going to get a word in edgewise. She wanted to tell Raven she could break her neck moving it that way, but that would probably be stupid.

"While we're at it, just who the hell are you to tell me how I should feel, or where I should be? Damn it, I'm not a child, and I've proven that again and again."

Shade opened her mouth to agree, but Raven didn't pause.

"You think I've never slept with anyone before you? That I'm..." Raven made quotes in the air, "innocent?"

"Um." *Where had that come from?*

"Or that I'm weak? That I'm not good enough for you? Because I'll tell you something else, I keep up with the big dogs just fine, baby. Just fine." Raven got up from the table and took Shade's plate along with her own to the sink, mumbling something about not staying on the porch.

"I'm not done." Shade wanted to protest, but she didn't want to argue with Raven while she was in full fight mode. Especially now, as she continued to yell at her in Spanish, and she couldn't understand a word of it, but Raven's gestures and tone made her opinion perfectly clear.

It was kind of cool. Raven was gorgeous when she was spitting mad. But she'd had enough. "Stop it!" Shade yelled. "Just stop for a minute and let me talk."

Raven whirled from the sink, her eyes flashed anger, but her mouth closed, and she looked at Shade expectantly.

"First of all, I want to make something perfectly clear. I've never thought I was too good for you. You have that all wrong."

"But—"

"No," Shade said. "It's my turn. Raven, you have me set up like a doll. My house is clean, you cook, you heal, and soothe me."

"But—"

"And *I'm* not finished yet," Shade said. "It's perfectly obvious to me you're not a child, and while that argument served me in the past, it isn't working now. You humble me, Raven, flat out humble me."

Raven's expression softened. "So?"

Shade shook her head. "There are things you don't know about me, bad things that would change your mind about who I am, and what I stand for, in a heartbeat. The darkness never goes away, Raven. It never goes away." And knowing that made Shade sad. She wished she'd made different choices, handled herself better. She couldn't erase her past. She couldn't erase who she was, even if she wanted to. There was nothing inside Shade that wanted to hurt Raven.

And as sure as Shade knew the sun would come up tomorrow, eventually, she would do just that.

"There you go again," Raven said. "Putting up that barrier between us. Why do you keep shutting me out? I've proven to you I want to be here. That I *can* be here. Do you think I don't know about your drug problem?"

Shade sat resolute. She didn't want to argue anymore, and she certainly didn't want to talk about her addiction. She wanted and valued Raven above anyone or anything else in her life right now, and that's why she couldn't let herself have it. Raven deserved someone who could make her laugh. Romance, flowers, and dancing. Shade didn't have it in her to provide any of those; she wasn't built that way. "Raven, I would only bring you down with me in the end. You've already got scars because of me. I won't ever forget that. I have nothing to give you."

"I know you think you're making a noble sacrifice," Raven said. "But you're wrong, and I think it's stupid. When I go, I'm not coming back, and one day you're going to realize I was the very best thing that ever happened to you, and then you'll remember—it was you who threw what could have been away. I will not beg for your attention."

Shade limped to her recliner, kicked back, and stared at the ceiling, avoiding any more eye contact. She heard Raven walk down the hall to the guest room. That was almost too easy; she'd expected more of a fight. In the end, Shade won. She'd saved Raven, got her independence back, and could do whatever she wanted, whenever she wanted to do it. This was a good thing, she told herself. Her head ached, her stomach twisted in knots, and she felt sick, but she could fix that.

What did she want? To go up, down, or sideways? Just how many pills would it take to erase self-loathing this time?

She closed her eyes when she heard Raven approaching the living room. Shade waited for her to say something, but the next thing she heard was the front door closing quietly.

Oh God, what the fuck have I done?

❖

Hot tears slipped down her cheeks, and Raven stood in front of her house wondering if she even wanted to go in.

She didn't want to explain. She didn't want to discuss anything. She just wanted to curl up on her bed and cry it out. Her heart felt shattered, and she needed time to deal with her decision. She'd known she'd needed to walk away. The nudge, the whispered reminder of her mother's warning in her ear, the message was clear.

It was time to leave Shade to heal her own damn demons.

Raven simply couldn't, and wouldn't, kill them all for her. But wasn't it Shade's darkness that attracted her for so many years? What did that say about her?

Before she could turn back to her car, the front door opened, and her mother appeared and held out open arms. Raven didn't hesitate. She rushed into them before the sobbing started.

She welcomed the comfort and safety her mother provided, and she let her lead her into her room, and into her bed. As if the cat had radar, Blanca was by her side in a second, purring in her ear.

"Do you want me to stay, mija?"

"No, Mama. I just want to sleep right now, gracias."

"Bueno, I'll be in to check on you later."

"Love you."

"Rest now, Raven."

She turned on her side, pulled the comforter over her head, and brought her knees to her chest. She let her grief come in stages. She refused to charm herself to feel better, or ask her mother to heal her. She wanted to walk through the pain by herself. It was the only way she would make it to the other side.

❖

Somebody shook Shade's shoulder, hard. "Wake up."

"What?" Shade opened her eyes and saw Jordan leaning over her. She blinked, but when she opened her eyes, she was still there. "What?" she repeated.

"You're an asshole." Jordan turned and went into the kitchen. From her vantage point on the recliner, Shade saw several grocery bags on the counter.

"Where's Sunny?"

"Just me."

What the hell was going on? She vaguely remembered taking more pills, enough to shut her fucking voices up, and now she didn't even know what time it was.

She stood up, took a moment to balance herself, and followed Jordan. "Did you draw the short straw, or what?"

"Fucking A," Jordan said and slid her sunglasses down to look at her. "I don't know—or care—where any of this stuff goes."

Shade sat at the table and put her aching head into her hands. "I'll put them away." She reached for her cell phone on the table, hoping Raven had called while she was passed out. She was still foggy, though. How long had it been since she'd left?

"She's not going to call you."

"What are you talking about?" Shade had lost count of how many narcotics she'd taken. Her head was swimming, and her words were slurred. She was so fucked up, she couldn't read Jordan, whose thoughts appeared to be in a foreign language, which was weird because Jordan didn't speak anything but English.

Worse, she knew that Jordan knew just how high she was. That would never do. "Well, thanks." She hoped that the dripping sarcasm would get rid of her, but to Shade's horror, Jordan sat across from her and smiled wickedly.

"No problem."

Now what? "Don't you have to go home?" Shade asked.

"Nope." Jordan pulled out another chair and propped her feet on it. "We've got all night."

"To do fucking what?" Shade was confused. She and Jordan were never alone. Ever. At least not without either Sunny or Tiffany acting as a buffer. *What the fuck is going on?*

A knock on the front door startled her.

"Stay there," Jordan said. "I'll get it."

Shade wanted to throw up. She was suspicious and didn't trust Jordan, or anything else about this visit.

Jordan high-fived Kat when she opened the door, and motioned her in. Now Shade really knew something was going on, and she wanted no part of it. If this was going to be a mere visit, Sunny and Tiffany would have come as well.

"Leave me alone. Go away."

"Not happening, buddy," Kat said.

"Why are you here?" *Please, let them go away.* Shade got up and stumbled toward her bathroom, and she heard Jordan stomping right behind her. Jordan was quicker and she blocked Shade before she could enter.

"Consider it an intervention." Jordan opened her drawer, grabbed the bottles, and threw them over Shade's head to Kat, who caught them and raced to the other bathroom.

When Shade heard the toilet flush, she wanted to pass out. "What the fuck are you doing? Those are mine. I need those!"

She tried to square her shoulders, to stand up to Jordan, but before she could take a swing, Jordan put her arms around her to prevent it. "We are trying to help you."

"This is so *not* fucking helping." Shade was weak, and no match for Jordan's strength. She couldn't even draw up any psychic power to shoot at her.

"Where's the rest?" Jordan asked.

She was so calm about ripping away her security, Shade wanted to slap her.

Kat appeared, and they muscled Shade onto the bed. "Where's the rest?"

Jordan opened the nightstand and found her other stash. "Is there more?"

"Please," Shade said. "Please don't." She watched helplessly as Jordan went back into the bathroom to flush this batch. "Fuck you."

"Hey," Kat said and knelt in front of her. "We're going to help you through this, okay? You don't have to go through this alone."

"I've always been fucking alone."

"That's a lie," Jordan snapped, leaning in the doorway of the bathroom, looking every inch the cop she used to be.

Shade glared at her, thinking she was going to kick her ass or kill her. As soon as she was able to.

"Get mad!" Jordan continued. "It's better than this pathetic whining. I really thought you had more fight in you."

"Can we have a little compassion here?" Kat asked. "She's our friend. She deserves some."

"Don't you think Raven deserves our *compassion*? She's at home with a broken heart, and we find this asshole all fucked up and out of it in la-la land? Do you think that Raven *deserved* that?"

"Of course not," Kat said. "But we're still not here to attack Shade."

Shade watched the two of them argue and felt strangely detached. She had sent Raven away, had accomplished what she set out to do. Then she tried to kill the pain of what she'd done to both Raven and herself. It was business as usual, really. Why the need for good cop, bad cop?

When Kat got up, and she and Jordan began shouting at one another, she knew she had to stop. Her life was so out of control. And she didn't know how to fix the chaos she'd created. Her answer for everything had always been more. More drugs, more sex, more anything, please, to drown her self-hatred.

More had just run out. And at this point, more would never be enough again.

The thought of Raven crying broke Shade's heart, and it reached into the hard knot of anger and resentment she felt toward the world.

She tried to convince herself it wasn't all her fault because she'd warned Raven not to fall in love with her. She'd reacted from a place of fear, because when she'd seen her that morning in the kitchen, Shade had discovered she absolutely loved her too. She was terrified, and she had absolutely no idea what to do next. Her argument was weak, and it didn't hold any value any more. Shade was sick of justifying herself. She was sick, period.

Shade had never asked anyone for help, ever.

But I did. Lacey's voice whispered in her heart, the same place she'd tucked her into last night. The truth hit Shade hard, and she knew this was another moment of choice. She took a deep breath. "As much as I don't want to admit it, Jordan is right, I'm an asshole, and I need..." The word stuck in her throat, and she gestured instead.

"Say it out loud," Jordan said. "So I can be sure I heard it."

"Help. I need help. Are you happy now?" Shade wished she had something handy to throw at her.

The last thing Shade expected was for Jordan to walk over and sit next to her on the bed. She bumped her shoulder and sighed. "That's the first step."

"I want to call Raven," Shade said. "I want to apologize to her."

"Not right now," Kat said. "I don't think it's a good idea. Let her be for a while."

Jordan bumped her again. "Sunny, Aura, and Tiffany are going to take care of her."

"So you had this planned already?" She felt stripped naked, but strangely, now that the cards were tumbling down, she also felt relieved everything was out in the open.

"Aura had a vision," Jordan said. "And she told me to tell you, you weren't fooling anybody."

Shade didn't know if she'd ever felt so embarrassed. "Of course she did."

Jordan grinned at her in that evil way again. "I convinced them they were all in denial."

"Yay you." Shade glared at her, but her heart wasn't really in it.

Kat sat on the bed on her other side. "We have an intake for a treatment center in Eastern Washington."

Jesus, she had enough of her own crap. She would never be able to sit in a room full of people full of pain similar to hers. It would suffocate her before she could get better. "Oh hell no, I can do it here." Shade's stomach twisted again as she told another lie, and she instantly backed down. "I don't know if I can do this."

"Sure you can," Jordan said. "We're going to help you."

"You don't understand." Shade hated the whine in her voice.

"I understand more than you think I do. My mother was an addict. And I lost her to drugs when I was too young to understand. I spent years working the streets, watching people kill themselves on this shit. Doesn't matter which drug it is, it all kills you in the end."

"You're better than this, Shade," Kat added.

And therein, thought Shade, lay the major problem. She didn't know if she *was* better.

Or even if she could be.

CHAPTER FIFTEEN

Four months later...

Shade pulled in the driveway and stared at her front door. She hadn't been home since Jordan and Kat hauled her off to that extended-stay treatment facility. There, with professional help, she used her visiting days to work through *other* things with Aura, who made the eight-hour each way trip, once a month. There were some things Shade just couldn't share with the recovery team—not if she wanted to stay out of a psych ward, anyway.

Then, when she was done there, she spent another month in Kat's Seattle condo and tried to figure out where she wanted to go from there, and more importantly, continued to discover just who she was—without drugs.

She attended meetings every day, and told her story until she was blue in the face. At least the ones she *could* tell. And she missed Raven every day.

Every goddamn day.

The treatment center she'd gone to was too far for a casual Saturday drive, and Shade's only connection to home was Aura. She found she could stand without her sisters. That was a hard lesson, because she hadn't realized that the whole time she was feeling tough, and thought she was protecting Sunny and Tiffany—it was the other way around. They protected and enabled her.

That was horrible to swallow. And oh so humbling.

Kat and Tiffany came to see her in Seattle, along with Sunny and Jordan. Shade had found she enjoyed rediscovering who they were now, today, without all the anger and darkness she had always surrounded herself with. She also respected their boundaries when they refused to talk about Raven.

It was part of Shade's recovery. She owned years of other fuck-ups she had to deal with first, before she could even contemplate seeing Raven. She needed to be whole first, without baggage, or at least well on her way.

Tiffany, bless her heart, let it slip one day that Raven didn't work at SOS anymore. Shortly after Shade went into treatment, she'd gone back to her family's store. None of them questioned her decision. They all understood.

Shade had a close call with a relapse only two weeks ago. Jordan called to tell her the police had finally found Beenie. Well, her body anyway. She'd overdosed after writing a confession, and a heartbreaking P.S. at the bottom begging Shade to forgive her. She said she'd felt compelled to do the things she'd done, but she couldn't understand why. Only the SOS team could fully understand the compulsion, and Shade felt sorry for the woman who had very nearly killed her.

Now that she was clean, Shade shouldered her part in Beenie's death. She wished her spirit would have come to her. Shade would have sent her straight to the light. The entire sequence of events over this last year, including being in a coma, led to her life being irrevocably changed.

Those dark times led her to hope. Not the fleeting, whispering traces she'd experienced previously, but a full, hands-on experience that allowed her spirit to fly.

She'd bought another car, a little red sporty number. She'd told Jordan to fuck off when she said Shade was experiencing an early mid-life crisis, but all of their bickering was good-natured these days.

The purchase left her bank account much lower, and she planned on going back to work. There were some clients she would have to let go, and she was okay with that. Clients with darker, less than noble needs. She had a clearer sense of right and wrong, and while she fucked up in the past, she didn't have to repeat the pattern.

Spirits regularly showed up at meetings. And while that freaked her out in the beginning, she now realized it was her purpose to help the still suffering addicts, dead or alive. She took the time to gather them afterward, and counsel them. Most of them believed they couldn't cross over because of things they'd done during their lifetimes. The ones who refused to leave, although few, were the spirits who chose to stay to cause trouble. Those with harmful energy, she dismissed and banned—until they were ready for help.

All that remained to be seen about her willingness to stay drug free was her ability to be in Bremerton, and be in her house. On her own.

Might as well get it over with, she thought. Shade walked up to the door, with barely a hitch in her stride left over from her accident. Her limp had gone away right after she arrived in the facility. Another clue that she was on the right journey, as Angel had predicted.

She unlocked the deadbolt and stood on the threshold.

No one knew she was coming home today. It wasn't as if she wanted to announce it, or have a welcome home party. Shade took a deep breath and walked into her house, where most of her ghosts still lived. Where she'd been so casually cruel to so many, both living and dead.

Would she be able to stay here? She wasn't sure yet. She took another hesitant step into the entry, and a chill raced down her spine when she saw the items. Shade took slow steps over to her chair.

A black guitar case sat on her recliner along with a small package. Shade ran her finger along the ribbon, then held the present close to her face.

Oh God, it smelled like her.

Raw emotion hit her senses, and she stopped to let it flow all the way through. It hurt, yes. But hey—the only way out was through. She finally understood what that sentence really meant.

She smiled sadly, moved the case, and sat down. Shade carefully unwrapped the paper to save it, not caring that the old Shade would have thought it a wussy thing to do. There was no note attached, but she didn't need one.

Raven's energy was all over it. She'd made her a bracelet of wrapped leather and beaded cords, surrounding a small charm that said, *Believe.*

Shade put it on and wanted to cry. She opened the guitar case, and did.

❖

Raven was in the back office, making notes on her vendor charts, when she heard an internal bell ring.

Shade was back in Bremerton, and her presence tripped the spell Raven had placed in the entry hall of Shade's place. It wasn't the first time it had gone off, but Raven had no problem identifying whose energy passed over it. The time she'd spent at SOS created permanent signatures for all the women. The trauma they'd survived together, the intensity of emotion, were all imprinted in Raven's mind.

She'd had a dream Shade was coming home three nights ago. She'd had time to pick up the guitar, and the Believe bracelet had been made nearly a month ago.

Into both gifts, she poured pure, positive energy, and folded in some healing intentions. While she was at it, she made an effort to leave behind her youthful yearning for Shade, along with her wish that things could have ended differently.

When she'd first entered the house, Raven's heart felt echoes of her pain. It was far more intense than she thought it would be. She thought she'd buried it deeper. But like something living that sinks in the water, it rose back to the surface after the struggle, and stared at her with dead eyes. She left the case on Shade's recliner, with the wrapped gift next to it, and quickly left the house.

She'd mourned deeply for Shade, and experienced the death of her own idealistic expectations. But gradually, she was able to discern a different point of view of their time together.

And it wasn't all Shade's fault.

Raven had craved her darkness, was insanely attracted to her unavailability, charged in to save her, and then expected her to change.

Shade hadn't written, hadn't called, hadn't made any effort to contact her at all, and Raven knew she'd been living in Seattle for weeks. That information uncovered the hope she thought she'd given up.

And now, the ringing bell revealed much more. Wave after wave of emotion hit her until she felt dizzy from the onslaught. She reached for the phone and then quickly drew her hand back.

"Mija?"

Of course, her mother would feel it too, and come to check on her. "I'm good, Mama."

"I just wanted you to know I'm here if you want to talk."

"Gracias." Raven felt none of the resentment she used to when her mother interfered. Her mother had been her rock when she fell apart. She remained a steady, soothing force available to her when she reached for it. And when Raven was ready to hear them, her mother had the words to help her through to the other side.

Her mother never judged Shade, or said I told you so.

It was a rite of passage between a mother and an adult daughter, one that took Raven into another transition of maturity, and attempted to leave her devastating crush behind.

She'd seen it clearly the day she chose to leave, when she'd had enough. A premonition hit that she'd always live on the dark side with Shade, and enable her to keep herself there. As much as Raven wanted to stay, it wouldn't have been healthy for Shade, and it would have been miserable for her.

In principal, she believed individuals entered someone's life, and then left after you learned whatever lesson was needed in order to grow spiritually.

It sounded good in theory, but right this moment, she felt as if she stepped back in time, and the wound was fresh again. Raven knew it diminished her personal authority to recall only the pain. She tried to remember to forgive Shade, and herself, for the soul experience, and bring her power back, but she wasn't having much success.

She ordered herself to get it together and turned her back to the phone. As soon as she did, her hand itched again, and she ran out of the office.

Her mother could probably use some help in the front during the afternoon rush. It would be a good distraction. She was right. People were crowding the aisles, and the line to check out was ten deep. Raven took over the register while her mother answered customers' questions and directed them to the correct shelves.

After she finished her last transaction two hours later, she was relieved to find there was no one else waiting. But before she could take a deep breath, her cousin Lyric walked in and headed straight for her.

Raven waved and leaned on the counter.

"What's wrong with you?" Lyric asked.

"Nothing." *Everything.* "Why?"

"Because I know your face," Lyric said.

Raven sighed. "I don't want to talk about it. I'm fine."

Lyric shrugged. Raven loved that about her. Lyric never pushed, but it was usually because she wanted to talk about herself. It was part of her charm.

"Well, then. Get your stuff and let's go get ready."

"To go where?"

"Don't tell me you forgot. You *promised* me."

"You're such a drama queen," Raven said. But she had forgotten. She'd promised Lyric she'd go on a double date. "Was that tonight?"

Lyric rolled her eyes at Raven. "You know it's the only way I could get a date with Caroline while she's in town. Her college friend joined her at the last minute, and you said you'd go with us and keep her company."

Caroline was a traveling bank manager who came into the Bremerton branch every few months. She was blond, skinny, and Raven was sure, in the end, she was going to break Lyric's heart.

It wasn't anything Caroline had done in the past. She was sweet enough. So maybe Raven was projecting her own experience onto Lyric's life.

Still, she couldn't think of anything she wanted to do less than spend an evening with two giggling former college roommates while Lyric fawned over Caroline.

And God, she was being unfair. She had promised her, and was only feeling this way because of—that person she wasn't supposed to be thinking about.

"Let me get my things," Raven said and tried not to feel like an ass when Lyric's face lit up with gratitude.

Raven retrieved her coat and bag, and then took a moment to disarm the bell in her mind. Shade was home safe. That was what she'd wanted to know, and now she did. She tried to be positive and told herself she was going to have a good time.

It didn't work.

❖

Shade kept her promise and checked in when she arrived. Her sponsor, Wendy, stayed on the phone with her while she checked any former stash locations Jordan might have missed.

When she looked in the last probable spot and found nothing, she chuckled. Jordan may not be a cop anymore, but she didn't miss a detail. Shade assured Wendy that all spaces were accounted for, and that she would go to a local twelve-step meeting.

After she disconnected the call, Shade wandered the rooms aimlessly, feeling weird and disconnected. The times she remembered as fun now seemed desperate, and she hated to say it, but quite a few of them were depraved as well. She shuddered inwardly and reminded herself that she, as a person, was not her past. The things she'd done did not define her.

There weren't many happy memories here, and until Raven came along, Shade wasn't even sure the house was ever cleaned thoroughly, and she'd lived there for eight years.

Raven's touch was still everywhere. Shade wondered why she hadn't retrieved her crystals from around the house when she dropped off those amazing gifts.

The guest bathroom still smelled of her, feminine and bold at the same time.

Shade missed her, and had thought of her every day while she was gone. At night, she dreamed of her and wrapped herself in Raven's scented hair.

But Shade had promised herself she wouldn't go to her unless she could stand tall and proud. She didn't want Raven to fix her, Shade wanted to be whole *for* her. Raven deserved that.

Shade had learned a lot about herself in the previous months. The lectures were familiar, as she'd heard them from Aura, Sunny, and Tiffany in the past. But there was something about being called out on your shit by strangers, sitting still, and listening—because you no longer wanted the alternative. The pain of using was finally greater than the pain of not.

The house felt closed in, and Shade went to the back door. She stood and looked out, unable to comprehend it was her yard. She made a note to ask who'd mowed the jungle down, because it was beautiful out here. There was new yard furniture and a cherub fountain.

Angel chose that. Ah, it was Tiffany's family who'd done the work. Gratitude and love swelled in her chest. It was just like them to do this. Kat was big on outside spaces after living in a condo for so many years, and just having grass to mow made her happy.

Shade sat in the loveseat swing and rocked back and forth, enjoying the sun peeking through the clouds, and wondering if she should call Raven, or wait. A light flashed in her eyes, and Shade looked down at what caused it. The Believe charm on her bracelet caught the sun and sparkled at her.

Shade smiled and thought it just might be serendipity. She'd take it, whatever it was.

She pulled out her phone again and dialed the number she'd memorized.

"Whispering Winds, how may I help you?"

"Um, hey. Hi. Is Raven around?" Shade held her breath. She was certain Raven's mother knew it was her. The pause lengthened, and Shade wondered if Juanita had hung up on her. "Hello?"

"No, Shade," Juanita said. "I'm going to tell you the truth. She's out on a date."

"Oh." Shade felt like a donkey had kicked her in the chest, and was going to ask if she could leave her a message, but Juanita hung up on her before she could.

Well, that hadn't gone as well as she thought it would. Shade went back into the house.

"And why should it go your way?"

Shade turned slowly to face the corner, where the voice had come from. Her body was hidden in the shadows, but the voice was unmistakable, as well as the sarcastic, condescending laughter that followed. She'd practiced with Aura, several times, what she would do if her mother showed up, now that she was on the path to healing.

"Hello, Mother." Shade swallowed her revulsion and took a deep breath. "Have you come for help?"

The look of abject shock and surprise on her mother's face was a pure bonus. Shade calmly smiled at her.

"Who are you?" her mother asked and sneered. "Nobody, that's who."

"You don't have any power over me, not anymore."

Shade tuned out her spitting fury and the remarks aimed to hurt her. She refused to engage.

"Are you done?"

Her mother continued to spew hatred.

"No?" Shade asked. "Okay. I've had enough. You're not even real, and I'm done." Shade flicked her wrist, and the corner was instantly empty.

God, that felt good. Aura had finally gotten through to Shade. Her mother, Travis, and so many other dark spirits like them stayed around because Shade kept them alive and near—subconsciously to punish herself.

She was a long way from forgiveness at this point in her recovery, but she was willing to concede there was no longer a need to listen to her mother's garbage. She shook off the encounter and disconnected her energy from it. Her mother wouldn't get any more from her.

Instead, she closed her eyes and thought about Raven. Shade hadn't given her a reason to stay; she'd only provided a free ride on the rollercoaster of misery that was Shade's world. Where there wasn't room to laugh, because everything was centered on her misery, her addiction, her, her, her.

Now she was all alone.

Shade recognized the downward spiral of self-pity and stopped it. That was so not allowed. She wasn't going to feel sorry for herself and stand in the corner.

Raven is dating? Hmm. She hoped the other woman was ready for a challenge. Because Shade wasn't going to walk away, or disappear into the night gracefully.

Not a chance.

For the first time in her life, Shade stood comfortably in her power, free of shadow and doubts. It was time to fight the good fight for something she believed in.

❖

"I'm not wearing that!" Raven yelled at Lyric. "And you can't make me." The dress in question was a strappy, thin, red wrap-around that left Raven's entire cleavage bare and clung to her curves without mercy. "It screams I'm available, and take a number." *And I bought it to wear for Shade.*

Lyric begged a little, but gave up when Raven wouldn't budge. Instead, she chose a black tank dress with a modest neckline, and with a sweater, her outfit looked as if she were attending a business meeting.

When they arrived at the hotel's restaurant, it appeared Caroline's friend, Brittney, was wearing the same exact dress Raven had refused to, only in blue, which matched her eyes.

Raven thought she looked better in it, then chided herself for feeling resentful. It wasn't Brittney's fault Raven was here.

Over dinner, Brittney turned out to be quite charming, and sweet to talk to. Raven grudgingly admitted she was having a good time. The table was full of flirtatious energy flying in all directions. They talked about current events, charities, and each had a funny customer story. The dinner went by quickly.

After a drink, Brittney focused more on Raven. She twisted a lock of her hair, leaned forward, and at every opportunity, pursed her lips in a sexy pout.

Raven was flattered, and considered it for a half of a second. But it was never going to happen. Brittney wasn't at all her type. She didn't have dark hair, wasn't tall, or on the slender side. There wasn't any mystery in her eyes, and she was as easy to read as a morning newspaper.

Curious, she probed Britney's mind slightly and got an image of her naked and twisting on a bed, while Raven serviced her. That was her exact thought, *serviced.*

Raven looked a little deeper and saw Brittney on the phone with her wife, Tess, assuring her she was going straight to bed after dinner.

She was so done with this farce. Raven wasn't into casual sex, especially with a pillow-princess, married woman who wasn't her type. So, really—why *was* she here?

Lyric handed the waiter her credit card. "More cocktails, ladies? Dancing?"

Raven shook her head, and Lyric kicked her under the table. Raven ignored her. "You're going to have to go without me. I have an early morning. It was nice to meet you, though, and thank you for the lovely time."

Brittney stood, as if to argue, or stop her, and Raven held out a hand. "Maybe next time, Tess, your wife, can join us." Raven smiled wickedly, turned, and walked away from the table. She wasn't worried about Lyric. Raven had taken a moment to peek into Caroline's thoughts, and saw quite an energetic threesome planned.

She stopped before getting into her car, took a deep breath, and searched for Shade's energy. She traced it back to the bell and discovered it was gone. Did that mean she'd left town? Or was there some other, worse, reason she couldn't feel it?

It could be either, and Raven didn't want to run through any more possibilities. She wanted only to go home, get in her comfy clothes, and read a book.

If she told herself that a hundred times, would she believe it?

Absolutely not.

Chapter Sixteen

Shade knocked on Sunny's door and noticed that she and Jordan replaced the clear glass with a beautiful stained glass panel. The change brought up quite a few moments of nostalgia, good ones, of Shade living here while loving Sunny.

She reached for the gratitude for the experience and felt none of the loss she had previously attached to the house, or to Sunny herself.

The door opened, and there she stood. Sunny poured out her light, and Shade drank it in as the gift it was. "Hey."

"Well, hello. You're late as usual. Come on in. We're all waiting for you."

Shade checked her watch. "I am not! It's five till."

"I'm just teasing. But really, on time means being at least fifteen minutes early."

"No one told me that," Shade said. "Ever."

"We're in the dining room. I'll bring you some water."

"Thanks." Shade watched her walk away and felt out of place.

"There you are," Kat said and clutched Shade's arm dramatically. "Please, *please* be on my side today."

Shade laughed. "For?" She picked up on Kat's playful energy, but sensed desperation underneath it.

"Just say yes."

"Okay." If Shade didn't agree with Kat, at least she hadn't said yes. If there was one thing she was good at, it was semantics.

Tiffany came around the doorway of the dining room, and a wave of tenderness stopped Shade's forward motion, and she held out her arms. Tiffany hugged her, curled tightly into her side, and she tightened her arms around her. "I'm so sorry, Tiff."

"For what?"

"Being so much trouble all the time."

Tiffany stepped back, tucked a lock of hair behind her ear, and shook her head. "I have you so beat there. You," she said, "addiction. Me, homicidal, dead ex-husband and blood curses. I win." Tiffany took her arm and led her into the dining room.

Shade let her think she'd won, because it didn't cost her anything to let her. Besides, she was happy that Tiffany appeared to be coping so well. "You're so goddamn cute," Shade said.

Aura was lighting candles around the room, and the area smelled of sweet sage. The scent of home. Shade hugged her and sat in her usual spot at the long, polished table. She had so many happy memories centered around it, and today none of them were tainted by the darkness she'd carried.

Sunny, herself, and Tiffany had started Sisters of Spirits here, with Aura's guidance. Shade looked at each of them in turn, and they each looked back at her expectantly.

"We're waiting on you," Kat said. "You called this meeting."

"Oh, right." Shade got up from the table and crossed to the whiteboard set up in the front of the room. "I need. Uh…"

"You can do it," Jordan said. "Spit it out."

"Okay, smartass. I need help. Again."

"Of course," Aura said. Shade knew she could always count on her.

"Sounds serious," Sunny said. "Are you okay?"

"I'm in," Tiffany interrupted. "Whatever you need."

"Me too," Kat added.

Shade looked at Jordan, who smirked and nodded.

"Okay then." Shade's scalp tingled and she pointed at Tiffany. "Stop that, I'm getting to it."

"Quit stalling already," Jordan said.

Shade resisted the urge to flip her off. "Now, don't laugh. I need your help, because I want to learn how to be romantic."

She waited for the hilarity to die down, and tapped her foot impatiently.

"I'm sorry." Jordan coughed into her hand. "I thought I heard you say you wanted to learn how to be romantic."

"Stop it!" Sunny hit Jordan's shoulder and smiled brightly at Shade. "I think it's sweet."

Tiffany couldn't stop giggling, and Shade was reminded of her previous voyeurism of her sex life. Actually, Tiffany might remember it better than Shade did. *Now that was funny.*

Kat, the newest member of the sisterhood, hadn't known Shade's reputation personally in this life, but had been her student in a bygone century.

Aura clapped her hands to quiet the group. "That's my girl," she said. "Go on."

"You can't teach an old dog new tricks."

"So not true, Jordan," Sunny said. "Just last week you learned how to—"

"Point taken," Jordan interrupted her, and turned red.

Sunny winked at Shade. She could have looked into Jordan's thoughts, but had a good idea of what Sunny had been talking about. It was a tantric move Shade had taught her years ago. Shade was kind of impressed with Jordan, since it took some serious stretching to get it right.

She saw the actual memory behind her eyes, saw herself with Sunny, and stopped.

And waited.

There wasn't any grief or resentment attached to it, just a fond remembrance of how young they had been, and it reassured Shade that she had truly let go.

"I find it hard to believe you need any help with the ladies," Kat said. "Your prowess is legend."

Shade laughed. "Romance and sex are two different things. I have complete confidence in the latter."

Sunny blushed, and Shade turned her back to the group to change the direction of the conversation. She printed out the word *Ideas* on the top of the board and then drew a line underneath it.

"Write down the flowers you sent this morning," Aura said. "Oh, and the card."

Shade looked at her.

"What?" Aura smiled. "I'm your mother. I know these things."

The warmth of love behind the statement filled Shade to the brim, and she nodded.

The room was getting hot, and Shade rolled up her sleeves.

"That's a cool bracelet," Tiffany said. "Our Raven made us all one, with different charms. Mine says Family."

"Me too, mine has a butterfly, and a silver love charm. Raven said she was going to make an entire line of them for the store." Sunny raised her arm and showed off her bracelet.

Shade rolled the beads between her fingers and saw Raven while she was making hers.

Hers was the only bracelet that held Raven's tears. Shade promised herself she would turn every single one of those tears into laughter.

"Okay, brainstorm with me here."

Raven was a few minutes late, and her mother had opened the store. When she entered, she was met by the smell of roses. In a crystal vase on the retail counter were at least three dozen red roses laced with baby's breath. She walked over to see who they were for, but she knew.

She reached out and ran a finger softly across the petals while inhaling deeply. Her heart pounded while she opened the card with shaky fingers.

Thank you for everything. Love, Lacey.

That surprised her, but the thought was wonderful, and her spirit lifted. "They're beautiful," she said out loud.

"Sí," her mother said.

Raven startled, as she hadn't known she was behind her.

"Can I give you some advice?"

The fact she'd asked instead of told her was another reminder of how their relationship had grown. Raven nodded and turned the vase this way and that.

"I know that you want to run to her, mija. I'm also aware of how deeply you still feel about her. But this time, make her work for it. Let her prove to you that you're worth the attention."

"But—"

"No, mija. She also needs to prove to herself she needs to work for it. Last time was too easy for her, and she'll never appreciate you as much as she would if you make her chase you."

"We've already had sex, Mother," Raven said. "There isn't any mystery there."

"Oh, my ears! That's not what I'm saying. That was then, and you both skipped the courtship, the fun and importance of it."

"I thought you didn't want me to go back to Shade."

"She called yesterday."

"What? Mama, you didn't tell me?"

Her mother gestured toward the flowers. "My point exactly."

Raven wondered why Shade didn't call her cell, but remembered she'd switched carriers, and while she still had Shade's number, she had no way other than the store to contact her.

"Besides," her mother continued. "She'll have to prove to me she's worth having my baby girl, that she's changed her ways."

"Isn't that my decision?" Raven didn't want to argue with her, but she needed to stand her ground.

"Sí, at the heart of it. But because I hurt with a mother's pain right along with you, I need time to heal as well. I'm not going to jump up and down and welcome back the woman who broke your heart."

Raven coughed to smother a laugh as she pictured her mother doing just that. "You're right."

Her mother dramatically placed a hand over her heart. "Qué? What did you say?"

Raven smiled. "I said, you're right, and I won't settle for anything less than the best."

Her mother cried happy tears and hugged her before she went back to the office.

Raven moved the flowers to the center of the store, on top of a display, where she could see them from anywhere in the retail area.

Show me what you got, babe.

❖

"This is all we have for the list?" Shade asked. "It's pathetic. Flowers, candlelight dinner, dancing, back rub, and a surprise puppy." She paused. "Well, I kind of like the last one." She looked around the room again. "Jordan. What did you have?"

"Way to call me out," Jordan said. "Well, I carried her up the stairs after she fell."

"It was your fault," Sunny said. "I thought you were a robber."

"That's it?"

"Well, there was that time when the lights went out in my apartment building, and I made out with her."

"Jesus, that was when you were under oppression. Sunny, is that all she has? Because that makes me want to cry for you."

"Let me think. I have something, I'm sure. Wait, she makes me green smoothies in the morning."

Shade shook her head. "Okay, no help from either of you. Kat?"

"Which life? The time I chased her through the woods after dancing naked around a fire, or this one, where we lived through a murder?"

"Point taken," Shade said. "You guys are pitiful. No wonder I was the only one getting any action."

"We were aiming a little higher," Jordan said.

"Touché," Shade said and gave her a quick nod. "I'll give you that one."

"These are some good ideas," Aura said. "But I have a better one."

"I'm all ears," Shade said. "Because I can do any of these with my eyes closed. It has to be fantastic, over the top, and she has to love it."

"Oh, it's perfect." Aura smiled. "I saw it."

Shade grinned. "Now, *that's* what I'm talking about. Give it to me."

They chattered around the table, outlining the plan. The mood was enthusiastic and happy. Shade thought she couldn't have come up with a better solution than asking her family for help.

This was going to be epic.

When they were done, Kat stood up and cleared her throat. "Before we go, I have something I need to do right now, here in front of all of you."

Tiffany looked surprised. "How come I don't know about this? I know everything that's going on."

"I helped her," Aura said. "Just a bit."

Kat took something from her inside coat pocket, turned Tiffany's chair to face her, and then got on one knee.

"Oh!" Tiffany gasped. "Oh," she said again when she saw the ring, and began crying.

"Will you marry me? I promise to love you and Angel forever. Again."

Tiffany couldn't speak, but nodded vigorously while she held out her right hand.

Shade caught Kat's eye for a second and she winked at her. The table erupted with excited cries and tearful congratulations.

"Yay!" Sunny said. "We have so much planning to do. Mom, who can we get for the flowers?"

Shade realized her own eyes watered a bit, and she was happy for all of them, but was anxious to begin her own new life.

With Raven. If she could catch her.

Shade said her good-byes and left quickly. She finally had a plan, and she wanted to get everything into place.

❖

Raven recognized the young boy from the neighborhood when he rushed into the store. He waved an orange envelope and rushed over to her, out of breath and clearly excited.

"Some lady outside paid me to bring this to you!"

"Did she now?" Raven asked and tried to look out the front window.

"Oh, no," he said. "She's gone now. I saw her leave. Here, take it."

Raven took the package that felt like a CD. She took five dollars out of her pocket and held it out to him. "Thank you," she said.

"More money, thanks!" The boy rushed out, probably afraid Raven would change her mind, and she laughed.

She tapped the envelope against her palm and debated whether to open it right away. *Who am I kidding?* She ripped the side and looked at the plastic cover.

Play me.

Nothing else, just the two words. Raven excused herself from the counter and went into the back office where her laptop was sitting on the desk.

Her hands trembled slightly as she put the disc in.

"Um, hi. Raven. I wrote this for you. I have words and stuff, but I'm not a very good singer. Thank you for giving me back the gift of music. Um. So, anyway, here goes."

Raven's heart lurched in her chest at the sound of her voice. It was different somehow, but still all Shade's.

There was a small pause, and guitar music poured from the tiny speaker. She didn't need the lyrics, she could feel the energy behind the melody. The dark chords turned even darker before they lifted and soared. The guitar's strings sang straight to her soul. Within the notes, she felt the words Shade hadn't been able to give to her.

Her eyes filled with the aching beauty of it and the force of Shade's love for her.

When the guitar music faded out, she heard a click, then Shade speaking again.

"Well, I hope you liked it. I, uh, I'd love to see you tonight. Could you please call me?"

There was another pause.

"I love you, Raven."

The timer on her music program showed the recording was over.

Raven wasn't going to play any games, or waste any more time. She'd heard all she needed in the music, and in Shade's voice.

She reached for the phone.

CHAPTER SEVENTEEN

S hade's heart pounded against her ribs. She was nervous and hoped she hadn't forgotten any details for the evening. She looked down at her white dress shirt and black slacks. Oh shit, she had even worried about looking like a waiter when she'd bought them. It was too late to change now.

She took a breath and knocked.

The door opened in a flash, and Juanita stood in front of her. "You clean up nice," she said. "Raven's not done yet. Come in."

The creepy smile scared Shade a bit, but she entered. She felt Juanita trying to slip past her thought guard. "You don't have to sneak," she said. "Go ahead." Shade dropped her mental shield, and let her look. She showed her what was in her heart. Shade knew it was pure, and she wasn't worried about acknowledging how she felt, but she *was* going to stop her before she saw what she'd planned for the night. "Enough," she said.

"Bueno. You realize it's going to take me some time, sí?"

"I'm sorry, I really am." And she was. "I'll make it up to you."

"You make Raven happy. That has some weight. But words are cheap, and only time will prove to me you've changed."

"Of course." She heard heels clicking on the wood floor. The butterflies in her stomach seemed to kick into high gear, and she prayed she wouldn't get sick right there in the hallway. She didn't think she'd ever been this nervous in her life.

Raven turned the corner of the hall, and Shade felt struck by lightning.

Ohmifuckinggod. Shade looked around quickly, but she was almost certain she hadn't said it out loud.

Raven smiled seductively at her, and Shade knew that she, at least, had heard her first reaction. Her tongue stuck to the roof of her dry mouth, and when she tried to say hello, nothing came out but a grunt.

Juanita glared, and her expression told Shade she had heard her inside voice as well. She shook her head in apparent disapproval, and disappeared into the kitchen, leaving Shade alone with Raven.

Her hair was loose and flowing around her shoulders, her lips full and red, matching the slinky dress that accentuated every beautiful curve on her body.

"Ack," Shade said.

"I'll take that as you like it?"

She nodded. Raven's scent enveloped her, and Shade was paralyzed by it. She felt like an ass. Where were her smooth moves and confidence? She felt as if she'd never been on a date before. Well, really, she admitted, there weren't many actual dates. Hookups was a better word. Pure panic began to take over when she realized she didn't know how to behave at all, because she couldn't remember the last time she'd been with a woman, and she hadn't been fucked up in one way or another. "Nnng,"

Raven pressed her cheek to Shade's. "You look fabulous."

Shade shook her head. "Nn-ng."

Raven stepped back and then turned around in a slow circle, giving Shade an additional view of the way the dress dipped low, revealing the dimples on the small of her back, before draping around her hips, and the material left little to the imagination. It fit her like a second skin, hugging her ass and the tiny strip of a red thong underneath it.

Shade desperately attempted to speak normally. "Ff-f." *God help me. I may have swallowed my tongue.*

Raven picked up a silver, lace shawl from the hall tree and wrapped herself in it, leaving her shoulders bare.

"Hnk."

"Really?" Raven asked, then yelled into the kitchen. "Mother, stop it!"

Shade heard laughter, and a quick exchange in Spanish before the gleeful giggling returned. She was more than relieved that her inability to speak wasn't her own doing. "Thank you," she whispered. "Can we go now?" Shade turned the handle and hoped this was a warning and not a sign of things to come with Raven's mother.

After she closed the door behind them, Raven grabbed each side of Shade's collar and tugged her face down to her. "Here," she said. "Let me help you with that."

Shade nearly lost her balance, but steadied herself by pulling Raven's hips closer.

She slid perfectly against her and molded to her body with a rush of warmth. Shade didn't have any time to think before Raven's lips met hers.

They were soft, sweet, and oh so incredibly sexy. A half growl, half purr started at the back of her throat, and the kiss started a chain reaction of heat that started from her toes and rose to the top of her head.

Raven hadn't even opened her mouth. She hadn't done anything but touch her lips, and Shade nearly forgot they were standing on her mother's porch.

If this is what a simple kiss was doing to her, what was going to happen later?

Raven leaned back and wiped red lip gloss from Shade's mouth with her thumb, and then dabbed at the rest with a small tissue she'd pulled from her purse. After wiping her thumb, she smiled up at her.

Shade knew she would always remember this moment—Raven radiant on the porch under the glow of a full moon. And she would cherish it forever because she also knew her life could really begin in this minute, on the porch, under the full moon, with a perfect kiss.

The night was still young, and Shade had plans to add many more memories to it.

"Ready?" Shade held her arm out, and Raven tucked her hand around her elbow while Shade helped her down the stairs to the car.

Shade opened the door for her, and was rewarded by the sight of bare, beautifully tan thighs as Raven folded herself into the low passenger's seat.

"Nice ride."

"I feel like I'm riding in a roller skate sometimes."

"But it's hot," Raven said. "Or you wouldn't have bought it."

"Seems I'm taking a liking to things that are—spicy," Shade whispered. "Muy caliente."

"Your Spanish is improving."

Shade chuckled. "No, I just know 'hot' in any language."

"Ooh la la."

"My point exactly." Shade was enjoying the banter, the easy flirting, but the pace didn't match the high rate of her pulse. In the depths of Raven's eyes, Shade saw herself—the person she could become, the woman she wanted to be.

She shut the car door, and the sound felt like a period on the end of a long sentence that was once her past. Shade jogged around to the driver's side.

Raven crossed her legs, and something sparkled in her strappy high heel. Shade faltered when she threw the car into first, and spun the tires before they pulled away from the curb. She didn't know why some women wore such high heels, but right then, she was grateful to be the one to witness how amazing they looked on Raven's feet. Shade's gaze shifted upward and stopped at the splendid shadow of Raven's cleavage.

"Watch the road," Raven said.

"Huh? Oh yeah, sorry." Shade was going to kill them both if she didn't stop staring. She deliberately looked at the road.

"I'll make you a deal," Raven said. "You pay attention to your driving now, and I'll let you look later."

The promise projected images in Shade's mind, and almost distracted her as much as her bare skin had. "Jesus, Raven. We have a long way to drive." And to Shade it felt as if two blocks would be too long. "And I've never wanted anything as much as I want you right now."

"Where are we going?"

"Seattle."

"That *is* a long way." Raven's tone was teasing, and smooth as butter before it turned serious. "Sometimes, the very best things worth having, take some time."

Shade detected the nuance of unsaid words. She'd lived an instant gratification lifestyle for so long, it would be an integral part of her recovery to learn patience. "Something tells me we're not just talking about—"

"No," Raven interrupted. "We're not."

"Let's start with this. I am so sorry for the way I treated you."

Raven touched Shade's shoulder. "You don't need to—"

"Yes, I do. I was mean and ungrateful." Shade wanted to look at her expression, but she knew how Raven was feeling. She felt the flash of hurt. "When I cut through all the bullshit, mine, not yours, I realized after being beat over the head with it that I was terrified of what you represented to me."

"Why? I'm an excellent catch."

"My point exactly." Shade chuckled. "You were everything I thought I didn't deserve. Honestly, after Sunny and I broke up, I convinced myself I had reached way too high."

"But—"

"Let me get it all out, okay? Hang on." Shade changed three lanes and followed the next Seattle sign before moving over two more, keeping herself in the fast lane. "Okay, where were we?"

"Sunny."

"No, this isn't about Sunny. It's about me. And you." Shade wanted Raven to understand that above all. "I used the breakup as an excuse not to be involved in my own life. Of course, I was heartbroken then. But really, the breakup validated how I felt about myself to begin with. It allowed me to justify my bad habits and behavior."

"Raven, you saw what happened to me as a child, as much as I wish you didn't, I'll be forever grateful for your help."

"I'm not sorry," Raven said. "Though I'll freely admit your father telling us it was our second trip freaked me out a little."

"I know, right?" Shade laughed. "I'm not even anywhere near processing that yet."

"Me neither," Raven said.

"If you let me, I'll make it up to you every day."

"Go on," Raven said.

Shade finally let herself glance over at her. "You take my breath away."

Raven fanned herself dramatically. "Oh? And?"

"You're amazing and pure."

"Have you fooled, don't I? I'm not as good as you think I am. You're under the mistaken impression I'm a nice girl."

"Sweetheart, you are."

"Take that back!"

"Really? God, you're adorable. Okay, make me."

"I'll remember that." Raven leaned toward her and blew hot breath against Shade's neck before pulling away. "Later."

Shade swallowed hard. "You win."

"Win what?" Raven laughed.

"Um, everything?"

"So you're smart now, too?"

"I'm learning." Shade relaxed a little bit. Not that she wasn't still nervous, she was, but Raven's energy was accepting. The edge thrumming along her nerve endings was a raw sexual buzz. She had so much to tell Raven, and entire conversations flitted out of her brain before she could voice them. Not only was Raven a complete distraction, she was an incredibly strong force in the small car, and her scent filled Shade, making her dizzy from the wanting of her.

The city lights of Seattle became visible in the night sky, and Shade was grateful they were closer. She couldn't wait to put her arms around Raven again.

It wasn't just the fierce physical attraction, though that was stellar. Traces of Raven's energy had remained with Shade for the last six months. A loving, healing presence living within her broken spirit, a bond that reassured her daily, and had given her hope while she was gone.

Shade knew they needed to talk, that Raven needed to hear her story, and she didn't think that an "I'm sorry," was quite enough. But they would get to that.

Right this moment, they were dressed to the nines and on a real date. Shade cared, really cared, about what Raven thought of her today.

Her new sports car hugged the curves of the freeway and drove like a dream. Life was excellent. She glanced over at Raven and saw that she'd either just licked her lips or reapplied her lipstick, because her mouth looked luscious, wet, red, and ready to kiss again.

Shade prayed the drive would go faster. When they hit Seattle traffic, she headed toward the city center and concentrated on the drive. She didn't have quite the bird's eye view she had in her van, so it took more finesse. The way everything in her life did now, it seemed.

❖

Raven kept quiet during the maneuvering it took to get through Seattle's downtown streets. After their kiss, and brief flirting, she hadn't known what to say when Shade kept trying to apologize.

She didn't want her to be sorry. Everything happened for a reason, and the Universe had played out this situation to get where they were today. She would admit to dressing with torture in mind, and she was happy she hadn't worn the dress when Lyric wanted her to on that disastrous double date. It had the exact effect she was hoping for.

Truthfully, Raven had forgiven her the moment the roses came. Lyric had called her a few names in jest, "whupped" being one of them.

Raven had wonderful dreams of Shade and their future, but nothing was ever set in stone, people had free will, prophecies could change, and Shade could relapse and become the person she'd been once more.

"I can only promise you today."

Shade's soft statement brought Raven out of her thoughts. She hadn't realized she was broadcasting so clearly. "Can you explain that to me?"

"Sure," Shade said. "Let's get settled first, okay?"

Raven smiled at her. "Of course." She watched Shade walk around to her side of the car. Her belly buzzed pleasantly, and the sensation headed due south. Shade looked hotter than she'd ever seen her.

When Raven took her hand for help out, the contact of their skin crackled with sharp electric jolts.

"Sorry," Shade said. "That happens a lot lately. I feel as if I'm bursting with it."

"You are." Raven stood and nearly tipped over on her heels, but Shade was standing close and pulled her against her body, laying a strong hand on Raven's lower back to steady her.

"Thank you." Raven felt Shade's heart beating against her palm. The temperature between them rose until she was sure her skin would ignite from the heat. She looked up into Shade's eyes, which were focused on her like lasers. Raven shivered from the intensity and knew when they made love this time, it would be unforgettable.

Shade grinned at her, and Raven knew she'd read her mind again. Did she think it was unforgettable? It would be beyond description. Raven inserted naked images of the two of them doing naughty things.

Shade's breathing increased until it was heavy, almost harsh. "Please pull back."

Raven managed to shield her emotions, but it was several moments before she felt steady. Shade's power was raw, and Raven had been unprepared for the undiluted rush of it.

"I'm sorry." Shade rested her forehead against Raven's.

"For what?" Raven asked. "Sharing? Get over it." She smiled up at her. "Let's save it for after dinner, shall we?"

Shade groaned.

Raven raised an eyebrow. "You better get some protein in you, old lady."

Shade laughed, and Raven reveled in the genuine sound before Shade put her arm around her and steered her toward the restaurant. "I'll take that challenge, little girl."

Shade's intimate tone had the hair rising on her arms and neck, and Raven didn't know how she was going to make it through dinner.

Chapter Eighteen

Shade was aware of the entrance she and Raven made at the front desk, and she stood taller, never taking her hand off the small of Raven's bare back. Both men and women stopped in their tracks to look at them. The impact of their desire triggered her shoulders to pull back proudly. Raven's pheromones were filling the restaurant already, mixing with her own desire.

Raven sighed happily before following the waitress, and Shade watched the extra twitch in her hips, knowing it was for her alone. She strode confidently behind her, though all she really wanted to do was let out a primal scream that Raven was hers.

Well, as much as Raven would let her possess.

Just as Shade had the thought, Raven looked over her shoulder at her and winked.

The gesture felt connected to her nerve endings, and shot straight between her thighs, where the sensation continued to tingle until they reached the table.

Their seats overlooked the water, where they could see parts of downtown lit up along with the boats in the harbor.

Red candles flickered on the table, providing intimate lighting in the dark space, illuminating Raven across from her in a beautiful glow. Raven held her forefinger over one of them, and the flame jumped an additional inch.

"Show off," Shade said, then promptly matched her action with the other candle, causing the fire to dance toward hers.

The waitress cleared her throat, and when Shade looked up at her, she saw the woman's eyes full of curiosity. She dropped her energy, and Raven stifled a laugh behind her hand.

"Can I get you anything to drink?"

"Water, please for me," Shade said.

"Me too," Raven said.

"You don't have to—"

"I'm fine." Raven smiled up at the waitress. "Thank you." The dismissive finality in the tone of her voice had the waitress backing away from the table. Shade was impressed that Raven could pull it off without seeming to be cold. It was a skill she'd never mastered, or even thought about, before.

As soon as they were alone, Raven pressed her finger against Shade's lips to quiet her. She flicked her tongue against it, and Raven stuttered. "I'm sorry," Shade said. "I missed that. What were you saying?"

Raven leaned back in her chair. "Dios, you're so hot." She turned and looked around the room. "There are several ladies here that want your attention. I can smell them."

Shade's gaze never wavered from Raven's face. "Don't want them. I want you."

"Good." Raven smiled sweetly. "Because I'd hate to rip their faces off. I just got my nails done."

Shade grinned. She loved that about her. You never knew what was going to come out of her mouth, or if you should duck. It was exciting to match wits and temper with her. "I've missed you."

Raven's face softened. "How come you never called me or wrote?"

"I needed to get better. Believe me, I wanted to." Raven's hurt energy made Shade sad. "I never intended to hurt you."

"I know that. I do," Raven said. "When I finally calmed down and went over the details, I can see where you lied, and where you didn't."

"I'm an addict. I have been since I was thirteen years old."

The waitress dropped off their water. "Are you ready to order?"

"Not yet," Shade answered without looking at her.

"I'll check back."

She watched Raven open the menu and stare. Curious, she opened her own. "What is this stuff?" she whispered loudly. "The only thing I recognize is the lobster."

"There are no prices," Raven whispered back.

"Don't worry about it," Shade said. She'd checked before she came. She wanted to bring Raven to the best restaurant in town to impress her, and they never had prices on their menus. Well, that's what Kat told her anyway. Shade had never been in such a fancy place.

"Me either," Raven said. "I would have been happy with Chinese food."

"I agree. Let's just get the lobster."

"Okay," Raven answered. "But I hate to put a bib on."

Shade looked around the room again. She couldn't see anyone else wearing one. "I think the bibs are only for crab, so we're okay. I would hate to see you cover up as well."

Raven had that knowing look on her face and sent another naked image. But Shade could sense Raven was still anxious under the flirting. Concerned about where she stood, and worried about what Shade said about living one day at a time.

Shade meant it when she told her she loved her. The only other living human beings she'd said those words to were Aura, Sunny, Tiffany, and Angel. When the waitress came back, she simply pointed to the lobster and held up two fingers.

Raven stared expectantly at her, the candlelight flickering in her dark pupils. Shade took a deep breath. "Ready for the gruesome details?"

When Raven nodded, she inhaled again, drawing additional energy from her heart chakra. "Where do you want to start? When I got to treatment or from the beginning?"

"I want to know everything," Raven said softly.

Shade took a quick peek and found only Raven's compassionate energy along with a need to know the details. She deserved the whole story, all the good, bad, and ugly. If she chose to stay with

Shade and build a life with her, she needed to know everything that could affect her decision.

"First of all, babe," Raven said and leaned forward. "I can also hear your thoughts. We are bonded through our experiences. There isn't anything you can tell me that will change my mind about loving your spirit, the essence of who *you* are. *Nada.*"

The tables in the restaurant were far enough away from each other for discretion, but Shade felt a slight pressure in the air. Raven smiled at her. "Just a little privacy shield."

"Wouldn't it just be easier to let you see it all?" Shade asked.

"I need your words," Raven said. "How you perceive your journey. How I would see it would be completely different. It's okay, go ahead."

Shade was grateful for her willingness to listen without judgment. At this point, no one had heard the whole story except her sponsor in the twelve-step meetings she attended. Shade cleared her throat and started at the beginning.

"You saw what happened. Life didn't get any better after that. After my father showed himself to me, all kinds of dead people showed up. I'm pretty sure I lost my mind for a while, and spent almost a year in a psych ward. When I got out, it wasn't long after I found drugs could ease the pain. At first, I used my mother's, or got them from the men she made me..." She hesitated and Raven jumped in.

"Ssh. We don't have to go there right now."

"Right. Okay. Anyway, I started getting into other trouble at school. They sent me to counselors, whom I thought at the time were full of crap. The adults in my life talked about how evil drugs were, don't do it, it will ruin your life. But when I got high for the first time? I knew they were liars. For me, getting high was about feeling better, to not hurt, to breathe in and out, and not feel the agony of existing with no purpose, no love, and an ability to see the dead."

"I can't imagine how horrible it was," Raven said. "To feel that level of hypocritical betrayal from all sides in your life."

Shade nodded. "That's an excellent way to put it. So, you know I met Dr. Skye when I turned eleven. I was in yet another institution, this time by my mother's request after I physically fought with her. I'd had enough, and I had recently discovered I could throw my hate at her, psychically, and it would knock her down. She totally freaked and committed me. I kept trying to convince those freaking dumbass doctors that the dead wouldn't leave me alone. Their answer was to strap me down, keep doping me up, and try to make me change my story."

"Another betrayal." Raven nodded. "And they believed your mother's deception."

"Yes." Shade swallowed the lump. There was still major healing needed in this area of her life. "Anyway, the State mandated that I see another psychologist, and my mother had to go along with it. Not because she wanted to, but because I was her cash cow and she wanted to keep the welfare, and the other source of her income, you know."

"I do. God, Shade, I'm so sorry you went through all of this. I hate that I don't have the words to make it better."

"I've learned over the last few months, it's all work I have to do myself. It helps to talk about it. And I want you to know how I got to the point I was with myself and my addiction."

"Okay," Raven said, "but we can stop anytime you want."

Shade took her hand. "Let me get it all out. I tend to throw rugs over the elephants in the room, and call it good."

Raven laughed. "Good one."

She let the momentum of the story continue. She was far from done and wanted it out of their way. "I broke into the drug cabinet one night and tried to overdose. I was so tired of being screamed at, called delusional, and being forced back to my mother's house."

Shade heard Raven's sharp intake of breath, but continued on. "Dr. Skye, in my eyes, was just like the rest in the beginning. But over time, somehow, he gained my nonexistent trust. He never gave up on me, even when I was violent and hateful. He cut the meds they had me on, and saw me three times a week. Eventually, I told him about the dead people, and he told me about his extraordinary wife and daughter, who was the same age as me, and how gifted they were."

"Aura and Sunny."

Shade nodded. "One day, he signed me out for a field trip, and I met Aura for the first time. God, I can remember the first time she touched me. That first jolt of energy that was both magical and soothing. I hadn't known, not really, how cold my heart was before that day."

Angry energy assaulted her from the other side of the table, and Shade stopped talking. Before she could ask Raven about it, the waitress fussed around their table, making certain they had everything they needed, and left quickly.

"First of all," Raven said when they were alone again. "It breaks my heart to think that an eleven-year-old child would think she had a cold heart, and take responsibility for it. None of what happened to you was your fault. And if your mother was still alive, not one person in this world could save her from me."

Shade sat back from the force behind the words. She was a little awestruck Raven could go from loving to murderous in three seconds flat. That she did it *for her* was mind-blowing. She was humbled, and she didn't know what to say.

Raven smiled at her sweetly. "You were saying?"

Shade looked down at the lobster tail, several of what looked to be lima beans, and three asparagus spears on her plate, drizzled with a dark sauce, and a small dish of melted butter. She tried not to grimace while she swept the beans to the end of the platter.

She needn't have held back. Raven was doing the same thing across from her.

They both laughed. "Guess we're going home hungry, huh?" Shade said.

Raven's eyes caught hers. "We already knew that."

Heat flushed between Shade's thighs, and she crossed them in an attempt to relieve the sudden pressure. She had been near flash point on Raven's front porch before they left. Apparently, her lust had merely been sleeping while she was talking.

She inhaled Raven's spicy, clean scent, and since her mouth was watering, sincerely hoped she wasn't drooling.

Raven's seductive smile did little for Shade's patience. She had no hunger left for the food on her plate, she was more interested in having Raven. The closest place was the car, and she calculated how fast she could get her there, raise Raven's dress, and put her mouth on her. Christ, could she even do that in the seat of that small fucking car?

Shade felt a cool breeze swirl around her, calming the sexual agitation, and she relaxed her shoulders. "Did you just *do* that?"

"We have all night," Raven said. "I'm not going anywhere, and neither are you."

Shade paused. Raven ran right into her darkness, took care of business, and strolled right out again, not even breaking a sweat. She knew that being *this* connected to Raven would require complete trust—for both of them.

"About the car," Raven said, and waved her fork. "Rain check. It does have a sunroof?"

Shade nodded and wondered if Raven's capacity to mesmerize her would ever end. She knew she loved her now, and anything else she discovered would be additional gifts.

"Say it," Raven whispered. "Please."

"I love you." Shade gave her the words, out loud, and found herself fighting the tears that burned in the corners of her eyes. She felt completely humbled by the wave of feelings that rushed over her. And for the first time she could remember, not one of them included regret, guilt, or shame. How freaking cool was that?

"So," Raven said. "Can we continue the story? I want to know why you thought you had to go through this alone."

Shade hesitated while she thought about the question, not because she was thinking of excuses, but because she really didn't know. She'd been alone her entire life until Sunny. And Sunny walked away because Shade suffocated her in darkness. "After Sunny," she said. "I was lost. If she couldn't love me, there must be something wrong and broken, because she lights the world, you know? She loves everyone."

"She loves you," Raven said. "But her path is different. That's when I met you, and I knew that you were for me."

"I don't and can't for the life of me see why," Shade said honestly. "I was so fucked up."

"When I was young, I couldn't see that part." Raven leaned closer. "I saw *you*. The spirit that you *are*, without outside interference, void of any behavior, or preconceptions. And when I heard your music, I knew without a doubt that I was right. That beautiful song you wrote for me uncovered all of the bullshit. With each note, you became clearer to me, and all of the feelings I had for you, minus our recent time together, came flooding back."

"I don't deserve you."

Raven flipped her hair over her shoulder. "Not then." She laughed. "But the truth is, this is the *you* that does. I feel it in my soul. Does that make sense?"

It did. And with a clear head, Shade might even come to believe it. All she knew for certain was that the drugs kept her disconnected from her source of power. A person's birthright is always Love. She'd hated herself for so long, she couldn't find it any longer. "I'm truly sorry I hurt you, Raven."

"I know you are. But you were sick, sí?"

"Sí."

"I'm not perfect either. I have a hot temper, I'm impulsive, and I can be selfish. I'm not one little bit ashamed of being high maintenance either."

"No!"

"Shut up!"

Shade laughed. "You're perfect for me."

Raven looked at her, her expression serious and calm. "And you're strong enough for me in every way." She grinned slyly. "Except when I kicked your ass in the office."

"Hey now," Shade said.

"I was incredibly turned on afterward. You?"

Shade nearly choked on the piece of asparagus she was chewing. She coughed and pounded on her chest. Raven took a tiny bite of lobster, a drop of butter slipped down her chin, and landed between her breasts. Shade tracked the movement as it disappeared into her dress.

"Stop staring," Raven said. "Get back to the story."

Where was she? Oh yeah, after Sunny. "After I went to your mother for a spell, when I came back the next time, I had her put it on me instead. One that ensured I wouldn't fall in love with anyone else. I never wanted to hurt like that again. And on the other side of the coin, I didn't want to hurt anyone else."

"How ironic," Raven said. "That's the exact time my mother warned me about necromancers."

"Was that sarcastic?" Shade asked.

"Of course it was." Raven took another dainty bite. "She agreed to such a spell to keep you from me. And she never foresaw the fact I would become gifted in such a way."

"Now that's a mind fuck."

"It is." Raven dabbed her mouth. "One could argue it was destiny."

"One could." Shade felt a burst of happiness. She wasn't unlovable or alone in the world. Never had been. The fault was in the way she'd perceived reality and how she chose to cope with it. For Shade that had meant building a wall that surrounded Lacey, and encased all of her hurt and pain.

Raven waved her hand. "Please continue."

"Okay, so armed with the spell your mother put on me, that's when I dove deeper into drugs and alcohol. I can't remember much of that time, but I do remember when Sunny found me and put me to work at Sisters of Spirits. I thought in some sick way that she still wanted me to be there for her, that I only had to be patient. I cut back on the hard drugs, but never much on the drinking.

"After Jordan, and that whole scene, that's when it got really bad, and someone gave me opiates for the first time. You can hear the war story later. I want to focus on where I am now. The fucked up thing about drugs is, by the time you know you're addicted, there isn't anything you feel you can do about it. It's near impossible to think past the cravings for more. And more. Then you need it just to feel human, and not feel like your body is falling apart. After that, it takes more to feel the effects, it never works as well as the first times, but at least when you're doing it, you don't feel as if you want to die."

"Was your detox horrible?" Raven asked. "When you went to treatment?"

"Yes. And part of the reason I didn't contact you. Jesus, I hated Jordan and Kat in the beginning. It's the hardest thing I've ever done, and I don't wish it on my worst enemy." The stabbing cramps in her back and belly, the chills, then sweats, and inability to sleep or eat. Even the thought of taking a shower was excruciating, because the force of the water hitting her skin felt like needles. She'd ended up lying in bed, jerking and rocking, and wondering why a person could be put on earth to suffer like this. She hated herself, she hated everyone else that wasn't addicted, and she wanted to curl up and die.

Shade blinked away her memory, and saw Raven staring at her with tears in her eyes.

"I had no idea," she said. "Yet, you kept me out of your mind. I couldn't reach your energy."

"I didn't want you to witness that, Raven, and truthfully, I didn't think I'd ever be well enough for you. I believed I was irrevocably broken. By the time I realized I could get well, I didn't want to come back until I had something to offer you."

"You broke my heart. I'm not going to sugarcoat that at all," Raven said. "You could have explained that to me then. I might have been able to help."

Shade shook her head. "No. It was my fight to win, my wreckage to clean up. I had to do it alone. By the time I was clearheaded enough to realize what I'd done, I thought it might be too late, that the damage had been done. I was afraid of rejection, and my sponsor told me it was in your best interest that I wait."

"I can understand that." Raven pushed her plate to the center of the table. "I don't like it, but I can accept it."

"So here we are."

"Yes."

Shade watched Raven's body shift as she uncrossed her legs under the table, and a shiver skittered down her spine when her foot caressed her calf beneath the tablecloth. She inhaled sharply at the contact.

"Pay the bill," Raven said.

CHAPTER NINETEEN

Raven whimpered when her back hit the wall in Kat's condo, but she didn't allow her lips to break contact with Shade's. The sensation of her tongue being sucked was glorious, but her body cried out in other places as well. Shade's shoulders pinned her to the wall. She'd filled out since she'd last been with her, and she was stronger. When she couldn't draw a breath, she finally pulled back to gasp for air. "How's your back?" she managed to ask.

"Fine." Shade spun her away from the wall. Raven teetered on her heels and grabbed a hold of Shade's hips for balance while she kicked them off. Then she gathered strength to push her away, but Shade came right back like a rubber band.

"Wait." Raven put her hand on Shade's chest. "Go over there."

"Where?"

"You should see the look on your face." Raven laughed. "There." She pointed to the couch. "And open the curtains. I want to see the city. Where's the bathroom?"

"Down the hall, second door on the right."

Raven had always heard how beautiful Kat's condo was, but this was the first time she'd been there. The moon was full tonight, and she wanted to revel in its power. As much as she thought she loved Shade before, tonight she'd discovered another pocket in her heart, just waiting for her to find, and the intensity of her feelings was a little frightening. She hadn't known it was there, and how can you prepare for something you've never felt before?

Her panties were soaked, and she realized while looking in the mirror that the back of her dress sported a wet spot. She took them both off, and then her bra. Just being naked in the same place as Shade had her insides quivering, and her body screaming to be near her.

Raven fluffed her hair and licked her lips. She heard Shade in the kitchen, and the clink of ice cubes into glasses, and shivered. Her nipples ached, and she felt the need to be filled up. Fire burned inside her core, and a wave of desire hit her so hard, she had to put her hands on the bathroom counter to steady herself. This wasn't an ordinary call of desire. Raven felt she might faint if it wasn't answered, that she'd break if she wasn't held together by Shade's arms.

She was also ready to give Shade as good as she got.

❖

Shade took the glasses of ice water back to the living room and then opened the drapes. The lights of the city competed with the luminosity of the full moon. Standing here, seemingly on top of the world, she felt powerful. Better than any drug she'd ever tried, high on spirit. She could manifest her destiny, be the person she wanted to be.

Be the woman Raven needed. She turned when she heard the click of the bathroom door. She hadn't turned on any lights in the room, yet she could see clearly.

Raven came down the hall, naked, and the water glass slipped from her hands to drop on the travertine floor. Incredibly, it didn't shatter, and Raven smiled.

Like a goddess, she walked toward her, full of magic and seduction, and Shade would do everything in her power to worship her, body and spirit. Her eyes burned and she memorized every detail of this moment, permanently etching Raven into her soul.

Raven stopped in the middle of the room, her hands down at her sides, her head bowed for a moment, as if in offering. Shade crossed to her and wrapped herself around Raven until there was no space between them but her clothes. It was incredibly erotic and Shade trembled.

She let one hand drift to Raven's ass, to squeeze and attempt to draw her closer. Raven's head tilted back, and Shade felt her hair tumble around her arms. Raven arched her back and pushed her hips nearer yet, and Shade felt her heat through her pants.

With her other arm, she straightened Raven until their chests were also pressed together, and their hearts beat in tandem along with their breath. She exhaled into Raven's ear and followed it with a swirl of her tongue before she blew gently again. Goose bumps rose on Raven's body, and Shade felt her shiver against her. She continued the trail her tongue started until she reached Raven's mouth and licked her lips softly before pressing into the kiss. Her head spun with sexual exhilaration.

Raven kissed her back with the same intensity, followed her lead, and gained momentum as Shade's tongue entered her mouth, and she tasted her again.

Pure and sweet.

Mine.

Shade was ready to drop her to the floor, had even put her foot behind Raven's to do so, and stopped herself. Instead, she used her body to back her up, down the hallway and into the bedroom.

Raven's teeth nipped at her lips, and each time, the tiny pain shot a lightning bolt between Shade's thighs. When they were at the doorway, Shade placed a hand between Raven's legs, and stumbled when she felt smooth, naked skin. Raven was on fire, and so wet.

For her.

She ran her fingers between Raven's labia, soaked her hand, and stumbled. She leaned against the doorjamb and watched Raven climb onto the bed. As soon as she turned to look back at her, Shade sucked the tips of her own fingers while Raven watched.

"Omigod, that was sexy." Raven stared at her. Shade watched her breasts sway gently with the effort it was taking her to breathe.

"What do you want, beautiful witch?"

"Everything."

Shade unbuttoned the white shirt slowly, unzipped her pants, and let them drop to the floor. "Okay, if you think you can handle it."

"Hope you held on to your walker." Raven laughed.

"Brat, you did not just say that!" Shade pounced on her.

The sound of laughter died quickly and was replaced with a sweet, heavy breath in her ear, and tiny whimpers from Raven's throat. Shade didn't feel as if she could get close enough. She wanted to melt into her warm skin and share her heart. She wanted to live inside her spirit.

She growled in the back of her throat. The surge of their connection intensified her need to take her. She sat up and repositioned herself between Raven's thighs. "Wider," she said, and pushed her knees farther apart. Shade moaned. Raven was completely exposed to her, wet and glistening in the moonlight, her lips full and open, ready for her attention. She lowered herself, inhaling her scent, and then blew softly on her folds. "Every part of you is gorgeous," she whispered.

She watched Raven's flesh shiver, and gently fanned her breath again across her clitoris, fascinated when she saw it twitch.

"Shade. Please, baby."

Shade swiped her tongue lengthwise, tasting every inch she could reach, and she knew she would never get enough of her. Raven pulled her knees up to her chest, giving Shade more to look at, more to taste, and when her hips tried to move, Shade pinned them to the bed.

She sucked her engorged clit, and Raven cried out. "Now, Shade. Fuck me now."

Shade's own hips ground against the mattress, and she tried to find a pressure point to ease the throbbing of her own clit as she entered Raven's heat with two fingers. She felt her inner muscles instantly clamp around them, and Raven's body rocked against her hand and face.

Nothing existed but Raven's scent and flesh, and her cries spurred Shade to give her more. She stroked inside her, both hard and soft, and continued to lick and suck after Raven's first shattering climax had passed, and she brought her to another.

Shade felt she could stay there all night, bring her more, and listen to her cries of pleasure, while she trembled and came against her mouth.

But Raven rolled to her side. "Enough."

Shade turned onto her back and sighed. She was happy, sated by Raven's satisfaction. She wiped her mouth and chin with her hand, and before she realized what was happening, Raven's hands grabbed her under the arms and pulled her up the bed toward the pillows.

Shade was flat on her back. "I'm good," she said. "Cuddle with me." She wasn't really, she had come rubbing herself on the blankets, and had another orgasm the last time Raven did, but both had done little to relieve the pressure that still pounded insistently.

"Don't do that," Raven said softly. "Don't shut me out."

"What?" Shade was confused. She'd been completely invested in Raven's pleasure. What was she doing wrong?

Raven's hair fell in a curtain around her face, and she covered her with butterfly kisses. "It's my turn to love you."

Shade's throat closed with emotion. She couldn't remember the last time she'd been on her back and open to receive anything.

"Good," Raven said. "Then you'll only remember me."

Shade didn't know what to say, but Raven appeared to be waiting for permission. Shade felt vulnerable, and the corners of her eyes burned so she closed them. Raven licked the tears that escaped, then sucked Shade's lower lip into her mouth. Shade felt paralyzed, and unsure.

"Do you trust me?"

Shade nodded without hesitation. "Yes."

Raven straddled her hips, and she rested her weight above Shade with her forearms. Her breasts swayed in her face, and Shade reached up to gently knead their softness. Raven shifted again so she could nibble on one. Shade looked up at her face and saw the pleasure ripple across Raven's features, and her hips pressed down.

Raven pulled away and cradled her breasts. "Do you like these?" she asked.

Shade reached for Raven's ass.

"Uh, uh." Raven scooted backward on her knees until she was between Shade's thighs, and spreading them for her to kneel between.

God, she was turned on. Shade's muscles tightened, then trembled with excitement. When Raven whipped her hair back, held it to one side, leaned over, and flicked her tongue across her clit, she nearly lost it again. "Jesus, Raven. Stop it. I'm going to have a heart attack."

"No, you're not." Raven got back up on her knees, and twisted her own nipples into tight little points, before sliding her left breast along Shade's labia.

The softness of her skin and the hardness of her nipple was a juxtaposition of sensation she'd never felt before. What was even more exciting, was how erotic it looked, as Raven's tit slid across her flesh. When Shade saw her own wetness covering her dark, full areole, the wave of lust that hit caught her by surprise, and her head fell to the pillow. "That feels so fucking amazing."

Pressure built in her entire body, and her muscles tightened in response. Raven's lips closed around her clit, and Shade felt the edge of her teeth as they scraped against her. She panted and whimpered, and the intensity of her orgasm shattered her consciousness.

Then she was aware of Raven holding her, her soothing voice and gentle caresses as she experienced several more.

From behind closed eyes, she watched their energy braid together in several more variations; colors and emotions flew across the night sky of her mind and she felt complete.

Shade felt Raven's magic brush against her senses, the gentle brushes of her astral wings as they wrapped around her.

And they flew together into the night.

Epilogue

Eighteen months later...

Raven screamed.

Shade's blood turned to ice in her veins. She'd cut her client off in the middle of his sentence, apologized, told him to make another appointment, and ran out of her office and down the stairs.

Sunny met her at the bottom of the stairs, and Jordan was right behind Shade. Kat was already in the car, and they raced outside.

"Wait for me!" Tiffany yelled.

"Hurry!" Shade held the door open, then slammed it when Tiffany got in. Everyone was talking at once, but Shade didn't hear a word. She huddled in the backseat of the new Sisters of Spirits mobile unit and tried not to let her mind race to the worst possibilities.

Raven screamed in her head again, and she started shaking with fear.

Sunny and Tiffany both held her, but even with their healing force, the intensity of their shared bonds of energy, Shade couldn't pull herself together. She felt like a stunned bunny, paralyzed with indecision.

When she felt another wave of pain, she nearly doubled over. "Would you fucking drive faster?" she snarled at Kat.

"There's our Shade," Tiffany said. "Come on back. Raven needs you."

Kat screeched into the parking lot, and as a unit, they ran into the hospital. Shade looked helplessly at Sunny when they reached the front desk.

Sunny wrapped her arms around Shade and held her tight. "I love you. Now go. I'll take care of this."

Shade wasn't going to wait for the elevator. She ran up the stairs two at a time. Her adrenaline gave her the strength to overcome her fear.

When she shot through the door, she was met with a wall of people. She tried to push through them before she realized they were her in-laws.

Juanita grabbed her arm and pulled her along. "She's going quickly. Go to her now."

Nurses handed her a name tag, and she ran down yet another hallway.

An intern motioned her to the room Raven was in, and Juanita came in behind her

Her wife was in excruciating pain, covered in sweat, and her hair lay in wet tangles around her face and neck. Shade felt the next contraction as if she were experiencing it herself and nearly dropped to her knees. She looked helplessly at Juanita. "I thought first babies took a long time to come!"

"Why would I let my daughter suffer and go through that?"

"But I almost didn't make it. You could have warned me."

"Hush," Raven said. "You're here now. I waited for you." Her face tightened, and she blew out several quick breaths in succession. Shade felt the band of pain inside her abdomen. She thought fracturing her spine hurt, but it didn't come close to what Raven was going through.

Time sped up, and Shade lost track of what was going on around her, because her focus was on Raven, holding her hand, and wiping the tears on her face, while Raven's mother held her hand on the other side of the bed. The doctors and nurses were all busy, and Shade ignored them.

A nurse slid a high steel stool closer to her, and Shade balanced against it, never taking her eyes from Raven's while they breathed as one.

"Time to push."

"Thank the baby Jesus," Raven said, and after three excruciating attempts, Raven fell back against the bed.

Shade felt the wave of relieved energy surround Raven, but she couldn't tear her eyes off the blood. God, there was so much, it made her dizzy, and then everything went dark around the edges before she felt herself fall.

When she saw Juanita and a nurse standing over her, she felt humiliated, and batted them away from her so she could stand up again.

"You all right?" one of them asked her.

Damn it, she missed cutting the cord while she was flat on the floor. Friends and family were beginning to crowd the small room. Both her father and Raven's were grinning at her from the corner of the room, near the ceiling.

Shade looked over at the bed and saw Raven smiling at her while she held their tiny infant daughter, Hope. The force of their love lit the room. She wiped the tears from her cheeks and pushed her shoulders back. Everything she'd gone through in her life was worth it in that second—because it led her to this moment. The moment her life was truly complete.

"I've never been better."

About the Author

Yvonne is currently living in Texas with her partner and their dogs. During the week, she's a writer, but on Friday nights, she's a rock star. Or maybe she's a karaoke queen. Same thing, really. When she was a kid, her mom constantly asked her, "Where do you come up with this stuff, Yvonne?" The answer was—and is—always the same. "I don't know. I just make it up as I go along."

Her first book, *Sometime Yesterday*, won the 2013 Golden Crown Literary Award for Best Paranormal Romance in addition to being a finalist in the Lambda Literary Awards.

The Awakening: Book One in The Sisters of Spirits Trilogy, won the 2014 Golden Crown Literary Award for Best Paranormal Romance.

Books Available from Bold Strokes Books

Pedal to the Metal by Jesse J. Thoma. When unreformed thief Dubs Williams is released from prison to help Max Winters bust a car theft ring, Max learns that to catch a thief, get in bed with one. (978-1-62639-239-7)

Dragon Horse War by D. Jackson Leigh. A priestess of peace and a fiery warrior must defeat a vicious uprising that entwines their destinies and ultimately their hearts. (978-1-62639-240-3)

For the Love of Cake by Erin Dutton. When everything is on the line, and one taste can break a heart, will pastry chefs Maya and Shannon take a chance on reality? (978-1-62639-241-0)

Betting on Love by Alyssa Linn Palmer. A quiet country-girl-at-heart and a live-life-to-the-fullest biker take a risk at offering each other their hearts. (978-1-62639-242-7)

The Deadening by Yvonne Heidt. The lines between good and evil, right and wrong, have always been blurry for Shade. When Raven's actions force her to choose, which side will she come out on? (978-1-62639-243-4)

Ordinary Mayhem by Victoria A. Brownworth. Faye Blakemore has been taking photographs since she was ten, but those same photographs threaten to destroy everything she knows and everything she loves. (978-1-62639-315-8)

One Last Thing by Kim Baldwin & Xenia Alexiou. Blood is thicker than pride. The final book in the Elite Operative Series brings together foes, family, and friends to start a new order. (978-1-62639-230-4)

Songs Unfinished by Holly Stratimore. Two aspiring rock stars learn that falling in love while pursuing their dreams can be harmonious—if they can only keep their pasts from throwing them out of tune. (978-1-62639-231-1)

Beyond the Ridge by L.T. Marie. Will a contractor and a horse rancher overcome their family differences and find common ground to build a life together? (978-1-62639-232-8)

Swordfish by Andrea Bramhall. Four women battle the demons from their pasts. Will they learn to let go, or will happiness be forever beyond their grasp? (978-1-62639-233-5)

The Fiend Queen by Barbara Ann Wright. Princess Katya and her consort Starbride must turn evil against evil in order to banish Fiendish power from their kingdom, and only love will pull them back from the brink. (978-1-62639-234-2)

Up the Ante by PJ Trebelhorn. When Jordan Stryker and Ashley Noble meet again fifteen years after a short-lived affair, are either of them prepared to gamble on a chance at love? (978-1-62639-237-3)

Speakeasy by MJ Williamz. When mob leader Helen Byrne sets her sights on the girlfriend of Al Capone's right-hand man, passion and tempers flare on the streets of Chicago. (978-1-62639-238-0)

Venus in Love by Tina Michele. Morgan Blake can't afford any distractions and Ainsley Dencourt can't afford to lose control—but the beauty of life and art usually lies in the unpredictable strokes of the artist's brush. (978-1-62639-220-5)

Rules of Revenge by AJ Quinn. When a lethal operative on a collision course with her past agrees to help a CIA analyst on a critical assignment, the encounter proves explosive in ways neither woman anticipated. (978-1-62639-221-2)

The Romance Vote by Ali Vali. Chili Alexander is a sought-after campaign consultant who isn't prepared when her boss's daughter, Samantha Pellegrin, comes to work at the firm and shakes up Chili's life from the first day. (978-1-62639-222-9)

Advance: Exodus Book One by Gun Brooke. Admiral Dael Caydoc's mission to find a new homeworld for the Oconodian people is hazardous, but working with the infuriating Commander Aniwyn "Spinner" Seclan endangers her heart and soul. (978-1-62639-224-3)

UnCatholic Conduct by Stevie Mikayne. Jil Kidd goes undercover to investigate fraud at St. Marguerite's Catholic School, but life gets complicated when her student is killed—and she begins to fall for her prime target. (978-1-62639-304-2)

Season's Meetings by Amy Dunne. Catherine Birch reluctantly ventures on the festive road trip from hell with beautiful stranger Holly Daniels only to discover the road to true love has its own obstacles to maneuver. (978-1-62639-227-4)

Myth and Magic: Queer Fairy Tales edited by Radclyffe and Stacia Seaman. Myth, magic, and monsters—the stuff of childhood dreams (or nightmares) and adult fantasies. (978-1-62639-225-0)

Nine Nights on the Windy Tree by Martha Miller. Recovering drug addict, Bertha Brannon, is an attorney who is trying to stay clean when a murder sends her back to the bad end of town. (978-1-62639-179-6)

Driving Lessons by Annameekee Hesik. Dive into Abbey Brooks's sophomore year as she attempts to figure out the amazing, but sometimes complicated, life of a you-know-who girl at Gila High School. (978-1-62639-228-1)

Asher's Shot by Elizabeth Wheeler. Asher Price's candid photographs capture the truth, but when his success requires exposing an enemy, Asher discovers his only shot at happiness involves revealing secrets of his own. (978-1-62639-229-8)

Courtship by Carsen Taite. Love and justice—a lethal mix or a perfect match? (978-1-62639-210-6)

Against Doctor's Orders by Radclyffe. Corporate financier Presley Worth wants to shut down Argyle Community Hospital, but Dr. Harper Rivers will fight her every step of the way, if she can also fight their growing attraction. (978-1-62639-211-3)

A Spark of Heavenly Fire by Kathleen Knowles. Kerry and Beth are building their life together, but unexpected circumstances could destroy their happiness. (978-1-62639-212-0)

Never Too Late by Julie Blair. When Dr. Jamie Hammond is forced to hire a new office manager, she's shocked to come face to face with Carla Grant and memories from her past. (978-1-62639-213-7)

Widow by Martha Miller. Judge Bertha Brannon must solve the murder of her lover, a policewoman she thought she'd grow old with. As more bodies pile up, the murderer starts coming for her. (978-1-62639-214-4)

Twisted Echoes by Sheri Lewis Wohl. What's a woman to do when she realizes the voices in her head are real? (978-1-62639-215-1)

Criminal Gold by Ann Aptaker. Through a dangerous night in New York in 1949, Cantor Gold, dapper dyke-about-town, smuggler of fine art, is forced by a crime lord to be his instrument of vengeance. (978-1-62639-216-8)

The Melody of Light by M.L. Rice. After surviving abuse and loss, will Riley Gordon be able to navigate her first year of college and accept true love and family? (978-1-62639-219-9)

Because of You by Julie Cannon. What would you do for the woman you were forced to leave behind? (978-1-62639-199-4)

The Job by Jove Belle. Sera always dreamed that she would one day reunite with Tor. She just didn't think it would involve terrorists, firearms, and hostages. (978-1-62639-200-7)

Making Time by C.J. Harte. Two women going in different directions meet after fifteen years and struggle to reconnect in spite of the past that separated them. (978-1-62639-201-4)

Once The Clouds Have Gone by KE Payne. Overwhelmed by the dark clouds of her past, Tag Grainger is lost until the intriguing and spirited Freddie Metcalfe unexpectedly forces her to reevaluate her life. (978-1-62639-202-1)

The Acquittal by Anne Laughlin. Chicago private investigator Josie Harper searches for the real killer of a woman whose lover has been acquitted of the crime. (978-1-62639-203-8)

An American Queer: The Amazon Trail by Lee Lynch. Lee Lynch's heartening and heart-rending history of gay life from the turbulence of the late 1900s to the triumphs of the early 2000s are recorded in this selection of her columns. (978-1-62639-204-5)

Stick McLaughlin: The Prohibition Years by CF Frizzell. Corruption in 1918 cost Stick her lover, her freedom, and her identity, but a very special flapper and the family bond of her own gang could help win them back—even if it means outwitting the Boston Mob. (978-1-62639-205-2)

Edge of Awareness by C.A. Popovich. When Maria, a woman in the middle of her third divorce, meets Dana, an out lesbian, awareness of her feelings brings up reservations about the teachings of her church. (978-1-62639-188-8)

Taken by Storm by Kim Baldwin. Lives depend on two women when a train derails high in the remote Alps, but an unforgiving mountain, avalanches, crevasses, and other perils stand between them and safety. (978-1-62639-189-5)

The Common Thread by Jaime Maddox. Dr. Nicole Coussart's life is falling apart, but fortunately, DEA Attorney Rae Rhodes is there to pick up the pieces and help Nic put them back together. (978-1-62639-190-1)

Jolt by Kris Bryant. Mystery writer Bethany Lange wasn't prepared for the twisting emotions that left her breathless the moment she laid eyes on folk singer sensation Ali Hart. (978-1-62639-191-8)

Searching For Forever by Emily Smith. Dr. Natalie Jenner's life has always been about saving others, until young paramedic Charlie Thompson comes along and shows her maybe she's the one who needs saving. (978-1-62639-186-4)

A Queer Sort of Justice: Prison Tales Across Time by Rebecca S. Buck. When liberty is only a memory, and all seems lost, what freedoms and hopes can be found within us? (978-1-62639-195-6E)

Blue Water Dreams by Dena Hankins. Lania Marchiol keeps her wary sailor's gaze trained on the horizon until Oly Rassmussen, a wickedly handsome trans man, sends her trusty compass spinning off course. (978-1-62639-192-5)

Rest Home Runaways by Clifford Henderson. Baby boomer Morgan Ronzio's troubled marriage is the least of her worries when she gets the call that her addled, eighty-six-year-old, half-blind dad has escaped the rest home. (978-1-62639-169-7)

Charm City by Mason Dixon. Raq Overstreet's loyalty to her drug kingpin boss is put to the test when she begins to fall for Bathsheba Morris, the undercover cop assigned to bring him down. (978-1-62639-198-7)